# UNDERCOVER PROTECTOR

Melinda Di Lorenzo

Recycling programs for this product may not exist in your area.

ISBN-13: 978-1-335-45629-8

Undercover Protector



This edition published by arrangement with Harlequin Books S.A.

For questions and comments about the quality of this book, please contact us at CustomerService@Harlequin.com.

**Printed in U.S.A.**

Amazon bestselling author **Melinda Di Lorenzo** writes in her spare time—at soccer practices, when she should be doing laundry and in place of sleep. She lives on the beautiful west coast of British Columbia, Canada, with her handsome husband and her noisy kids. When she's not writing, she can be found curled up with (someone else's) good book.

**Books by Melinda Di Lorenzo**

**Harlequin Romantic Suspense**

***Undercover Justice***

*Captivating Witness*
*Undercover Protector*

*Worth the Risk*
*Last Chance Hero*
*Silent Rescue*

**Harlequin Intrigue**

*Trusting a Stranger*

**Harlequin Intrigue Noir**

*Deceptions and Desires*
*Pinups and Possibilities*

To those who have overcome, and to those who are still fighting the battle.

# Chapter 1

All around Nadine Stuart, thick, black smoke pressed in. The scent of charred wood and plastic mingled in the air, making her choke. She could hear voices, too, and even if she couldn't work out what they were saying, she knew they were urging her to run. But her feet were leaden, her mind sluggish. And the longer she stood still, the less motivated she felt to move.

*It's the lack of oxygen.*

The thought made sense, but its cool logic seemed out of place in the chaos.

She drew in a breath and willed herself to go. To move. Before it was too late. But the only thing that sped up was her heart in her chest. It thundered so hard that it hurt. Above her head, a dangerous crack resounded, and she knew if she looked up, the ceiling would be crashing down.

She squeezed her lids shut.

A scream built up in her throat.

Her mouth dropped wide.

She threw back her head.

And with the exception of her pulse, everything around her went still. Ever so slowly, Nadine dragged her eyes open. Then she blinked, and reality came flooding in. There was no smoke, no scream and no paralyzing terror. Instead, there was disinfectant-scented air, soft white light and the steady hum of medical machinery.

*The hospital*, she thought.

Though to be more accurate, it was the Whispering Woods Acute Care Facility. The mountainside tourist town was too small to have a real hospital, but the influx of outsiders twice a year—summer and winter—necessitated something more formal than a simple clinic. Nadine wished she could be thankful for it, but she'd been stuck in the same bed for seven days. Being under lock and key for that long was more than enough. And the unpleasant icing on the unpleasant cake was that the nightmares—an off-and-on staple for nearly the last decade—seemed more frequent here in the yellow-walled room.

She sighed. If she'd been back home in Freemont City, she would've simply discharged herself.

*Except Freemont's not really home anymore, is it?*

Nadine swallowed, wishing she could simply shove off the reminder. It wasn't like she'd left anything behind. Her things were boxed up or sold. Her old job belonged to someone else. And her ex was probably in bed, his arms wrapped up around his current fling.

*And you washed your hands of that life on purpose.*

That much was true. For six months after her breakup with Grant, she'd walked around in a daze. She'd done her best to be there for her cherubic students with their sweet questions, but, really, she hadn't been able to get into a proper teaching groove. So when a lawyer had shown up on her doorstep and informed her that she'd inherited her childhood home in Whispering Woods—a shock because she'd assumed that everything her mom owned had been spoken for a year prior when she passed—she hadn't even hesitated. Kismet, she'd called it. Especially when the teaching position at Whispering Woods Elementary had fallen into her lap, too.

Except in the month or so since she'd arrived in town, she hadn't accomplished much in the way of teaching. And she'd accomplished even less in regard to cleaning out her inherited apartment. Instead, she'd watched her half brother get shot. She'd been caught up in some decade-and-a-half-old crime that somehow *also* tied to the decade-old accident that she couldn't remember. And, according to the few people who knew what was really going on, the police weren't even aware of her brother's murder. It was as chilling as it was concerning. Thankfully, the corrupt cop who'd killed him was also dead, and though she was responsible for the event that caused his death, the local authorities investigating had ruled it an accident. But now Nadine was stuck in a hospital bed with an IV in her hand and a generally bad taste in her mouth. And of course there was the wannabe guard at her door. A detective from Freemont with his own ties to the crimes in question.

Her eyes drifted to the narrow blinds of her interior window. She could just see the man's slumped-over form on the bench in the hall. So far, Detective Anderson Somers hadn't budged much from his spot. She was pretty sure he'd been living off vending-machine sandwiches. Maybe the same watery coffee dispensed there, as well.

Nadine let out a heavy breath and looked away. If his presence didn't bother her so much, she might've felt a little sorry for him. She doubted that being her watchdog was as exciting as his usual day-to-day work.

*He probably hates it here as much as I do.*

But even with that acknowledgment, she could barely manage to drum up more than a trickle of empathy. Because Anderson Somers's presence was the real reason she couldn't discharge herself. It was he who'd insisted to the doctor that Nadine needed the extra recovery time. He'd said it all in a too-nice voice, reeling off some medical jargon about head injuries, smiling like he cared. He had a nice smile. Even teeth. And it always touched his eyes. So the doctor had bought it. Of course.

Nadine narrowed her own eyes at the window. What, exactly, had the detective said to the staff at the care facility about his relationship with her? she wondered. What would make them think he could speak on her behalf? She was truly curious, but she wouldn't dare ask.

Like he could feel her eyes on him, Anderson shifted in his seat, his head lifting enough that Nadine could see his shaggy blond mop. She quickly sank back against her pillow and squeezed her eyes shut, hoping he hadn't caught her staring. A second later, she worried that maybe he had, for her door whooshed open and soft footfalls tapped along the floor, then stopped not far from the edge of her bed.

Nadine feigned sleep, inhaling and exhaling at a carefully measured pace. At a count of ten, the steps receded, and then the door shut. When she lifted her lids and peered through her lashes, she saw that the bench outside was now empty.

*Hmm. So he's been sneaking away when I sleep.*

For some inexplicable reason, the idea bothered her as much as the fact that he'd been watching her around the clock. She narrowed her eyes again. Then pursed her lips. And finally smiled as a realization occurred to her. This was the perfect opportunity to free herself. From both the detective's scrutiny and the doctor's.

Nadine slid her legs out from under her covers, then swung them over the side of the bed. She waited for a reaction of some kind. A yell from the nurses station, or for Anderson to suddenly pop his head in and shoot her one of his too-sympathetic smiles. But there was just the same silence as there had been when she was tucked nicely under the blankets.

So she took it a step further. She reached over to her automatic IV unit and pressed the off button. Then she waited some more. No alarm sounded. No one came running.

"All right, then," she murmured to herself.

With her eyes on the door, she took ahold of the tape that held the plastic tubing to her hand and pulled it off. Then she pressed her pinky finger firmly against the port and tugged out the tube itself. It came free with ease—no mess, no pain. It was almost too easy.

Nadine breathed out. Maybe she should've felt a bit of guilt as she shouldered into her sweatshirt. Or as she grabbed her shoulder bag. Maybe she should've admitted that it was a bit unreasonable to go running out of the care facility like she was doing. But she wasn't going to let either thing stop her. No way would being stuck where she was get her any closer to getting justice for her brother. Or any closer to filling in the gaps in her memory. She needed to be moving. Looking. And in order to do those things, she couldn't be kept under guard in a hospital bed.

She cast a final look over the room, slid her feet into her slippers and slipped out into the hall.

As Detective Anderson Somers rounded the corner in the hall that led to ward 3B, he just about dropped his coffee. A woman who looked an awful lot like Nadine Stuart was moving very quickly in the other direction.

Blond hair, almost shaved up one side and a shock of bluntly straight locks on the other. *Yep.* Brown eyes, a little guarded and a lot defiant. *Uh-huh.* Then she turned her head just enough that he could see the distinctive scar along the line of her cheek. It was her. No doubt. Complete from the rosebud mouth to the sheep-print pajama bottoms.

For a second, Anderson was too startled to do much more than stare. What was she even doing awake, let alone scurrying through the hall? It was two in the morning. He'd barely seen her out of the bed since she'd been admitted the week before, and less than five minutes earlier, he'd checked in on her to make sure she was asleep before he took off to grab some coffee that wasn't vending-machine swill.

"Were you faking it, princess?" he wondered aloud.

She must've been. It wasn't like she'd made it a secret that she wasn't happy being cooped up. Imprisoned, she'd called it at one point. So it shouldn't be much of a surprise that she would—

"Dammit," Anderson muttered, his brain catching up to the fact that she was on the run just as she disappeared into one of the elevators at the end of the hall. "You *were* faking it."

He took a final, irritated sip of his coffee, then set it down on the lip of a nearby trash bin and strode after her. When he reached the elevators, though, his mood grew even sourer. The lights over the first set of doors—the ones that had swallowed Nadine—were burned out, so he couldn't tell if she'd headed for the lobby or the underground exit or some other escape route entirely. The second set of doors had been hung with an out-of-service sign. To top it all off, as Anderson turned to the final set, a team of frantic nurses pushed by him, wheeling a gurney and a crash cart. He jumped out of their way. Even if it wouldn't have been tacky to join them in the elevator, there wasn't room.

With a frustrated grumble, he spun toward the stairs. At least shoving the heavy door open provided a much-needed release of annoyance. Slamming his feet into the concrete steps was pretty good, too. As he moved down them as quickly as he could, he tried to calm his mind.

He considered himself to be a patient man. More than reasonable. Since the moment his partners had asked him to keep tabs on Nadine Stuart, however, both his patience and reason had been sorely tested. From her snippy comments and looks full of distaste to her need to call him by his title—Detective with a capital *D*—every time no one else was in earshot, yeah, she was definitely putting him about as close to the edge as he ever got. It was the whole reason he'd moved from keeping vigil *inside* her room to acting a glorified bodyguard *outside* of it instead.

He kept reminding himself that she'd been through some tough things in the last little while. Things that could break a person. Losing her brother violently. Being thrust under the very dark microscope of Jesse Garibaldi—the same man who was responsible for his own father's death fifteen years earlier.

Jesse Garibaldi.

Just thinking that man's name was enough to make Anderson grit his teeth.

Fifteen years, he and his three partners had been chasing the man. They'd finally found him holed up here in Whispering Woods.

Holed up? No. That's not quite right.

The evil man wasn't in hiding. He was in plain sight. Ruling the town through money. Using the people in it to further his own agenda.

Anderson knew just what it felt like to be on the losing end of that particular stick. He wouldn't wish it on anyone. Smart-mouthed Nadine Stuart included.

Somehow, though, being forced to chase the woman through the medical center dulled his ability to be quite as sympathetic as he should be. What kind of person ran from help? She had to know unequivocally that Anderson wasn't a threat. Hell. She was the only person in all of Whispering Woods who was fully aware of his agenda.

It made little sense to buck against his protection. All the stubbornness in the world wouldn't keep her safe if Garibaldi got ahold of her.

Anderson had reached the landing that led to the lobby then and paused in his run. Going out that way was the straightest shot to freedom. It meant going past the information and intake desk, but it was still the quickest route out. Would Nadine be most interested in speed, or would she try to do something trickier? If he had to guess, he'd say she was the kind of woman who'd go for clever. Of course, she'd also probably assume that Anderson wouldn't be far behind. He weighed the options, then eyed the door and made his decision.

"Lobby it is," he said, his voice echoing through the stairwell.

He pushed through and found the wide space almost empty. The only person in sight was a solitary woman sitting behind the desk with her nose buried in a book, and she didn't even glance up as Anderson walked straight up to her. He fought a need to grit his teeth at the lack of security and told himself that a care facility like this one wasn't *supposed* to be under lock and key. It was the reason his own presence was a necessity. Still, he would've felt a little better if he thought that Nadine had met with a bit of a challenge.

He cleared his throat and fixed a polite smile onto his face. "Excuse me?"

The woman lifted her eyes and aimed a bored stare his way. "Yes?"

"Sorry for the interruption, but did you happen to see a blonde woman come by in the last minute or two?"

"People come and go all the time."

"This one would've been in pajamas."

"Pajamas?"

"With a sheep theme."

"Are we talking about a patient?"

Anderson pressed his lips together for a moment before answering. Sounding the alarm about a patient on the run seemed a bit over the top. He somehow doubted it would help Nadine want him around, too.

"Just a woman with a strong love of casual wear," he said.

"And casual wear is now sheep-themed pajamas?" The woman lifted a dubious eyebrow.

"Guess it is."

"Then, no."

"No?"

"I haven't seen a blonde woman in casual wear come by in the last one or two minutes."

"You're sure?"

"Every person who comes in or out has to walk right past me."

"True enough. Thanks anyway."

Fighting a need to curse, he turned back toward the stairs and stopped. From where he stood, he could hardly *see* the first set of elevator doors. He was standing up. If he'd been sitting down like the woman behind the desk, he doubted he'd be able to see them at all. It'd be easy enough to exit the elevator and veer to the right instead of the left.

"What's at the other end of the hall?" he asked.

The woman let out a sigh. "What?"

Anderson pointed. "If I went down there instead of past you."

"Staff lounge."

"Any way to get out?"

"Are you sure this isn't about a patient?"

"Yes," he lied.

She sighed again. "There's an exit. But in order to get to the exit, you need to get into the staff lounge. And in order to get into the staff lounge, you need a passkey. So unless your friend in the pajamas is a staff member, she couldn't have gone that way."

Anderson forced another smile. "Thanks again."

His cop's gut was rearing its head, telling him that Nadine would've found a way. He didn't waste time questioning his instincts. Moving quickly, he took long, decisive steps across the linoleum. In seconds, he reached a door clearly labeled with a Staff Lounge sign. There he stopped and studied the locking mechanism. It was a simple, magnetic swipe system. With a quick glance around, he yanked his wallet from his pocket and chose a card at random, then jammed it into the slot. The light above the handle flickered but stayed red. He yanked his card free and threw the door a glare.

"Card get demagnetized?" said a voice from over his shoulder.

Anderson turned and nodded at the man who'd appeared behind him. "Guess so."

The man smiled. "Happens to me about twice a week. Gotta love overpriced technology that only works a quarter of the time. Here, I'll let you in with mine."

"Thanks."

A heartbeat later, he was standing inside the supposedly secure staff lounge, his eyes on the glass door at the rear of the room. Through it, he could see just what he needed to.

*Nadine Stuart.*

She was planted on the edge of the sidewalk in the taxi zone, her head down, her cell phone pressed to her ear. Anderson walked toward the door, watching as she hung up, stuck the phone into her bag, then fixed her eyes straight ahead. When she started to cross the narrow strip of pavement in front of her—presumably toward the bench she had in her sights—a navy-colored car on the same side of the road started to move, too. First at a crawl. Then a little faster.

Worry hit Anderson like a truck.

He threw himself against the door, slamming it open so hard that he half expected it to shatter or at least crack. He didn't stop to check if it did. He dived forward. He wrapped his arms around Nadine's waist. And he pulled her out of sight and out of harm's way a heartbeat before the navy car screeched through the spot where she'd just been standing.

# *Chapter 2*

Nadine's chest compressed and the air blew out of her lungs as her body flattened between Anderson's solid form and the concrete pillar behind her. Vaguely she was aware that just ahead on the other side of the bushes where they now stood, a car had first careened to a halt, then peeled out. But, mostly, the man pinning her to the spot took her attention.

His arms were firm around her waist, his hands warm on her hips. If she'd been able to breathe, she might've demanded to know what he thought he was doing. As it was, all she could do was work to draw in a gasp of air as she glared up at him. His ocean-blue eyes stared back, no apology for the intrusion touching them. She wondered why she hadn't noticed before how intense and stormy his irises were. She felt like she was being sucked in. Drowning. But maybe in a good way. If that was even possible.

After what felt like a lifetime but what really couldn't

have been more than few seconds, he finally released his hold on her. Physically, anyway. His gaze still held her.

"Are you trying to get yourself killed?" he demanded gruffly.

She sucked in a trickle of oxygen, then managed to exhale a single-word reply. "No."

"Could've fooled me."

She tried again. *Inhale. Exhale. Inhale. Speak.*

"How do you figure?" It was better, if only slightly.

"You snuck out of the hospital and—"

"Care center."

"What?"

"It's technically not a hospital."

"So?"

"So if you're going to throw around accusations, you should get your facts straight first."

"Are you *helping* me argue?"

"Someone has to. Clearly."

His mouth twitched just a little. "Okay. You snuck out of the *care facility* and—"

"Sneaked," she corrected.

"Really?"

"Well. It's the more correct word. *Snuck* is acceptable, but if you want to sound smart…"

"So I seem like I care if I sound smart?"

"Do you really want me to answer that?"

"Fine. You *sneaked* out of a *care facility* where you're supposed to be on bed rest with IV fluids because you suffered a head injury. In the middle of the night. Does that cover my concern about the death wish?"

"I asked to be checked out days ago," she replied. "And they were going to let me go until *you* talked them into keeping me. My leaving isn't a death wish. It's a preservation of my sanity."

"In your attempt to preserve your sanity, did it slip

your mind that it's not safe for you to be walking around alone?" he countered.

"I live here. I need to be able to cross the street without a bodyguard."

"Someone just tried to run you down, Nadine."

"Accidents happen."

His mouth set in a flat line for a second before he answered. "You really think that was an accident?"

Her heart fluttered nervously, but she brushed it off. "Of course."

"It's the middle of the night. The spot where you crossed was well lit. There were no other cars, no other people and no *reason* for whoever that was to come tearing through like that. Think about it for just a second."

She swallowed. She'd been so wrapped up in her escape that she hadn't been paying much attention to what was happening around her. Had she even noticed the car before it zoomed past? Would she have seen it at all if it weren't for Anderson? And if she *had* seen it, would it have been too late?

*And what about the most important question?* added a pushy little voice in her head. *Is Anderson right? Was the swipe in my direction purposeful?*

Now that he'd put the idea forward, she couldn't deny that it was a possibility. She'd seen what Jesse Garibaldi's men—or one of them, anyway—was capable of. Her brother's death was proof of the ruthlessness. And that didn't even factor in the pipe bomb and fire that had killed her father and scarred her for life.

Unconsciously, she lifted her fingers and ran them over the puckered marks that followed the curve of her cheek. And unexpectedly, Anderson's hand joined hers. She was too surprised to pull away. Even when he tipped her face up so that their eyes locked again, she didn't move. Or maybe she couldn't.

"Now that you're thinking about it," he said softly, "and you see that it might be true, do you understand why I might think you're putting yourself in danger by running out like that?"

Nadine drew a breath. It annoyed her that he was right. It got her back up just enough that she couldn't help but shake her head, and the motion dislodged Anderson's grip. For a second, his hand hung in the air. Then he dropped it and shook his head, too.

"No?" he said. "Really? You can't even acknowledge that staying here might be safer for you?"

"It doesn't matter if you're right or not," she replied. "What matters is that I'm being treated like an incompetent invalid. I'm the one who found Garibaldi's underground storage unit. Didn't your partner tell you that?"

"Of course he did. Brayden told me—and the others—everything before he and Reggie left for Mexico." He shot her a *look* as he said it.

She refused to be embarrassed. When "everything" happened, Nadine hadn't known that Brayden Maxwell was an undercover detective searching for Jesse Garibaldi. All she'd been sure of was that Reggie Frost—a waitress at the local diner—had witnessed her brother Tyler's murder. Nadine had just been protecting herself. So, yes. "Everything" *might've* included knocking Anderson's friend on the head, a little bit of breaking and entering, and a small run-in with Reggie. But it also meant she'd kept her identity a secret, eluded a trained professional and only come forward because she wanted to.

Her reply came out strong. "So if you know *everything*, then why am I being kept tied to a bed in a hospital?"

He scratched at his chin, his face showing his frustration clearly. "Look, Nadine…"

"Yes, Detective?" There was more than a hint of sarcasm in her reply.

"It's just plain safer for you to be in one spot."

"My apartment is one spot."

"Your apartment is also private."

"Isn't that better?"

"No. The hosp—care center, I mean, is full of people around the clock. Approaching you there would be a dangerous move for Garibaldi." He spit out the man's name with a grimace, then added, "We know that he doesn't want to expose himself publicly, so staying here..."

"But for how long, Anderson? There are only fifteen long-term rooms here, and if I had to guess, I'd say you can only talk the doctors into believing I'm more injured than I am for another few days at most. And after that, you can't expect me to just hide. The school is waiting for me to come back. People will start to talk. It's not like it's a secret that I'm here. You're protecting me and exposing me at the same time."

He had a funny look on his face, and she had a feeling he might've missed everything she'd just said.

"What's wrong?" she asked.

"That's the first time you've said my name."

"Is there something you'd *rather* be called? You don't look like much of an Andy, but if that's what you want..."

"No."

"Then what's the problem?"

"You've been calling me 'detective' for a week."

She crossed her arms over her chest. "Not when anyone can hear."

"No," he agreed. "When anyone can hear, you don't call me anything at all."

"We're getting off topic."

"You're right. We are. We need to be talking about you going back upstairs."

"No. We need to talk about the fact that I'm going home."

"You can't go home, Nadine. Garibaldi's men could be watching your apartment. Waiting for a wrong move."

Fear made her shiver. "I don't want to stay here."

He lifted his hand again, reached it toward his face, then dropped it to his side instead. "First, let's go back upstairs. If you really think you can't stay here, I'll call the team. I'll see what they say. We'll find a solution. I promise."

"You promise?" she echoed doubtfully.

"Do you think I like the idea of living my life on a bench outside your room? 'Cause I really don't. I can't get any further in my case if I'm playing watchdog. And I'd really like to build on what Brayden found out about Garibaldi."

"So go work on it, then."

"And leave you unprotected? I don't think so. That's not how I work. Whether you think so or not, keeping you alive is more important to me than making progress on the case."

Another snarky reply popped into Nadine's mind, but a trickle of conscience kept her from saying it aloud. She'd been right when she'd surmised that the detective had things he'd rather be doing. But she hadn't really considered it in terms of a sacrifice on her behalf.

"Okay," she said. "I'll go back up. But I don't want the IV. And I want to know that you're going to keep that promise."

His face cleared, a charming smile making an appearance. "I will."

"Don't be smug."

"I'll try not to be."

"*That* sounded smug."

"Sorry."

"Can we just go?"

"Yep." He stepped back and swept an arm out. "Ladies first."

Nadine snorted. She moved ahead of him anyway. But as they came out from their secluded spot, she stopped abruptly. The care center's lobby was jam-packed, and the wail of distant sirens cut through the air.

It took Anderson only a second to figure out that the facility was in the process of being evacuated. A couple of administrative staff held clipboards and were checking off names and filtering people through to frazzled-looking medical personnel. Mobile patients to one spot. Those in wheelchairs to another. He cast a glance toward Nadine. Whatever was going on, he was damned sure it had something to do with her. Which meant he needed to get her as far away as possible.

He grabbed her elbow and started to steer her away from the building.

"Well," he said, "I guess you're going to get your wish and not be stuck here any longer."

She let him guide her for all of five steps before she planted her feet so hard that his fingers slipped from her arm. "Wait."

"Seriously?"

"Don't you think we should find out what's going on?"

"It's an evacuation."

"An evacuation? Why are they still inside, then?"

"They must be confident that whatever's happened, the lobby is secure," he said. "And they could be doing a full head count before they escort them all outside. Easier to keep everyone straight if no one can wander off."

Nadine's gaze swiveled sharply to the scene. "A head count?"

"Yes."

"So they'll figure out that I'm gone."

"Presumably. But I'm more concerned about making sure you're safe than I am about reassuring the staff that they've got the right number of patients."

"But it could be worse in the long run. I really think we should take a minute and ask what happened."

Anderson's teeth wanted to grind together, and he wondered if this new state of impatience was going to become permanent. "If I go over there and ask, will you agree to leave?"

She nodded. "It's not like I want to stay."

Now his teeth *did* grind together. "I'm going to walk you to the spot we were a second ago, and I want you to promise me you'll stay put."

Amusement made her brown eyes warm for a second. "Like a good girl?"

"Right. As if *that's* the role you're going for."

A laugh escaped her lips as his hand closed on her elbow again, and for a second, Anderson was surprised into stillness. In the week since he'd met her, he hadn't once heard Nadine laugh. It was a nice sound, and Anderson liked it enough that he almost forgot his irritation.

At least until she spoke again, her voice back to its slightly stinging tone. "Are we going?"

He jerked his head in a short nod of ascent. "Yep."

He guided her quickly to the other side of the bushes, shot her his best stern-cop look, then moved away again. Fast enough that she couldn't comment. As he strode toward the front of the building, though, he kind of wished he could hear that laugh of hers again. It was light and pleasant. Not quite musical. But almost.

Yeah, he definitely wanted to hear it again. Preferably soon.

He reached the automatic glass doors then, and they slid open. He tried to step through, smiling automatically as a woman in a nurse's uniform approached him right away and stopped him from going any farther.

"Can I help you, sir?"

"I hope so."

"Well, I'll try. But I'm afraid we've got a bit of situation and can't let in any visitors."

"Yeah, I figured that much out." He widened his smile. "I was actually *already* inside. Took a patient for a walk a short bit ago. Just a little worried about getting her back in."

"What's the patient's name?"

"Nadine Stuart."

The nurse bent to make a note, then lifted her head again and smiled back at him. "All right. She's accounted for."

"She is?" He couldn't quite keep the surprise from his voice.

She laughed. "That's a good thing. And her doctor himself noted that he saw her out here, so even better. We're actually taking everyone outside shortly so the police can do their thing. I'm going to suggest just sitting tight for now."

"Anything we should be worried about?" Anderson asked, relieved that if there had to be a head count error that at least it worked in his favor.

The nurse turned her head to the side like she was checking to see if anyone was listening before she leaned a little closer. "You're probably better to hear this from me anyway. Rumors from everyone won't be accurate."

"Definitely not."

"A patient saw someone in a mask sneaking around upstairs."

Anderson stifled a frown. "Scary."

The nurse nodded. "If it's true."

"You don't think it is?"

"Who knows? No one else saw anything. But the guy was adamant. Says Mr. Mask went right past his room on the third floor. So here we are."

"Well. Thanks for the tip."

"No problem."

He offered her a final smile, then turned on his heel. As he exited the door, he was glad to have left when he did—the siren was now at a high, and the familiar flash of blue and red appeared at the end of the block. He stepped up his pace to just under a jog and slid behind the bushes.

"All right, Nadine, I think we—"

His words died abruptly on his lips. The spot where he'd left her was empty.

"You've got to be kidding me," he muttered.

He turned back to the open space behind him, his head whipping back and forth in search of her. There was plenty to see—two police cars had driven up onto the shoulder of the road and the people inside were being moved, single file, to the exterior of the building. The one thing he saw no sign of was Nadine Stuart.

Cursing, Anderson swept his gaze wider.

Now seemed like a bad moment for to assert her need for independence. She might think she was taking advantage of the chaos, but the reality was that there were a dozen people who might see her and stop her. People who were—rightly—motivated to keep her from disappearing into the night. She sure as hell wouldn't want to be accosted by any well-meaning cops or doctors.

*Or by a masked lunatic roaming the halls.*

Anderson dropped another curse as a second possibility filled his mind.

*Maybe she didn't leave willfully. Maybe someone took her.*

Concern quickly overtook his irritation. He inched out a little farther, knowing that if he drew attention to himself—an out-of-place man hiding on the property—he'd risk sabotaging his whole case. The local cops wouldn't appreciate having their toes stepped on, and though his own boss had sanctioned the investigation, they were supposed to tread lightly until they had proof of Garibaldi's wrongdoings. Anderson knew he'd be walking a thin line if he got hauled in. He'd be asked questions he didn't want to answer.

*And that's not even factoring in Nadine.*

His jaw clenched with worry as he scanned the grounds and the crowd once more. Aside from the general confusion happening right then, he didn't spy anything that looked terribly at odds with the surroundings. No strange vehicles, no one lurking in the shadows. He breathed out, told himself that was a good indication that Nadine hadn't been grabbed, and he tried to focus on potential escape routes.

Where would *he* go if he was trying to escape notice and slip away? As soon as the question came into his head, he knew the answer. He'd try to blend in with the crowd. Take true advantage of the chaos so as not to stand out, then slip away the moment an opportunity presented itself. His eyes came to the group of people in the courtyard. Now that they were all outside and spread out a little, he could see that there weren't more than fifty of them. Ten or so medical personnel, half that many nonmedical staff, a few nicely dressed administrators, a few people who were casually dressed and appeared to be overnight visitors, plus two dozen patients in varying shapes, sizes and conditions. Anderson focused on the last group, ruling them out, one by one.

Nine were men. Six were kids. The remainder were women. A few were too old to fit the bill. A few were brunettes. One was on crutches, one in a wheelchair. Another, though, made Anderson narrow his eyes. The woman stood just outside of the main group, her shoulders slumped, a blanket draped over her head and squeezed at her chin.

*Bingo.*

He took one wide step toward the crowd. He started to

take a second, then stopped short as a hand landed on his arm. Instinctively, he spun, raising his fist as he prepared to defend himself.

# *Chapter 3*

By the time Nadine lifted her face, Anderson's balled-up fingers were already flying toward her face. She knew she should be pulling back or ducking—anything to protect herself from impact—but, instead, she panicked. She couldn't even squeeze her eyes shut; she just froze, waiting for impact. But it didn't come. His fist stopped just a hairbreadth from her cheek, so close that she could feel its warmth. It hung there for a long moment before it dropped down to close on her wrist. He pulled her back to the spot between the bush and the pillar and rounded on her.

"Nadine." Her name was almost a growl. "What're you doing?"

Her voice shook as she answered, "I was going to ask you the same thing."

He dropped his arm and he exhaled. "Where were you?"

Nadine held out her bag. "I dropped this when you saved me from the car."

"Well, I'm thrilled you're acknowledging that I saved

you. But I'm confused about why you thought it was a good idea to go grab the bag? *Now?*"

"I thought it would look suspicious just sitting there in the middle of the road."

"You could've been caught by the cops. Or by—" He cut himself off and shook his head. "We should leave."

But she wasn't going to just let it go—not with the way her heart suddenly jumped in her chest. "Or by who?"

"No one. Let's just go."

"By *who*, Anderson?"

"Whoever's after you, Nadine." His hand, which she just realized still clasped her wrist, gave her a little tug. "Let's talk about it in the car. I'm parked one street over and it'll only take a second to get there."

She dug her heels in stubbornly. "Did you see someone? Garibaldi?"

"*I* didn't."

"But someone else did?"

"A doctor saw you. Counted you in with the rest of the patients."

"That's bad?"

"Not specifically. But it means anyone could've seen you. C'mon." He dragged his fingers down, threading them through hers.

Heat jumped from the points where their skin met, startling her enough that she didn't resist when he pulled her along this time. Her hand even tightened on his as they slipped out of their hiding place. And she couldn't make it loosen. Thankfully, Anderson didn't notice. Or at least didn't comment as he led her away from the hospital.

"Why were you going *back* down in the crowd by the care center?" Nadine asked, trying to distract herself from how natural and reassuring it felt to be holding his hand. "The cops were already there."

"Because I was looking for you."

"But I was meeting you by the bushes."

"You were supposed to *wait* by the bushes," Anderson corrected.

"Didn't you think I'd come b—" She cut herself off as she clued in. "You thought I ran off on you."

"Is it much of a stretch?"

Nadine felt an odd warmth creep up her cheeks, and she silently scolded herself for blushing.

Aloud she said, "I told you I would stay."

She could swear Anderson was eyeing the pink in her face as he lifted an eyebrow her way. "Pretty sure you gave your doctor the same impression before sneaking off in the dead of night."

"Ha-ha."

He stopped in front of a midsize pickup truck, and when he freed his fingers from Nadine's to grab his keys from his pocket, she immediately experienced a pang at the loss of contact. It was accompanied by an urge to reach out and grab his hand again. She actually had to fight to shake off the need to do it, and she was suddenly glad that her cheeks were already heated. At least it provided a good cover for the new embarrassment tickling at her now. And the embarrassment only intensified as Anderson took a chivalrous moment to open the passenger-side door for her before he moved to get in himself.

"You don't have to do stuff like that," she said.

Anderson frowned as he turned the key in the ignition. "Like what?"

"Opening the door."

"You don't want me to be *polite*?"

"You can be polite without being so nice."

He pulled the truck out onto the road. "You're going to have to explain that one to me."

Nadine sighed. "I know you'd rather be working the case. You just told me as much a few minutes ago."

"I *am* working the case. You're my connection to Jesse Garibaldi."

For some reason, the statement pricked at her. "You know what I mean."

"No," he said, "I'm not sure I do."

"You don't have to pretend that I'm not an inconvenience by being thoughtful."

"Did it ever occur to you that I might just *be* thoughtful?"

"No."

"No?"

"Why would you be thoughtful toward me? I'm disrupting your investigation."

"You don't think all people need thoughtfulness, you know…just because?"

"That's not what— Ugh."

"Ugh?" His mouth twitched.

"I'm not saying this because I don't think people deserve respect in a general sense."

His tiny smile slipped away completely. "You think that *you* don't deserve respect?"

"No. I mean yes. Of course I deserve respect."

"Just not from me?"

She couldn't help but glare at him. "You are *seriously* a pain in the—"

"Hold on. I thought I was too nice."

"Now you're getting it."

His mouth quirked up again. "I'll work on that."

Fighting a huff—she already felt enough like a petulant teenager—Nadine focused her gaze out the windshield. But as she saw where they were, she realized they were going in the wrong direction.

"You've gone past the turnoff for my place," she said.

"We're not going to your place. If Garibaldi's feeling

bold enough to come after you at the care facility, I don't think he'd hesitate to send someone to your home, too."

In her need to tell Anderson to stop being so nice, the immediate threat had slipped to the back of her mind. Now she wondered how that was even possible.

"Is that what you were saying before?" she asked. "About someone else seeing Garibaldi?"

Anderson's hands tightened in the wheel. "A patient reported a masked man in the hall on the third floor."

"My floor."

"'Fraid so. Not much of a consolation, but I doubt it was the man himself. More likely one of his thugs."

"The same person in the car?"

"Or working with him."

She made herself straighten her shoulders and speak in a strong voice. "So what's the plan, then?"

"I've got a room at the Whispering Woods Lodge. We'll go there, I'll contact my partners and we'll decide from there what to do."

"You know that Garibaldi owns the lodge, right?"

"I do."

"So you don't think going there might be a little counterproductive?"

"That's the whole point. He won't be looking under his own nose."

Nadine shook her head. "But if he's looking for you now, too, he'll probably figure out pretty quickly that we're there."

"My room's booked under a pseudonym, and there's a conference of some kind at the hotel, so plenty of random names on the books."

"Were you also wearing a disguise when you checked in? Because if Garibaldi was casing the hospital, his guys'll know what you look like and it won't matter what name you used or how many people are staying there."

"Trust me," he said. "I've covered my bases."

"What does that mean?"

"Just that I've got a valid excuse for hanging around."

"What does that— You know what? Never mind. I don't think I want to know."

"Probably not."

But something about the way he said it doubled her curiosity. She couldn't quite pinpoint his tone. A little amused and a little...*something*...that made her want to blush again for no good reason. And of course the idea of blushing made her feel prickly yet again.

Fighting yet another sigh, she looked down at her hands. She could swear that just a short time ago, she'd been a happy, well-adjusted person. A favorite teacher. Now she was on edge, pretty much 24/7. It almost made her pity the big, blond cop who sat beside her now. He was definitely *not* receiving the best of her.

*Why does it even matter whether or not he gets nice me or not-so-nice me? I'm his* case. *He just said so.*

But for some reason it did matter. Especially now that she'd thought consciously about it.

She stole a glance at him from the corner of her eye, trying to figure out why she suddenly cared what he thought. He looked the same as he had for the last week. Blond hair, a little too long and several shades darker than her own. Strong jaw, dusted with a few days' worth of scruff. He had nice, even features. The kind that were deceptively ordinary. But Nadine knew better. The moment he turned on that warm, genuine smile and flashed those drown-in-me eyes of his, he became anything but ordinary.

"Oh!" The word popped out before she could stop it—an exclamation of understanding.

The eyes in question flicked her way. "You all right?"

She forced herself to nod. "Fine."

"You sure?"

"Yes!" she snapped.

"Whoa." He shook his head and turned his focus to the road, then added in a mutter, "Just checking."

She bit back an urge to apologize. At least her short temper served a purpose at that moment. It was the perfect cover for the realization she'd just made. Whether she liked it or not, the reason she cared what her wannabe bodyguard thought about her was the fact that she found him stupidly attractive.

Anderson kept his gaze fixed straight ahead. He sensed some kind of internal struggle going on with the pretty little schoolteacher.

*Oh, she's pretty now, huh?*

He acknowledged the silent, self-directed question with a mental wave of his hand. Yeah, she was pretty. It wasn't really much of a debate. Just because he hadn't taken the time to think about it much before now didn't make it untrue.

Her petite, almost waiflike frame contrasted sharply with the fierceness in her eyes in a way Anderson liked. Her dramatic hairstyle hinted at the fact that under her sharp edges, she might actually have a fun side. He couldn't deny being curious about it.

*And her scar...*

He had to hold his head rigid to keep from swiveling to look at it. Of all her features, maybe he liked the nongenetic one best. The puckered marking that sliced across her jawline screamed of a will to survive. Nadine Stuart had been through literal fire and come out alive. Prickly or not, that one thing made her a hell of a lot more than pretty in Anderson's eyes. It infused him with sympathy, too.

A decade earlier, she probably thought she'd been through the worst. Then came the last couple of weeks. Witnessing her brother get shot. Being dragged into the

Garibaldi investigation. Dragged in *again*, if he was being accurate. Now this. She was stuck under his watchful eye against her will.

"I'll only keep you here as long as I have to," he said as he flicked on his turn signal and guided the truck onto the last road before the turnoff that led to the lodge.

Her head jerked his way, and for a second, he actually saw a bit of softness in her chocolate-colored stare. Then she spoke, and her fierceness overtook her features.

"Don't start worrying about my comfort now."

He fought yet another stab of impatience. "I'm irritatingly nice. I can't help but worry about it."

A spot of color darkened each of her cheeks. "I thought you were working on that."

"I am."

"Good."

"But in the meantime…" He trailed off, unsure what he wanted to suggest.

"In the meantime, what?" she pushed.

Impulsively, he veered off the road, put the truck into Park under the cover of a decent-sized patch of bushes and turned to face her. "I dunno. But we're stuck together for the time being, Nadine. So we need to do something that's going to make the bit of time we have to spend together less…confrontational."

He expected her to argue. To point out the relatively *nice* way he put things. Instead, she nodded slowly.

"Okay," she said. "What do you suggest?"

"Let's start over."

"Start over?"

"Pretend that we're meeting for the first time and that it's because we want to."

"Are you sure that's—"

"Worth a shot? Yes."

She sighed. "Fine. Introduce yourself."

He felt a smile building. "I'm Anderson Somers. Thirty years old. Single. I've been a full-fledged detective with the Freemont City PD for about four years. Before that, I was a patrolman."

"Do you like being a detective?"

"Most of the time," he said honestly.

"Really? Only most of the time?"

"That surprises you?"

"I just kind of assumed that all cops were gung ho or whatever. And it also surprises me that you'd be honest about it."

"One of those nice-guy faults."

"Must make it harder to be a cop."

"Being honest?" He felt his mouth tip up even more. "Shouldn't that make me a better cop?"

"Don't you sometimes have to manipulate people?" she wanted to know.

"I prefer not to."

"And it works not to?"

"I think I'm pretty damned good at it."

"So then…when *don't* you like it?"

"I didn't say I don't like it."

"You said you like it *most of the time*. That means that sometimes you don't."

"Ha. Busted. The truth is, I really like the investigative end of things. It always fascinated me as a kid, to see how my dad got from point A to point B. But if I'm being really honest, until my dad was killed, I always thought I'd take after my uncle and become a firefighter."

Sympathy softened her voice as she asked, "Why didn't you?"

"You already know my story."

She shook her head. "Nope. I don't. We just met, remember?"

"Right. I forgot."

"So. Tell me."

"Not gonna let it go?"

"No." She said it softly enough that he thought she might, if he pressed it.

He decided not to. She did know already anyway—she'd heard it from his partner, Brayden, during their previous run-in with Jesse Garibaldi—and sometimes it just felt good to say things aloud.

"Fifteen years ago, my father—a detective like me—was killed. Murdered via pipe bomb. Along with two other men. Those men's sons, myself included, vowed to find out why, and we vowed to do it by the book."

He didn't realize he'd closed his eyes until he felt Nadine's warm grip on his forearm. "So you became a cop."

He lifted his lids. "I did. *We* did."

"What else?"

"Does there need to be more?" It wasn't a bitter question, just a serious one.

"I guess there doesn't have to be," she conceded. "You've already said a lot for having just met me."

"That's way truer than you know."

"What do you mean?"

"The guys and I don't typically share any of that info. Only a handful of people know about the case."

"Well, then, I'm glad I inspire that kind of trust after knowing each other for five minutes." She flashed him a smile that, if he didn't know better, Anderson might've called saucy.

He fought a chuckle at the unexpected expression. "All right. It's your turn."

"Ready?"

"As I'll ever be."

"Okay. Well. I'm Nadine Elise Stuart. Twenty-six. I like dogs."

"Dogs?"

"Yes. And sunsets."

"Okay..."

"Oh. And long walks on the beach, and—"

He cut her off with a groan. "Really?"

She blinked innocently at him. "What?"

"That's the angle you're going to take?"

"We just met. So I don't want to give away too much too soon."

The chuckle wouldn't stay down this time. Anderson let it take over, rolling through his chest, up his throat, then out into the truck. It felt good. And it felt even better when Nadine joined in, her musical laugh mixing pleasantly with his, making it easy to forget the pressing issues at hand. As his mirth tapered off, though, his gaze slipped out the window just in time to catch sight of a navy sedan as it whipped by. Maybe it was the same one that had tried to run her down, maybe not. Either way, it was a sobering reminder that in spite of the light conversation, they were far from safe.

# Chapter 4

The slightly buoyant feeling in Nadine's chest faded as they neared Whispering Woods Lodge. It was nestled into a man-made valley, its peaked, full log roof visible from the top of the very long block that led down to its enormous outdoor parking lot. And, usually, just that first glimpse of the rustically styled hotel made her want to go inside. Or it always had when she was a kid, anyway. She remembered how quickly it had been built. How everyone in town heralded Jesse Garibaldi as some kind of miracle worker. The man was still new in town then, his investments in tourism and infrastructure still a novelty. At ten years old, the awe of the town reinforced what Nadine already believed. Garibaldi's power was endless. Then, it had impressed her. Now, it made her shiver.

"You all right?" Anderson's warm voice cut through her worry.

"I'm okay," she replied. "Just thinking about when this place opened fifteen years ago. My dad worked for Garibaldi, so we got a front-row seat. It was amazing. Inspiring and hopeful and…" She shrugged. "I was ten. So it was pretty cool."

"It's *still* pretty cool."

"Except knowing what I do about Garibaldi makes it harder to enjoy it. Like it's got a taint. Does that sound funny?"

Anderson's mouth set into a line before he answered. "The man's a murderer, Nadine. Everything he touches—or *has* touched—does have a taint."

*Does that include me?*

The question sprang to mind unexpectedly, and she wasn't able to dismiss it as easily as it had come. After all, Garibaldi *had* touched her life. He'd paid for her and her mother's move from Whispering Woods to Freemont. He'd covered her many hospital expenses and the costs of her father's funeral. Then he'd paid for her entire education. If the man's taint extended to people, she was probably at the top of the list.

She opened her mouth—maybe to say something about it, maybe not, she wasn't sure—but stopped as she realized Anderson had bypassed the main lot and was headed for the underground one.

"I don't think we can park in there," she said. "Staff and VIP guests only. Unless they've changed that."

He turned a rueful smile her way. "Open the glove box."

She did as he said, and when she flicked down the door, a laminated parking pass fell straight into her hands.

"Is it fake?"

"No."

Anderson lifted up the pass and placed it on the windshield, then offered the attendant in the parking booth a wave as they drove through.

"See?" he said. "Perfectly legitimate."

"Well, then…which one are you?" she asked.

"Which one?"

"Staff? Or suite?"

"Not staff," he replied, his voice matching his still-rueful expression.

"You're in a suite?"

"Trust me," Anderson said as he pulled into a spot, "I didn't book it that way. It was an accident."

"Seriously? How does that happen accidentally?" She couldn't keep the surprise from her response, and she realized she'd been expecting him to say that he'd acquired the pass through some twisty, undercover police deception.

"I guess they were overbooked," Anderson said. "C'mon."

Nadine frowned as she let herself out of the truck. It was well-known that as the only real hotel in Whispering Woods, the lodge offered a good-sized chunk of reasonably priced rooms and an even bigger set of moderately priced ones. But it was just as well-known that their block of suites were luxuriously equipped and had a cost to match that luxury. She had a hard time believing that the lodge would just give him an upgrade. Especially by accident.

"What did you tell them?" she asked.

"Tell who?" he replied innocently, moving around to her side of the truck and gesturing for her to start walking.

She planted her feet and narrowed her eyes. "Why?"

"Why what?"

"Stop that. Why did they give you an upgrade, Anderson?"

He sighed and ran a hand over his shaggy locks. "Look. It just kind of happened."

"What did?"

"I was checking in, and the girl behind the counter was friendly. Chatty. You know those dolls where you pull a string to make them talk?"

"Yes."

"She was like that. Only her string got stuck and she just kept going."

Nadine fought a laugh. "That's not very nice."

He shook his head. "I didn't say it was a bad thing. It was just a very full five minutes. She told me all about her life and the guy she was marrying. Her high school sweetheart. And she wanted to hear about me. So I told her my cover story, which is that I'm here visiting a friend at the care center."

"Me."

"Yes."

"What does that have to do with the room?"

"When I said *friend*, the girl at the counter took that to mean something more."

"And you didn't correct her?"

"It didn't seem important. And actually…"

"Actually *what*?"

"Let's get to the elevator first."

Nadine started to argue, then caught the obvious embarrassment on his face and relented temporarily. "Fine."

"We should take the service elevator. We'll run into fewer people, and if someone from the staff questions us, we'll plead error."

"Are we really that conspicuous?"

"*I'm* not." He cast a pointed look toward her legs.

She looked down and spotted her hospital-issue pajama pants. "Oh."

"I did offer to get you some clothes a few days ago."

"Don't rub it in."

"I wouldn't dare. Let's go."

She let him lead her across the cement. They moved past a set of slick faux-wood doors that led to the main elevators, then around a corner and up to another, far more utilitarian setup—plain gray metal. Anderson tugged on the handle, then stepped back to allow her to pass through first.

"What, no further criticism of my politeness?" he joked as she stepped across the threshold.

"I've temporarily suspended my aversion to it."

"Glad to hear it."

"Don't be. I might change my mind once I hear what you have to say about what you told the girl at the front desk."

His expression turned sheepish, and he didn't speak until they were in the elevator and on the way up.

"Once the check-in girl had put the idea out there," he said, "it seemed like a better option. Being your boyfriend instead of your friend gave me a better excuse for my vigil outside your room."

Nadine had to push off yet another need to blush and instead asked, "But if you were my boyfriend, why would you be staying at the lodge in the first place? Why wouldn't you stay at my place?"

Anderson cleared his throat. "Exactly what *she* wanted to know."

"And what did you tell her?"

"The first thing that came to mind. That you and I had a fight."

"About what?"

"You want to know what our fictional fight was about?"

"I think I have a right to know."

"What makes you even think I told the check-in girl what it was about?"

"Because you got a suite, and you didn't get it just because you lied about being my boyfriend. And speaking of lying..." Nadine crossed her arms. "I thought you were Mr. Honesty."

"Mr. Nice Guy," he corrected. "And aside from the fake name—which was a necessity—and the fake fight—which was a knee-jerk-reaction kind of excuse—the girl filled in the rest on her own. I mentioned she was chatty, didn't I?"

She rolled her eyes. "And what did she fill in?"

"That I was getting ready to propose, and you ran off to Whispering Woods to avoid me."

"Well, that's a hell of a leap."

Anderson chuckled. "You have no idea. One second I was single guy, checking into a hotel for a few days, and the next, I was chasing after a woman who refused to marry me."

"I'm afraid to ask how that led to the suite," she said.

"Well. When you see *which* suite it is, you might be able to *fill in* a few things on your own."

"Can't wait."

"I'm sure."

The elevator pinged then and came to a smooth stop. But as the doors slid open and Anderson pressed an arm against one of them so she could go by, Nadine had a sudden urge to run. To shove the thick-shouldered man aside and run straight down the hall without looking back. And it wasn't fear that fueled the need. It wasn't even some unspecific kind of apprehension. It was *anticipation*. An unexpected tingle that licked warmly up her feet and hands, moved inward, then settled somewhere in her gut. It was a heady feeling. Dangerous. Unexpected. And directly related to her attraction to Anderson and the fact that she was about to be very, very alone with him.

Well, that…and the gold-plated sign that hung on the wall just in view.

*Honeymoon Suite.*

And it got worse. As Nadine forced her feet to move her out into the hall, a girl who couldn't be more than twenty or so bounced into sight, her ponytail wagging and eyes sparkling at the two of them. Even without an introduction, there was no doubt about who she was—the chatty storyteller who was trying to seal Nadine and Anderson into a fake engagement.

Anderson stifled a groan. In his mind, it was already awkward enough that he'd been forced to confess to having gone along with the assumptions made by the check-in girl. Now he was going to have to own it, too. Taking a breath, he forced a smile onto his face. Then he slung his arm over Nadine's shoulders as casually as he could manage and bent a little to whisper, "Can't say I didn't warn you."

"It worked!" the check-in girl squealed as she approached. "I told you it would!"

"You sure did," Anderson agreed.

She turned her eyes to Nadine. "How did he do it? What part convinced you? Tell me the room had something to do with it! It was the room, wasn't it? Wait—why aren't you wearing the ring?"

"The ring?" Nadine repeated, her voice almost faint.

"You don't have it? It's still stuck down that sink?" Her eyes flicked between them. "Wait. You haven't even asked her yet, have you? Oh! I let the cat out of the bag?"

"Little bit," Anderson managed to say.

The girl's smile only faltered for a second. "Well. It's a good thing I came up to change the flowers in the nook. Ask her now."

"Now?"

"She's obviously not going to say *no*. Otherwise she wouldn't have come to the suite. Or the hotel at all. Besides that, I'm the perfect witness. Not so much of a crowd that she feels like she *has* to say yes, but the perfect person to capture the moment if she says yes. Give me your phone."

"My phone?"

"How else am I going to record it for you?"

Anderson eased away from Nadine, dug the slim device from his pocket and handed it over. The girl's grin just about split her face.

"Okay," she said. "Don't forget to get down on one knee. You want it to be good."

Anderson shrugged helplessly at Nadine. Her eyes were wide, her bottom lip tugged in. She looked nervous bordering on terrified, and Anderson wondered how *that* was going to translate in the recording.

He leaned toward her ear again. "You're going to have to fake it a little better than that, honey. Even Little Miss Chatterbox won't be fooled if you look like I'm trying to push you off a cliff."

Her lips turned up in an almost passable smile. "I might be fighting an urge to strangle you right now."

"Just a few moments and one proposal and you can strangle away." He winked, then dropped to his knee and shot a genuine smile up at her. "Nadine Elise Stuart. For as long as I've known you, you've sparked something special in me. I can honestly say you know more about me than most people. I feel like it only took five minutes to get to that point. Literally. So between that and the fact I've never seen anyone look quite so sexy in a pair of hospital pajamas, I was wondering if you'd do me the honor of marrying me?"

Nadine's mouth worked silently for a second. Her gaze was a little soft, a little amused and a little something else that he couldn't quite pinpoint. Finally, she nodded, and Anderson tipped his head toward the check-in girl.

"Good enough?" he asked.

She lowered the camera phone. "Close."

"Close?"

"You need the kiss."

*Crap.*

"We're not really into PDAs," he said.

The girl shook her head. "This isn't public. This is just

the two of you, plus your own personal videographer. Posterity."

"Still not really—"

"It's fine." Nadine's hand landed on his shoulder.

He looked up again. "What?"

"It's fine," she repeated.

Anderson pushed to his feet It was hard to stop his gaze from flicking down to her lips before shifting up to her eyes. Although it hadn't been directly on his mind before, to say he had zero interest in kissing her—now that it had been put in his head—would be a lie. But to say that he wanted to force her into doing it was an even bigger untruth. In fact, the idea made his gut twist and ache.

"Nadine?" His voice came out a little hoarse.

She smiled, and he couldn't help but note that now her eyes moved briefly to *his* lips. "Let's just not make it something we wouldn't want our kids to see, okay?"

"All right."

He stepped forward, then stopped just far enough away that they weren't touching. He started to tell her he wouldn't do it—couldn't under the circumstances—but one of her hands came up to his cheek, stilling his mouth. Nadine's palm was warm on his skin. It sent a shock of heat straight through him, and articulate thought flew away as she used her fingers to guide his face down toward hers. Instinct kicked in quickly. Especially when Nadine pressed up to her toes, stumbled a little and bumped up against him. Then his hands came up automatically to steady her. To pull her body flush to his.

"Ready?" she breathed.

He tried to say that he was, but her face tipped up then, and her lips grazed his, and words were no longer an option. Action, on the other hand…that was a different story.

Anderson lifted one of his hands up and placed it on the small of Nadine's back. The other he brought to the back of her neck in a caress. Her hair brushed his knuckles, and as short as it was cut, it was still softer than silk. Her mouth was softer still. Warm, too, and not just yielding. Eager and willing. Her lips pressed to his firmly, then pulled away, then pressed again. She tasted so good—felt so good—that he wanted to keep it going. True regret filled him when the check-in girl's voice interrupted the kiss.

"That's *perfect*!" she crowed. "And I think I got it all."

Anderson dragged his eyes open and stared down into Nadine's chocolate gaze for another second before releasing her. As heavy as her lids looked, she didn't blink. It was impossible to look away, and he couldn't quite resist the need to drag his thumb over her lower lip.

"Nothing the kids wouldn't want to see," he murmured.

"Yes," she agreed.

"All right!" The ponytailed girl pushed in between them, shoving the phone at Anderson. "Promise her you'll get her a proper ring. No. Not just a proper one. The perfect one. To go with the perfect proposal and the perfect kiss. Did you hear that? He's going to get you something absolutely perfect."

"I heard it," Nadine said.

Anderson couldn't help but shoot her a surprised look. "You did?"

"Didn't you?" She lifted an eyebrow, undisguised mirth evident in her eyes.

"I guess I did."

"Oh, my gosh!" interjected the girl. "I can't wait to see it! But you better get going because those strawberries and champagne you just *have* to order will be up soon."

Then she flounced off in the other direction. Anderson shook his head in disbelief, then dragged his wallet out to free his key card, apologizing as he opened the door to the suite.

"That was…interesting. I'm sorry if—" He cut himself off as Nadine pushed by him, bent over and let out a strangled gasp, then collapsed to the edge of the couch.

He took a step closer, but she waved him off. Her shoulders shook, and for a second Anderson thought she was crying. He moved closer again, concern flowing in. When she lifted her head, though, he saw that tears weren't the case at all. She was *laughing.*

He frowned. "What's funny?"

She gasped out a sentence between laughs. "That—girl's—poor—fiancé."

"What?"

"She must just *steamroll* him. Can you imagine? Do you think he even meant to start dating her, let alone get engaged to her?"

He felt his lips twitch; it was good to see Nadine so relaxed. "Hard to say."

"Or maybe he's just like she is. Scripting his life aloud like that, too. I wonder what happens if their stories conflict?"

"God knows." He stepped past the couch and sank into the enormous chair on the other side of coffee table. "I really am sorry we had to go through all that."

"Which part?" she replied. "The running, the sneaking, the lying…or the kissing?"

"Yep."

"That's not really an answer."

"I know."

Nadine laughed again and leaned back, her gaze sweeping over the room. "It really is pretty swanky. Everything I imagined as a kid. We were supposed to take a tour not long after Whispering Woods opened, but I got the flu, and we never found the time to reschedule. I guess I never had a reason to come back. You don't really visit hotels in your own town, do you?"

"No, not so much."

"I used to dream about coming in here, though." Her eyes flicked around again. "I'm not sure if I wish I'd seen it before, or if I'm glad I'm seeing it like this for the first time."

Anderson surveyed the space himself. Aside from tossing his suitcase to the ground when he'd first arrived, he hadn't spent much time inside at all. He really hadn't taken the time to look around at all. Now he could see that it was tastefully decorated with boldly romantic coloring. Not rustically styled like the exterior of the lodge. Instead, the suite was…soft. Cream walls and cream carpet with pops of burgundy that added a touch of sexiness. He wondered absently what the bedroom looked like. Then his eye caught Nadine, and the wondering became a little less absent.

He cleared his throat and made himself ask in a teasing voice, "The honeymoon suite, specifically?"

Nadine shot him a dirty look. "No. Being a bride wasn't high on my list of fantasies."

"Not one of those little girls, huh?"

"My dad's driving job made him keep weird hours. His secret, second family took him away even more." She made a face and then went on. "When I was little, I thought all fathers and husbands spent that much time apart from their families. I didn't like it much and didn't want a life like that. But then I found out the truth, and it was even worse, so… Sorry. You probably don't want to hear all that."

Anderson shook his head. "Don't be sorry. I like to listen to stories about other people's abnormal upbringings. They make my own seem that much saner."

"Ha-ha."

"I'm serious. My parents were high school sweethearts who dropped out of school when they found out they were expecting me. They used to do what they called high-five parenting. My dad would work all night at the gas station while my mom and I slept. Then he'd come home, and she'd go to work at the grocery store. We moved around a lot because they could rarely keep up with rent."

Nadine winced. "That must've been hard for you. And them."

Out of habit, he shrugged off the sympathy. "It was just life. It wasn't until I started school that I realized ramen noodles and frozen vegetables and boxed cereal weren't the only things on the menu. A weird little light bulb went off in my five-year-old brain. I kept my mouth shut about it until third grade. Then I vividly remember coming home and telling my mom about some of the things the kids brought in their lunch boxes and how I wanted them. I'd worked out a whole plan on how unfair it was that they made me so different. She cried. That same night, we moved again. This time from our apartment to my grandparents' place. I thought it was my fault for wanting some packaged fruit snacks."

"But it wasn't. Of course."

"No."

Anderson looked down at his hands, recalling the confusion and misguided guilt. It wasn't a memory he normally shared. Or one he even liked to think about. He got the feeling, though, that it was doing Nadine good to hear it. Her face was open and interested, her body leaning forward. She'd been through a hell of a lot over the last little while. Anderson might not have been there when her brother was killed, but he was more than happy to try to make things a little easier for her now.

*And it feels good to get it off my chest, too*, he admitted to himself.

That was a surprise. One he didn't want to reason through right that second. Or even have time to think about. He had a case to concern himself with. A bad guy he needed to keep away from Nadine, a worse guy he needed to connect their current predicament to and fifteen years' worth of justice to serve out.

He brought his gaze up again with the intention of saying as much. But his mouth had different ideas.

"My mom never told me directly," he said, "but there were lots of whispers, and I heard them all. The day I came home and complained was the same day my dad left her a Dear John letter."

"Your dad left the two of you behind?"

"For about six months. My grandparents only took us in on the condition that my mom never have contact with him again. I learned that from the whispers, too. They hated him. Thought he wasn't good enough for her. So they weren't very happy when he turned up on their doorstep."

"But your mom took him back, just like that?"

Anderson laughed. "Not even close. It took my dad a month just to get her to talk to him again. He showed up every morning with a cup of coffee and a single rose."

"Persistent," Nadine stated.

"And apologetic. A lot."

"So what was his excuse for leaving in the first place?"

"Turns out his opinion of himself coincided with the one my grandparents had."

"He thought you and your mom would be better off without him."

"Exactly. But it turned out he was more selfish than he thought."

Nadine's brows knit together. "What do you mean?"

Anderson smiled. "He hated being away from us more than he wanted to make things better for us, apparently. So he came up with a plan—become a cop."

"I guess it would be hard for your grandparents to argue with that."

"Yep. My mom, too. She loved him, and when he told her he'd enrolled in the training program already…"

"What? She was powerless to say no?" Her smile softened the question.

He met her eyes. "Isn't that what true love is all about?"

"Powerlessness?"

"Yep."

"I *hope* not."

"You sure about that?"

"Why would anyone want to be powerless to say no?"

He leaned forward. "Because it's two sides of the same coin when you're really in love. All powerful and completely powerless at the same time."

"Do you know that firsthand?"

Nadine's face didn't change as she spoke, but the air in the room was another story. It shifted. Warmed. And Anderson couldn't help but wonder if the question held more meaning than a simple addition to the conversation.

# *Chapter 5*

As soon as the words were out of Nadine's mouth, she knew how they sounded. But she couldn't make herself take them back. Not even as the silent seconds ticked by. After all…was there anything wrong with wanting to know a little bit about the man she'd just kissed? About the man with whom she was—at least temporarily—sharing a hotel room?

*Sure*, said a voice in her head. *Nothing wrong with knowing a little about him. But the details of his love life? Whole different story.*

Clearly she was letting the fake engagement and the honeymoon suite go to her head. She hadn't even thought about Garibaldi or his masked henchman since the second Anderson's lips had met hers. Every ounce of worry had slipped away in those few seconds. So had any sense of reason. She shivered a little at the recent memory. Unconsciously, her tongue came out to touch her lower lip—the last spot his mouth had made contact with hers.

She noticed that his gaze dropped, following the motion. And she was suddenly sure that if she didn't speak, Anderson might dive over the hand-carved table in front of them and bury her mouth in another kiss. And there was no chance she'd stop him. Not after the way her toes had curled out there in the hallway.

She drew in a breath and, in a carefully detached voice, said, "You haven't answered."

"About whether or not I've been in love?" Anderson replied. "No."

"Not once?"

"I'd know, wouldn't I?"

"I guess so."

"What about you?" he wanted to know.

"Mmm," she responded.

After the briefest consideration, she decided there wasn't much point in lying. "I loved a man. But it turned out that he didn't love me back."

Anderson's expression went from curious to stiff. "Want to elaborate?"

"I don't know," she said honestly

For a second, he looked surprised. "You don't know?"

"It all fell apart about six months ago. I haven't really talked about it since."

"At all?"

"No."

"Not to a friend? A colleague?"

"No."

"Why not?"

"Because it's embarrassing, Anderson. I dated a man for two years. I lived with him for six months, and I trusted him. I thought we had a life together. Then I found out the jerk was having an affair. Multiple affairs over the years. And you know what he said when I caught him?"

She couldn't help but lift her chin in a challenge, daring him to make a guess.

But he just shook his head, his eyes stormy, and said, "Whatever his excuse was, it wasn't good enough."

The vehemence in Anderson's voice rendered Nadine momentarily speechless. She wasn't sure what to make of the unexpected fierceness in his eyes. Was the flash of protectiveness mere chivalry? Or was it something to do with her specifically?

*And why do I hope it's the latter?*

Taking a breath, she forced off the unnerving feelings tumbling through her chest. "It's not as bad as it seems."

He lifted a solitary brow. "You're defending him?"

"No. I— Well, not exactly." She shook her head, realizing how wishy-washy she sounded. "No."

"You sure about that?"

"I'm sure."

He studied her face like he was trying to be certain she was telling the truth, then issued a short nod. "All right. What was his excuse?"

"That he didn't realize we were exclusive."

"But you lived with him?"

"Yes."

"I don't buy it."

"Neither did I. Not when he first said it, anyway. I kept waiting for the other shoe to drop. There had to be something else."

She didn't realize she'd lifted her hand to her scarred cheek until Anderson leaned forward and his palm came up over top of hers. He slid his fingers over her knuckles and pressed the tips into the sensitive skin there. Nadine let him tug their clasped hands to her knee.

"You mean something about *you*?" Anderson asked gently.

"Something about me," she agreed. "Or something he

could *make* be about me. I knew it wasn't my fault that he slept around."

"Of course it wasn't."

"But I thought Grant would make it that way. That he'd say I'd been cold or distant or too focused on my job or too…something else. Except he never did. And the more I thought about, the more I realized he was right." It felt good to make the admission aloud.

But Anderson looked unconvinced, and his words echoed his expression. "How do you figure?"

"We never said it."

"That you were exclusive? Seems like kind of a given, considering your living arrangement."

"No. We never said the other stuff." Her face warmed.

Anderson's frown only took a second to clear. "Ah. No great professions of love."

"Exactly. And I guess it was kind of weird to go that long without exchanging the actual words. I mean, why hadn't we? Why didn't it ever come up? If someone had asked me directly if I loved Grant, I would've said yes, unequivocally. But when I really stopped to think about it—which I only did because of his claim that we weren't exclusive—it was pretty strange that I'd never told him. Not at the end of a phone conversation, not when he left for work in the morning…" She trailed off and shrugged helplessly.

"Is it what you wanted?"

"It's what I thought I had."

"That wasn't my question."

"I know."

He opened his mouth, then closed it like he'd changed his mind about whatever he was going to say, then squeezed her hand and asked, "So what happened after you found out?"

"I shoved everything I could into a suitcase, rented a

hotel room—far less swanky than this one—took a week off work and sulked."

"And your ex?"

"Was clueless. He sent me a text suggesting that we convert the office to a second bedroom and keep living together."

Anderson studied her for a second. "Can I make an observation?"

"Sure," Nadine said. "It's not like I haven't already totally embarrassed myself."

He shot her a look. "It's not embarrassing to have a relationship not work out."

"No. But it's pretty embarrassing to admit that your relationship wasn't a relationship at all."

"It just means it wasn't meant to be."

"Do you seriously want me to believe that's what you think?"

"What's not to believe? Too cheesy?"

"By far."

"That just means you weren't listening."

"What? When?"

"When I told you about my parents."

"I was so. I just—" Nadine cut herself off, midprotest.

Anderson jumped in right away. "You just what? Heard what I said, but then remembered how it ended? The part where my dad died?"

He didn't sound bitter, just matter-of-fact, but that didn't make Nadine feel any better. Because it was exactly where her mind had gone. And that actually made it so much worse.

She made herself nod, just once. "I really am sorry that your parents didn't get the long, happy ending they deserved."

He released her hand and folded one leg up and put his foot onto his knee. "It may not have been all that long, but it *was* happy. They were young when they met, and aside from that little blip where my dad left, things were good for them. Nearly fifteen years. Hell of a lot more time than people put in nowadays. And when my dad was killed, my mom tried hard to make sure I remembered the happy stuff."

"Did it work?"

"In some ways. It worked for me in that I remember my dad as being a great man. It worked for her in that when she met another great man three years later, she was able to remarry and give me a couple of awesome little sisters." His mouth tipped up, and his eyes shone fondly.

Nadine didn't really want to dampen his good spirits, but she couldn't seem to stop herself from blurting out the obvious contradiction. "But you're still *here* in Whispering Woods. If things worked out the way they were supposed to, then how come you still feel like you need to go after Garibaldi?"

"I've asked myself a thousand times how to reconcile the two things in my head. If my dad were alive, I wouldn't have my sisters. I wouldn't have my stepdad, Walt. But I could never call his death a positive thing." His voice roughened a little at the end, and he paused to clear his throat before continuing. "The only choice I have is to accept the past, try to give him the justice he deserves and move on with the future."

"You're a real romantic at heart, aren't you?" The question slipped out before Nadine could bite her tongue and keep it in.

Anderson smiled again, and this time the warmth in his eyes was directed right at her. "You make that sound like a bad thing."

"I guess it's just surprising."

"What? That a man can admit to having a softer side?"

"That, too. But also to hear about everything you've

been through and to know that you still have hope at the end."

"Now who's the romantic?" He said it in a teasing voice, but his gaze held something more serious, and whatever it was, it wrapped around Nadine in a way that made her tingle.

His hand came out again to reach for hers, and when his thumb traced the back of her hand, she dropped her gaze to watch the lazy circle it made. The tingle expanded to become a full-body buzz. And suddenly she *wanted* him to dive across the table. She even wondered a little why he hadn't done it already. He had to be able to feel the same tug that she did. She lifted her eyes again, and they immediately found Anderson's attention locked on her.

The strength of the need to feel his lips again startled her, and she jerked her hand away, breaking their connection.

She exhaled, trying to clear her head. "Are you going to place that call?"

Anderson shifted in his seat. "What?"

"To your partners? You know…about what to do with me?"

"Right."

He didn't move, and Nadine almost wanted to laugh. "Anytime soon?"

"Yep."

He dug into his pocket, but his gaze didn't leave her face. Even as he slid his fingers over the phone to dial automatically, he didn't glance down, and the heat in the air didn't dissipate. If anything, it rose. Like the only thing acting as a buffer between them was the slim electronic device and the vague ringing she could hear coming through from the other side. She counted them off.

*One ring.*

She was breathless for someone to answer and cut through the tension.

*Two rings.*

But also half hoping no one did.

*Three.*

Anderson's eyes were still on her, and almost hungry.

*Four.*

Surely no one answered after the fourth ring?

But then the greeting carried up loudly. "Somers. Nice to know you're alive and—no offense—but what the hell time is it?"

"Hey, Harley. Not sure. Middle of the night," Anderson said back, his attention turning momentarily to the call.

Nadine finally let out the breath she'd been holding unconsciously and pushed to her feet. "I'll give you a few minutes."

"Hang on, all right?" Anderson said into the phone, then fixed her with a concerned look. "You sure?"

"Yes. I should wash my face and make sure I'm not a complete disaster."

"You aren't."

The quick, utterly certain reassurance made her want to blush, so she hurried across the room, hoping he wouldn't see it. But when she reached the short hallway that led to the bathroom door, she paused, remembering something.

"Anderson?"

"Hang on again, Harley." He put his hand over the mouthpiece of the phone a second time. "Yeah?"

"You said you had an observation. But you didn't tell me what it was."

"I just noticed that when you were talking about Grant—even when you called him a jerk—you didn't sound mad that it was over."

"I didn't?"

"No. More like the *how* bothered you more than the ending itself."

"Let me guess…you think that's further indication that it wasn't meant to be."

He studied her for a second. "What do you think it means, oh ye of little faith in fate?"

"I *know* what it means. Grant was right."

"Nadine…"

"Hang on. Hear me out."

"I'm listening."

"Okay. First off, yes, he should've been faithful, and it's a little out there to believe he didn't understand that he shouldn't have slept with other women."

"No sh—"

"Hey!"

He shot her a smirk. "Sorry. I feel passionately about monogamy."

"I see that," she replied drily. "And I agree. But that wasn't my point. What I'm saying is that Grant and I *weren't* serious. If we had been, he might not have cheated. Or at the very least he might not have been so blasé about me finding out. So, no, I wasn't all that upset that it was over. I was just upset with myself for not seeing our relationship for what it was. And that, Detective, makes me mad."

Nadine spun quickly, wanting to avoid whatever argument Anderson might make, but his voice stopped her before she made it more than two steps.

"One other thing, Nadine," he said.

"What?"

"If you and Grant weren't meant to be, then fate probably has something far better lined up for you." He said it easily but firmly, then turned his face away and spoke into the phone again. "Hey, Harley. You still there?…Yeah,

I realize that I called you. Sorry. It was a long time…I know. I said sorry."

Nadine swallowed against the unexpected lump in her throat, then slipped into the hall and pressed her back to the wall. She really hadn't ever been a big believer in fate. But she had the unsettling feeling that Detective Anderson Somers had been thrown into her path for some bigger reason than just to act as a guard at her door.

Anderson's eyes lifted to the spot where Nadine had just been, pulled by some need to catch another glimpse of her. He was so focused on doing it that he completely missed what Harley Maxwell was saying on the other end. Which the other man was more than happy to point out.

"Someone drop something heavy on your head in the last few days, Somers? I just asked you if you wanted to get together to dance a tango, and you grunted a 'yeah,'" Harley said.

"Just distracted," Anderson replied, rolling his eyes and redirecting his attention as the sound of running water carried to his ears.

His friend immediately let out a loud groan. "You, too?"

"What?"

"My brother spent two days telling me he was 'distracted.' Then he hauled up and ran off to Mexico with a pretty waitress."

"I'm not running off with a waitress," Anderson said, finally pulling his stare away from the empty space near the hall that led to the bathroom.

"Only because you haven't met one yet," Harley countered. "But speaking of pretty girls…how's the cranky blonde?"

"Much less cranky since she sprang herself from the hospi—care center."

"Hospi-what?"

"It's—never mind. It's a thin line of distinction. And that wasn't the important part anyway."

"Whatever you say, my friend. How did she get out? Wait. You *are* with her, right? Because if you're not..."

"No, I've got her, Harley. We're in my hotel room."

His partner laughed. "Well. That explains the distraction."

"Shut up," Anderson grumbled, careful not to look around at the romantic decor. "We need to talk about what happened after she got out."

"So talk away."

"For starters, someone in a dark sedan tried to run her down just outside the care center. I've got a partial plate that I want you to run."

"All right. Hit me."

"It was 598 something."

There was a pause on the other end. "That's it?"

"I was a bit busy making sure Nadine didn't get killed," Anderson said.

"What about a possible make or model?"

"What...sedan doesn't cut it?"

"Ha-ha."

"Sorry, my friend. I haven't got anything else."

"You do realize that I'm not actually a magician."

"Don't sell yourself short."

"Ha. I'll do what I can, but you might want to wrap Ms. Stuart in bubble wrap while you wait. Could take me a while."

"Funny. Hey, Harley?"

"Yeah, man?"

Anderson's eyes drifted back to the empty space where Nadine had stood a few minutes earlier. The water had stopped, and he spoke his next sentence in a low voice, just in case she happened to be listening.

"I thought we decided that Garibaldi *wasn't* trying to kill her."

"We did." The frown was evident in Harley's reply. "And that conclusion was based on the fact that Nadine's brother told Brayden during his scouting mission that there was some kind of blackmail involved. I think her brother out-and-out said that she was safe so long as they managed to keep ahold of whatever mysterious piece of evidence they had on Garibaldi."

"So why the hell would he have someone try to take her out instead?"

"I dunno. Impatience?"

"Garibaldi's not stupid enough to get impatient. He's a long-game guy. I'd stake my career on it."

"You sure the attempt was purposeful?"

"Is that a real question?"

The other man sighed. "No, I guess not."

"I saw it with my own eyes, Harley. He took a moment. He targeted her." Anderson scrubbed a hand over his jaw. "Even if I had a doubt—which I don't—the whole building had to be evacuated just after the incident. Someone reported seeing a masked man in the halls."

Harley let out a low whistle. "Right after she sprang herself? Girl's got some serious good luck."

"Sure does. I'm just glad it happened the way it did. I'm thinking the car that tried to hit her had the masked man's driver at the wheel."

"So maybe the driver panicked when he saw her. Took matters into his own hands. Could be that the original intention wasn't to kill her."

"That'd be one hell of a panic. Killing a girl Garibaldi wanted alive would mean the guy wouldn't survive long himself. Besides that, the man in the halls was *masked.* You caught that, right? I don't think he was there to ask a few casual questions."

"Got an alternate theory?"

"Wish I did."

"Somers...does she remember anything else from before?"

Anderson dropped his voice even lower. "About the bomb and the fire when she was a teenager? Not that I know of. Her doctor said she might never fully regain the memories."

"He talked to you about her condition?" Harley sounded surprised. "Isn't that a bit unethical?"

"I might've led him to believe there was more to our relationship than bodyguard and bodyguard-ee."

"Of course you did."

"Hey, now. I'm doing the best I can with what I've got."

"I know, but..." The other man trailed off, and when he spoke again, his voice was a bit hesitant—like he didn't want to say what he was thinking. "What if that's why they decided to go after her like this?"

"What do you mean?"

"What if they know more than we do?"

"That's a given in some respects," Anderson said drily. "Garibaldi clearly knows what motivates himself. He's kind of an insider."

"Ha. I meant in regard to Nadine Stuart and whatever it is she's got locked in her brain about the blackmail. Garibaldi must have an idea of what it is, and he must know that it can implicate him pretty badly. He's never hesitated to kill in the name of protecting himself before."

Anderson saw where his friend was going with the idea. "You think that Garibaldi stopped seeing Nadine's blackmail as a threat."

"It's plausible, right? Maybe he eliminated whatever the leverage was. Or decided that so long as Nadine doesn't remember what it is, she can't tell anyone else. With her brother dead, she's the only threat."

Anderson's gut clenched unpleasantly. "So remove the threat."

"Sorry, man. I know it makes your job harder."

"I'll still keep her safe."

"I know."

"I just need to come up with a damn plan."

"Lay low. Keep her out of sight. Order some damn room service. Let me see if I can do anything with the plate number."

"Easy for you to say. She didn't slip out of a hospital room on *your* watch."

His friend laughed. "All right. Point conceded. She's not going to be content to be a bystander. What about probing her for some info about the blackmail? That was a part of the plan anyway, once she was feeling better, right? So start asking some questions. I'm assuming if she can pull an escape routine like that, she must be ready to talk a bit."

Anderson considered it for a second. He hated the idea of pulling a civilian into a case, even when the civilian in question was both a former victim and a continued target.

*But questioning her isn't out of the realm of reasonable behavior.*

She really was their only lead, and while his current priority was her safety, his ongoing case hadn't diminished in importance, either. Putting Garibaldi away was the primary reason he'd come to Whispering Woods—the only reason the small town was on his and his partners' radar. Being sensitive to Nadine's needs mattered, but it didn't give him an excuse not to attempt to get valuable information from her.

*So why does the idea bother you so much?*

He didn't have a definitive answer.

"You still there, buddy?" Harley prodded.

Anderson blew out a breath. "Yeah, man. Just thinking."

"And?"

"You're right. I should talk to her about it. See if she has any clue what kind of leverage her brother was talking about. If she doesn't, maybe she can at least give us a starting point. A place to look."

"Good."

"But that doesn't mean I have to—" He stopped abruptly as Nadine stepped back into the room.

It wasn't that he didn't want her to hear what he had to say, it was just that his tongue had stuck to the roof of his mouth. She'd bundled her petite frame into a one-size-fits-most robe, and her short blond hair was damp. Something about her freshly scrubbed, cozily wrapped appearance tugged at Anderson's heartstrings, and suddenly he knew why he was reluctant to put her on the spot. He'd known her for only a few days. Interacted closely with her for only a few hours and shared a single kiss, which was only meant to appease the excitable hotel employee. Yet somewhere in all of that, he'd managed to develop a distinctly unprofessional attachment to the prickly woman. And right that second, his instincts told him that it was only going to grow.

# Chapter 6

Nadine shifted awkwardly from foot to foot, her query about what Anderson meant when he'd said "leverage" sticking in her throat. She hadn't been eavesdropping, but the word had caught her ear as she stepped into the room. Now something in his expression made her mouth stop working. There was something warm, openly appreciative and utterly disarming about the way he was studying her. And her feet stayed planted to the spot, too, so she couldn't even turn and run.

Anderson cleared his throat like he was having trouble, as well, then spoke into the phone. "All right, Harley. I'm gonna hang up. Call if you get anything, and I'll do the same."

Nadine tried to get out a sentence, but all she managed was an embarrassing noise that sound like "erm."

One side of the detective's mouth turned up. "You, uh, lose something?"

"What?"

"Your clothes?"

"Oh." The blush she'd managed to keep under control while indulging in a quick shower was now back with full force. "I accidentally got them wet. They're hanging up. I was going to ask how you felt about me ordering up from the guest shop."

"Ordering up from the guest shop? Can't say how I feel about that since it seems like a made-up thing."

"Shut up. They've got some sweats and T-shirts there. Complete with the Whispering Woods Lodge logo. Unless you want me to sit around in a robe." Too late, she realized she'd left the door open for him to say that keeping her in the robe was *exactly* what he wanted.

But his eyes just raked over her once, and all he said was, "Clothes from the guest shop sound fine. And Harley also just pointed out that we might be hungry. Running from bad guys and pretending to be engaged tend to work up an appetite. For me, anyway."

"Is that a standard part of your job?"

"Eating?" he said teasingly.

The warm feeling in her cheeks increased. "No, I mean—you know what? Never mind. The food sounds good."

Anderson's face turned serious. "I'm just bugging you. And the answer is no, I've never had the occasion to create a fake occasion engagement, and I usually chase the bad guys down rather than hide in a honeymoon suite to avoid them."

Nadine exhaled and relaxed a little, realizing that his response—the middle bit, anyway—actually mattered to her. "So I'm really cramping your detective style, then."

His eyes crinkled up at the corners. "Little bit. But nothing some room service won't cure. Any food preferences? Allergies? Aversions?"

"I'm surprisingly simple."

"Oh, you think so, huh?" he teased.

She rolled her eyes. "I mean as far as food is concerned."

"Burgers and size-small pants work for you?"

"Extra small. And make sure they don't skimp on the mayo."

"Got it."

She moved to the oversize chair beside the coffee table, sank back into it and curled up her legs, only half listening as he placed their unusual order from the twenty-four-hour room service menu. She was both eager and apprehensive to hear what he had to say about the part of the conversation she'd just overheard.

*If he'll say anything at all.*

Her experience with police was limited, but she suspected they were tight-lipped about things related to their cases. Understandable, in most circumstances. Of course, she knew perfectly well that her circumstances weren't the usual. Most people didn't get a 24/7 guard outside their room after being in a supposed car accident.

*Because most people didn't intentionally run a corrupt cop off the road, resulting in his death, while simultaneously getting in the middle of a decade-and-a-half-long police investigation that had ties to their own choppy family history.*

Nadine plucked at the plush robe and tried, unsuccessfully, to brush off the run-on sentence of a thought.

It was true that things had ended badly for Officer Chuck Delta. And it was also true that he'd shot and killed her half brother, manipulated the crime scene after the fact, used his position to commit God knew what other crimes and worked for Jesse Garibaldi the whole time. Nadine didn't feel responsible for the man's death. He'd dug himself into the hole that was his criminal life. And Garibaldi... Well, the man behind the businessman facade was a whole other ball game. He'd taken Nadine's father's life. He'd tried to take hers, too. And she'd only just started to unravel the reasons why. There was no way she was just going to keep quiet and hide, no matter how badly Anderson and his partners might want her to.

Like he could read her mind, the detective interrupted her thoughts with a statement that confirmed her assumptions about his opinion on the situation. "I know you're probably sitting there trying to devise some method of getting me to tell you everything I know about Garibaldi. And I think you should know that I've developed an immunity to having anything stuck under my fingernails."

She couldn't muster up a laugh or even manage a lie; she just sighed. "I'm not going to be uninvolved in figuring out why my father and brother had to die."

He sat back studying her, his face unreadable. It was a little unnerving to be so silently and thoroughly assessed. And it made Nadine think—not that she'd been considering his worthiness until right that second—that Anderson was probably good at his job. His scrutiny made her want to squirm and blurt something out.

*And I don't even have anything to hide*, she thought.

She couldn't imagine what it would be like if she was trying to keep something from him. Impossible, probably.

But she tipped her chin up stubbornly, pressed her lips together, then said, "What's supposed to happen here? Am I supposed to succumb to some kind of cop wizardry?"

After a few more wordless moments, Anderson blinked, his stony expression dropping. "Works with the criminals."

"Which I'm not."

"You did kidnap my friend's fiancée," he pointed out.

She made a face. "Taking Reggie was a misunderstanding. She saw my brother get shot. And it's too soon for jokes, Anderson."

"Yeah, I know. Sorry." He sighed and ran a hand over his hair. "Look. There are few people in this world who know as well as I do what it feels like to be chasing a killer for personal reasons."

The statement stabbed a little at Nadine's heart. "I know. I didn't mean to—"

He put up a hand. "I'm not trying to make you feel bad. I'm saying that I literally understand what it feels like. I know the helplessness and the need for justice. I've been chasing it—chasing Garibaldi—for *fifteen years*. That's half my life, Nadine. I can't even guess how many of my waking moments I've spent trying to sort out what the hell happened and why. I've never been able to walk away from it. Maybe I couldn't even if I tried. So I really, truly get it."

By the end of the short speech, Anderson's voice had roughened with emotion. The hand he'd put up dropped down to his lap, and his gaze followed it. He stayed that way, and, without thinking about it, Nadine unfolded her legs, stood up and moved to sit beside him. She reached out and placed her own hand over his. For a second, he just sat still. Then his palm flipped over. As their skin met, his fingers closed to clasp hers tightly. And then it was Nadine who sat still, at least on the outside. On the inside, though, her pulse was thrumming.

Their pose was intimate. Familiar. Like an old friend—*or a lover*, said a little voice in her head—offering comfort in his time of need. It was disconcerting to feel such a strong connection to a near stranger. But Nadine felt no need to pull away, and after a few seconds Anderson at last cleared his throat and lifted his face to meet her eyes.

He shrugged, his expression tinged with embarrassment. "Apparently, I meant all that."

She gave his hand a squeeze. "I can see that."

"I don't have any interest in making you to do something I couldn't do myself. I'm not asking you to forget your need to find out what happened."

"But you want me to do what?" She was careful to keep

the question from sounding defensive. "Let it go for a while so you can do your job?"

"No." Anderson lifted their clasped hands to his mouth and dusted her skin with a kiss like it was the most natural thing in the world. "Something a little more complicated."

Nadine's heart fluttered nervously. "Okay."

"Don't say okay until you've heard what I want."

"Okay, er, you know what I mean. Tell me."

"What I want is for you to trust me."

It wasn't really what she'd been expecting to hear, and her surprise made her blurt out an honest response. "Trust is hard for me. I'm a woman whose dad led a double life and whose boyfriend thought being my roommate was an acceptable option after our breakup."

"I'm not asking you to jump in with both feet right away. I just want you to start with a little quid pro quo."

"Quid pro quo?"

He nodded. "You overheard that last part of my conversation with Harley?"

"You mentioned something about leverage and my brother," she said, embarrassed to admit that it had somehow managed to slip her mind in the last few minutes.

"And you're curious about what that meant."

"I was." She cleared her throat as she realized she'd just made it sound like she wasn't interested any longer.

If Anderson noticed, he didn't comment on it. "I want to preface what I'm about to say with a bit of an apology."

"Should I be worried?"

"No. I just don't want there to be any secrets between us. Part of that trust thing."

"All right." She felt cautious now, her heart beating unevenly for a different reason.

"We were up-front about the fact that I was sent here to act as a bodyguard, and you already know our overall goal is to put Jesse Garibaldi behind bars. Brayden told you all of that before he and Reggie left."

"Yes."

He released her hand and scratched nervously at his stubble. "He left out a few details. Or *a* detail, I guess."

"Just spit it out, Anderson. Listening to you jump around it is probably way worse than whatever you're going to say."

"Before your brother died, one of the last things he told Brayden was the reason that Garibaldi let you live. He said that your dad passed along something valuable—a way to blackmail Garibaldi."

She frowned, feeling like the revelation was a little anticlimactic. "But *I* don't know anything about something that could blackmail Garibaldi."

"That you're aware of."

"That I'm—oh. You think it's buried somewhere with the memory of the day my dad died."

"At the very least, it's a good possibility."

"And you think that you can help me retrieve that memory so that you can use it to gain the leverage yourself." She studied his face for a second. "And that makes you feel bad."

"I'm not a user, Nadine. Never have been," he replied, looking down at his hands. "Even having the odd criminal informant rubs me the wrong way. I guess I struggle with that whole greater-good piece. The other guys know it. They call me the *nice one*."

"Which I'm guessing is another reason they picked you to babysit me." She knew it sounded bitter and, sure enough, his eyes jerked up.

"Hey, now."

"I know it's not what you said. But it's what it boils down to, right? They sent the *nice one* to deal with the *difficult one*."

"Actually, that title belongs to our friend Rush. He's the fourth partner in our scheme." He smiled for a second before shaking his head. "And you're not difficult."

"I thought we were being honest."

"Nadine…"

"As you so kindly pointed out, I kidnapped a woman a week ago just to prove to myself she wasn't working with the man who killed my dad. I ran away from the care facility where you were making me stay for my own good. I obviously *need* a babysitter."

Anderson sighed noisily, put his hand on her shoulders and turned her gently so that she was facing him.

"You've been through a hell of time," he said. "You're *still* going through it. And it's lasted too long. All I want to do is to help you end it. Isn't that what you want, too?"

"Of course. But I don't want to be this massive inconvenience to everyone around me."

"Needing help from trained professionals isn't the same as being an inconvenience."

She started to argue, to point out that she liked being independent, then stopped abruptly as she clued in to the reason she was being so prickly. It was simple. She really hated the thought of being an unpleasant task instead of a choice.

*Especially to Anderson?*

She shoved aside the question and changed the subject. "You still haven't got to the quid pro quo part."

"I want you to tell me everything you *can* remember about the day your dad died, and everything your brother said to you during your last bit of time together. Somewhere in there—in your head—is the key to what Garibaldi's after."

He continued talking for a minute, assuring her that in exchange for the information she provided—whether it panned out or not—he'd keep her in the loop in regard to anything he and his partners found out about her father. He had a few caveats about ensuring that nothing would compromise the case, but Nadine was only half listening. The word "key" had triggered something in her memory. She didn't know what or why, but it felt like an answer, frustratingly out of reach.

Anderson paused in his speech as he noted a change in Nadine's expression. He knew what the look signaled because he'd seen the same one on many faces—both witnesses' and suspects'—in the interrogation room. The pretty blonde was experiencing an *aha* moment.

Trying to keep from getting too hopeful that it was something directly related to the case, Anderson reached out to touch her wrist and ask. He got only as far as opening his mouth, though, before a light knock on the hotel room door interrupted. Wishing he'd had a minute or two more, he moved from the couch to the door, where he verified through the peephole that it was room service. The staff member—not the exuberant girl from the front desk, thank God—set up the tray efficiently, handed over a plastic bag full of clothes, accepted the tip, then exited smoothly. It took under five minutes, but it was enough to change the tone in the room. The flow had been interrupted, and as much as Anderson wanted to push Nadine for a little bit more, he sensed that it was time to lighten the mood.

"Why don't you get dressed," he suggested. "I'll see if the honeymoon suite rental comes with any suitably romantic movies for us to watch while we eat."

"We don't have to watch a romance movie just because we're in the honeymoon suite."

"I know. But I want to."

Nadine lifted an eyebrow. "You *want* to?"

"What? We already established that I'm a romantic."

"But…romantic *movies*?"

"Let me guess. You'd peg me for an action man. Guns and ammo. Bombs and dudes jumping from helicopters."

"As a matter of fact…"

He let out an exaggerated sigh. "Always with the stereotyping. That's offensive to sappy policemen everywhere."

"What about car chases?"

"Nope."

"Slasher flicks?"

"Uh-uh."

"Political thrillers?"

"Not a chance. Trust me. I get all the pulse-pounding adrenaline I can handle at work. What I need is lighthearted drivel to take my mind off reality." He snagged the TV remote from the coffee table and leaned back. "Better hurry if you want a say."

"You're really serious, aren't you?"

"Deadly."

She shot him a half-amused, half-incredulous look, then grabbed the bag of clothes and hurried to the bathroom. As the door clicked shut, he started flicking through the prepaid channels in search of something just right. It took only a few seconds to find something that promised to make the viewer laugh, cry and laugh some more. He cued it up, then took the covers off their burgers as he waited.

He wasn't lying about his predilection for movies that kept things on the fluffy side. Violence and gore didn't appeal to him, and if that made him a giant suck, then so be it. But a bump and a muffled curse followed by a yell of "I'm okay!" drew his attention to the hall and prompted a silent question.

*Are you sure that's all this is about?*

He sighed again. He'd have to be an out-and-out liar not to admit that it'd been a long time since he'd found a woman as intriguing as he found Nadine Stuart. So sitting back and watching a movie with her—any movie, really—carried the potential for somcthing more than just a distraction from the swirl of dark things that clouded his everyday life.

The point was driven home as she stepped into the room, pausing to do a girlish, seemingly out-of-character spin right in front of him. "What do you think? They sent cozy pajamas."

Anderson couldn't find a grin. "I guess *they* thought you might not want to spend the whole night in clothes. Even comfortable ones."

She paused, midtwirl. "Wait."

"What?"

"*They* didn't send the pajamas. *You* did."

"Maybe."

"I can tell from that smirk on your face that you did."

"And I can tell from that smile on yours—or that *was* on yours a second ago, anyway—that you like them." He patted the couch beside him. "Come and eat."

She flipped her damp hair off her checks, made a face like she was going to argue, then shook her head instead and stepped over to sink down beside him. "Did you find a movie?"

"I did."

"So hit me with the damage."

"Well. It features a twentysomething starlet with really, *really* straight teeth, a low-cut shirt and a smart mouth. There's a dog. And a broken elevator."

"Hmm. Promising. What about the leading man?"

"Too good-looking to be believable, and therefore not important."

"Jealous?"

Anderson snorted. "Of a pretty boy in an overpriced suit?"

Nadine dipped a fry into her gravy, popped it into her mouth, then immediately grabbed another. "Uh-huh."

"I'm not jealous." He leaned over to snatch the fry from her. "But just for curiosity's sake…is that what you're into?"

"Who doesn't like a pretty boy in an overpriced suit?"

"Me, clearly."

She laughed, and Anderson reached out impulsively to thread his fingers through hers. Her laugh cut off abruptly as she stared down at their clasped hands, and he heard her sharp inhale.

"Are we really doing this?" she asked softly.

"Which part, specifically?" he replied.

"Pretending that you're not here to make sure I don't get killed by acting like we're on a first date."

"Is that such a bad thing?"

"Which part, specifically?" she echoed.

"Any of it," he said. "If you spend all your spare time dwelling on the bad things, you lose sight of the good."

"I know." She didn't look up, and Anderson didn't buy her claim.

He released her hand to bring his fingers to her chin, which he gently tilted in his direction. "Do you?"

"I do. I've managed to do a pretty decent job of living a good life in spite of everything that's hung over me for the last ten years."

"So what's holding you back from putting things aside for a couple of hours now?"

"Aside from the fear of being chased down and killed?" she asked drily.

"Aside from that, yes."

"I guess I'm just worried that this *isn't* spare time."

"We've got nowhere to be, and unless someone specifically knows we're here at the lodge, we're well hidden. On top of that, it's about four in the morning, and that's an impossible time to conduct any kind of stealthy investigative work. So as far as I'm concerned, this is definitely spare time. At least until it's light out." He dropped her chin and offered her an exaggerated wink. "And if we want to use it as a first date…that's fine by me. We do have a lot of ground to make up."

"What do you mean?"

"We're engaged already. So I figure we've got at least a year's worth of dates to cram in between now and the big day."

"Ha-ha. And you think the best way to start is with a terrible movie?"

"Terribly romantic movie," he corrected.

She met his eyes. "And if I want the bar set a little higher than that?"

"Then I suggest you come a little closer. I offer an epic cuddle service." He lifted his arm to the back of the couch and nodded toward the empty space.

She made a face—the same one that kept making him think she wanted to argue but couldn't muster up a good one—then sighed and slid over.

"Happy?" she said, her voice full of put-on grumpiness.

"Getting there. Just one thing missing."

"What?"

He pulled out the remote control from under his thigh and clicked the play button. "This."

"Of course."

"Yep."

She shuffled a little before tipping her head into him, and as soon as she was settled, Anderson brought his hand down to smooth her hair off her cheek, then pressed his chin to the top of her head.

"See?" he said after a few minutes. "This couldn't possibly be a waste of time."

She didn't answer, and a glance down told him why.

Her eyes were closed, her lips parted, the soft inhale and exhale of sound sleep making her chest rise and fall rhythmically. Anderson smiled. It felt good to have her tucked in beside him. Like she belonged there.

# Chapter 7

Anderson woke with a start, jerked out of sleep by something unwelcome and unknown.

In a nanosecond, his body went from still and out cold to still and on high alert. As he strained to pinpoint what had woken him, the hairs on the back of his arms were already standing up in anticipation of an intrusion. But he couldn't hear a sound. Careful to keep quiet, he breathed out, and, without opening his eyes, he took a mental inventory of his situation.

He was on the couch where he'd drifted off. Light seeped through his closed lids, making him sure the sun had come up. Everything seemed calm. Quiet. He started to open his eyes and sit up, but before he could get all the way there, the telltale click of the door unlocking hit his ears.

Anderson immediately slid his hand to his waistband in search of his holstered weapon. His hand came up empty. It took him a panicked second to recall that he hadn't grabbed the gun from the glove box of his truck before he and Nadine had made their stealthy entrance.

*Nadine.*

Panic hit him again, this time harder. He couldn't believe he hadn't thought of her first.

*No time to feel guilty.*

Where was she? His eyes swept the room as he pushed to his feet and inhaled. Her scent was all around. Faint but there. Her actual self, though, seemed to be AWOL.

*Damn, damn, damn.*

Up the hall, he could hear the door opening all the way now.

"Nadine," he called, his voice so low that it barely carried past his own ears.

Seriously. Where *was* she?

He darted across the room. The bathroom door hung open, its light off. He turned and strode in the other direction. He pushed open the French doors that led to the elaborate bedroom. The king-size bed sat untouched, and the second bathroom was as dark as the first.

There weren't enough *damn*s in the world to cover his confusion and concern, and he didn't have time to come up with a string of more creative curses. Whoever had opened the door was already inside. They were shuffling around out in the living area.

With a near-silent growl, Anderson grabbed the handle on the closet door, flung it open and stepped inside. It was a shoddy solution. The second place the intruder would look, straight after bending to peek under the bed. He wasn't interested in hiding, but it was also his *only* option if he wanted a chance to get a look at the invader and a chance to assess his chances of coming out on top in hand-to-hand combat.

*Hand-to-gun is the more likely scenario*, said a grim voice in his head.

He took a breath and forced off the thought. The person in the other room seemed to be taking their sweet damned time. He gritted his teeth. Thoroughness was a quality Anderson appreciated everywhere but in criminals. There, he preferred quick and stupid.

*And you still don't know where Nadine's gone to.*

He took the few minutes he had to reason through it. If someone had come in and taken her, he would've heard it. So logically he had to assume she'd left of her own free will. Maybe she slipped out to get some breakfast. Or maybe she'd woken early, found that the clothes didn't fit properly and headed to the Whispering Woods Lodge's gift shop for replacements.

*The why doesn't even matter*, Anderson said to himself.

The important part of the situation was the fact that at the very least she'd started out leaving on purpose. The real *question* was whether or not it'd stayed that way.

*If someone intercepted her between the suite and her destination...*

Anderson did a mental headshake. He'd deal with that when—if—it turned out to be true. If he didn't focus on saving his own butt, he wouldn't get a chance to worry about Nadine's.

And judging from the sounds carrying into the closet now, the intruder finally seemed to be making his way to the bedroom.

With his body tensed in anticipation of a need to go on the defensive, Anderson squinted at the half-inch space between the closet door and the frame. A flash of gray crossed his line of sight first. Then the outline of a short, squat person.

*Not exactly the look of a hired assassin.*

Of course, Anderson had experienced firsthand just how deceiving looks could be. As a rookie cop, he'd once pulled over a grandmotherly woman for running a stop sign and found a pound of marijuana on the passenger-side seat.

He continued to watch the figure move methodically through the room. Something about the movements made Anderson frown. They didn't give him the impression that the person on the other side of the door was searching for him or Nadine—or for anything else, for that matter. He ran a hand over his chin, puzzling it over.

*Why would a stranger come into the room if they* weren't *looking for us? It makes no sense. I can't think of a—*

He groaned quietly as the presumed intruder turned, revealing the simple answer. The gray flash was a hotel uniform. The short, squat stature belonged to a middle-aged woman who wielded an oversize duster with practice and purpose. Her role was obvious. Cleaning staff.

Anderson cursed himself for not considering the possibility in the first place. He'd requested no housekeeping when he checked in, but that was a week ago. He crossed his arms over his chest and tried to talk himself into waiting patiently. It wasn't what he *wanted* to do. In fact, if he hadn't been sure it would draw a hell of a lot of attention, he would've burst out of the closet and torn off in search of Nadine.

*Not in either of our best interests*, he told himself firmly. *Even if the minutes* are *going to tick by painfully.*

Thankfully, though, the minimal amount of time he'd spent in the room meant that the woman was able to power through the job. Before too much teeth-grinding time passed, the door was clicking shut again. The second it did, Anderson stepped back into the bedroom, then out into the living room. There he paused. He fought an urge to rip through the room frantically, and instead moved slowly, seeking out a clue as to where Nadine might've gone.

Almost right away, he found a note, written in tidy, teacher's handwriting that might've made him smile under different circumstances. As things were, the words did little to relieve his worry.

RAN TO GRAB SOMETHING FROM MY MOM'S. BACK SOON. N.

Though the note told him *exactly* where she'd gone, there was no hint as to why she'd left so abruptly. On top of that, her mom's place was the very spot her brother had taken his last breaths. Where he'd confessed to having something to use as blackmail against Garibaldi.

A chill crept through Anderson, and he couldn't shake the sudden, overwhelming stab of foreboding. Without stopping to question his gut, he snagged his truck keys and strode straight out of the suite without looking back.

Nadine lifted her eyes to her mom's place for the tenth time. She'd arrived via one of the lodge's dedicated taxis—which she'd guiltily charged to Anderson's room while mentally resolving to pay him back every cent—about thirty minutes earlier and hadn't yet been able to make herself approach the house. Instead, she sat on a public bench at the end of the street. At first, she'd sat down to assess the place. She wasn't naive enough to think that Garibaldi wouldn't consider having it watched. They were definitely well acquainted with it. If she wanted proof of that, she didn't need to look any further than the fact that his men had made short work of removing Tyler's body.

She blew out a breath and shoved aside the dark image that filled her mind. She hadn't taken the time to grieve his passing, and though they hadn't been close—barely knew each other at all, really—she could feel the sadness of loss on the periphery of her heart.

*Later*, she said to herself. *Right now you need to do* this.

She turned her attention once more to the home where

she'd grown up. So far, she'd seen nothing amiss. No out-of-place vehicles, no flashes of unexpected movement. But her rear end seemed frozen to its spot, and she couldn't say if it was fear of being caught, sorrow over all the loss or anticipation of being right that held her there.

*And I* am *right.*

The dream that had woken her at dawn was specific. A memory that fit perfectly with the sudden jolt of recognition caused by Anderson's offhand use of the word "key." She closed her eyes for a second, recalling the sleep-blurred images. In the dream, she'd been a child. It was her tenth birthday, and her father had been giving her a jewelry box. It was an ornate thing. Real wood, polished, stained and lacquered. Something not designed for a little girl with plastic bracelets and broken-clasped necklaces. The most important thing about it, though, was the fact that it needed a key to open it. When her father had handed her that key—both in real life and in last night's dream—he'd told her in a serious voice that it was so she could keep all their secrets safe. Not *her* secret. *Theirs.* The difference had never stuck out before. Now, though, it seemed like a significant distinction.

Nadine opened her eyes and focused her gaze on the window that had been hers as a kid. She'd only looked in the house briefly when she'd arrived back in town. Everything had been covered in a layer of dirt. Left exactly as it had been when her mom had uprooted them from Whispering Woods and moved their life to Freemont. Like it had simply been put on hold.

Nadine wondered if her mother had left it like that on purpose, thinking maybe one day they would return. Maybe its in-limbo status was one of the reasons it had taken nearly a decade for the paperwork to catch up.

She glanced around again, a lump of regret building.

Cleaning it out and going through everything had been

on her list of things to do, but being caught up in the continuing mess created by Garibaldi had delayed it.

*So what's your excuse now?*

She shook her head. The delay now was in her own head, and she needed to push past it so that she could move forward. And maybe help the case in the process.

Taking a deep breath, she cast another look up and down the street, then pushed to her feet and—with her head down and her shoulders hunched to make herself as invisible as possible—followed the sidewalk up the street. She didn't look up as she reached the house. She moved by feel, taking the steps to the second floor of the converted fourplex like she'd done a thousand times before. At the top, she realized her key was at home in the apartment she'd leased short-term. But when she put her hand on the doorknob, she found it unlocked anyway. Relieved, she pushed it open. And just inside, she stopped, puzzled by what she saw.

The grime was gone, the clutter reduced to manageable piles here and there. The reduction in untidiness left an unsettled feeling in the pit of Nadine's stomach. It was almost like someone had come in to look around, and instead of tearing the place apart, they'd put it back together again. She shivered and resolved not to waste time thinking about it.

"Just get the jewelry box and get out." Saying it aloud motivated her to actually do it.

Ignoring the way the hair on the back of her arms stood up, she stepped through the adjoining kitchen and living room and into the hall. She stared at the three doors that lined it. The first was her mom's. The second was the one and only bathroom. The last was her own. She drew another breath and counted off the thirteen steps that brought her to a halt in front of it, then pushed it open, flicked on the light and made a beeline for the closet. There she stood on her tiptoes and reached up to the shelf where she'd left the box years earlier. Her hands met nothing but empty space.

A lick of increased worry swept through her. Fighting it, she bent down and pulled out a small storage bin from the pile on the floor. She upended it, stepped on top and peered up to the top shelf. A conspicuous space—four-by-four inches—sat just in between an old shoe box and a small stack of books. The panic that hit was immediate. And dizzying.

On wobbly legs, Nadine lowered her feet to the ground.

Someone had clearly removed the jewelry box. And they hadn't even tried to hide that fact.

*Maybe it's a coincidence*, she reasoned. *Maybe Mom did something with it, or...*

She couldn't even make herself finish the thought. Her gut told her it wasn't true. In fact, her instincts were all but screaming that the key and the box were important in some way.

*So where is it?*

Worry pricked at Nadine again. If the jewelry box contained whatever blackmail item her brother had mentioned to Anderson's partner, and Garibaldi's men already had their hands on it, whatever it was, that could be very bad news for her. It could even be the reason she'd become a target.

*A target.*

And she was more or less out in the open. She had no weapon and no plan. And therefore no protection. Sweat made her palms slippery. Why hadn't she taken a minute to wake up Anderson? Sheer stubbornness was no excuse for risking her life. She wouldn't be any good dead to anyone.

*Except Garibaldi*, said a little voice in her head.

She couldn't quite shake it off, so she didn't try. She needed to drop her solo act, admit that she needed help and get back to the lodge as quickly as she could.

Feeling a modicum of relief at the silent admission,

Nadine spun and strode purposefully out into the hall. But she only made it a few steps before stopping again as a flash of something out of place on the floor caught her eye. It was flat and white and sticking out from under her mother's closed door.

*An envelope.*

With a slightly unreasonable glance up and down the hall, Nadine moved closer, then bent down. The little slip of white came free easily. She lifted it up, feeling uneasy.

A name was scrawled over the front in all caps. *HENDERSON.* Though there was something familiar about it, Nadine couldn't place it. But as her hands slid over the crisp paper, she had no problem figuring out what it contained. The shape of the key was unmistakable. But her skin wouldn't stop crawling, so she decided it was better to shove the envelope into the tiny pocket on the waistband of her yoga pants. She could deal with it after she got back to Anderson. If need be, they could return to the house together.

She started walking again, but her nerves made the tap of her feet on the floor sound ominous, and she had to forcefully swallow the fear that encouraged her to freeze to the spot.

*You've got this.*

But the second she reached the front door, she realized that what she actually had was a problem. A man-shaped one in a balaclava. He stood in the kitchen, a lit match in one hand and a pile of some unknown substance on the counter beside him.

For a second, Nadine was too puzzled to be afraid. What was he— *Oh.* He dropped the match to the pile, and it crackled. A slow, steady burn. One that would spread and destroy the house along with any evidence it might contain.

No sooner had Nadine made the conclusion than the masked arsonist lifted his gaze. It fixed on her, chasing aside anything but terror.

*Run!*

The urgent, self-directed command spurred her to move. She turned to flee. But it was too late. The man was on the move, too. He charged toward her, slamming her to the floor and knocking the wind out of her, cutting her attempt to scream to a squeak. And before she could recover from the impact, he'd twisted them up together. One hand pinned her arms behind her back, the other slammed over her mouth.

"Up," he ordered, his voice gruff and mean.

She had no choice in the matter anyway. He yanked her to her feet.

"Think you can follow instructions?" he asked.

She managed a nod.

"Good. Listen carefully. I'm going to let your mouth go. You're not going to scream. Not even for a heartbeat. And when we walk out of here, you're also going to keep holding my hand like it's the most natural thing in the world. I'm going to take off my mask, and you're not going to look at me. We won't be in a hurry. Two lovers who can't stand to be more than a few inches apart. And if you don't do what you should, I promise that I'll risk shooting you right here. Got all that?"

She nodded again, tears pricking at her eyes.

"Good," said her assailant. "At the very least, it'll prolong your life by a few minutes."

The dark words punctuated his rough shove toward the door.

Anderson took the last corner sharply, his anger and worry mixing to make him feel a little reckless. He tightened his hands on the wheel and braked, trying to calm himself. When he pulled the truck over, though, his eyes lifted to the converted fourplex where Nadine's mother had once lived, and all hope of gaining some serenity evaporated.

The petite blonde stood on the small patio that led to the door, a large, masked man positioned just behind her. As Anderson slammed the truck into Park, the man let Nadine go just long enough to pull off the balaclava. For a moment, he could swear he recognized the guy from somewhere. It made him frown, but dwelling on it wasn't an option at the moment. Getting Nadine to safety was the only priority.

He started to swing the door open, hell-bent on charging in and demanding her release. He was forced to pause, though, when he spotted an all-too-familiar silver flash between the pretty schoolteacher and her captor. The man had a gun.

Anderson cursed under his breath and took a moment to do a quick assessment of the area. A lone car sat parked at the other end of the block, kitty-corner to where he'd stopped the truck. It was a slick ride—a pricey sedan with low-profile rims and tinted rear windows. It didn't look like something driven by a thug.

*But Garibaldi's not your run-of-the-mill criminal, is he?*

The thought rang true. It was also obvious that the car didn't belong in the neighborhood. So there was a good chance that it belonged to the man who held Nadine. The guy's clothes matched the quality of the vehicle, too. A tailored suit, Anderson thought. Shiny shoes. Strange attire for a man on a kidnapping mission. There wasn't time to dwell on that, either, though.

The man was guiding Nadine down the stairs now, and when they reached the bottom, there was a possibility that he'd turn toward Anderson's truck.

*You need a plan, and you need it* now.

Thinking quickly, he decided his best bet was an interception. Even if he lost the element of complete surprise, he could retain an advantage if the man literally didn't see him coming.

Quickly and silently, Anderson grabbed his weapon, then opened the truck door and slid out. His feet hit the ground noiselessly, but he crouched down anyway, watching to see if Nadine's captor had taken note of his presence yet. Thankfully, the man appeared too intent on keeping his prisoner close to bother looking around.

Glad for the luck running his way, Anderson slunk away from the truck and made his way across the nearest lawn and its adjoining house. When he reached it, he pressed himself to the exterior wall and mentally mapped his way to the sedan.

Just a few houses up, there was a long row of privacy hedges that spanned several yards with no apparent break. After that, a six-foot fence with a gate that hung slightly ajar. Then an in-bloom bush covered in bright red flowers. Finally, there was the conspicuous car.

*Okay*, Anderson thought. *So long as the creep doesn't manage to coincidentally sync his glances with my movements, I should be fine.*

"Here goes," he murmured, then dropped his head and hit the road at a light jog—fast enough but not loud.

He hit the hedges without even breaking a sweat. He paused there for a minute, waiting until he was sure he hadn't been spotted before continuing on. When he was sure he was in the clear, he moved again.

The greenery flashed by as he crossed three yards, each one with a narrow path through its own spot in the bushes. Those he sailed by without pausing, just in case Nadine and her captor happened to pass by at the same moment.

At the end of the row, the fence he'd previously spotted rose up to block him in. Though the gate had been open on the street side, the side that lined the yard was a sold wall of tightly fitted panels.

Gritting his teeth, Anderson eyed the perimeter. It was apparent that the only way out was to double back and come out one of the paths. The idea sent more than a sliver of concern through him. It would be almost impossible to sneak out. The hedges were flush with the sidewalk, and even peering around to get a look at the street risked potential exposure. The last thing he wanted was to add any more risk to Nadine's already precarious situation.

*But not getting to her at all isn't an option.*

He turned with the intention of going back. As he did, a flash of movement caught his. His hand went automatically to his weapon while he crouched down defensively and zeroed in on the space where he'd spied the movement. His body wanted to go rigid. Out of habit, he took in and let out three deep breaths and forced himself to stay loose. At the third exhale, he just about choked. A dog—a Great Pyrenees, he thought—came wriggling out from between the corner of the fence and the bottom of the last hedge. The big animal, which had to weigh near to 150 pounds and whose white coat was covered in grime, gave Anderson a slightly guilty look, then wagged its tail and bounded up the yard.

Anderson watched, astounded, as the dog disappeared around the side of the house. Then, in what felt like slow motion, he shifted back to the spot from which the dog had crawled in the first place. There was no visible break in the bottom of the hedge, but for the animal to have come through as easily as it did, he knew there had to be one.

Moving quickly, he stepped forward, then dropped to his knees. A quick survey made him smile. There was a hole in the ground. A huge one. It led straight into the yard next door, defeating the entire purpose of the fence. With a silent thank-you to the big dog, Anderson flattened himself to the ground and pushed his way through.

# *Chapter 8*

Every part of Nadine—mind and body—was bucking against what was happening. What she was *letting* happen. The problem was that she couldn't seem to come up with an effective way to stop it. She didn't know if the man who held her would actually follow through on his threat to shoot her then and there. She had no idea what level of desperation he was at, but she couldn't take the risk. So she'd already considered and rejected anything that might tip him over the edge. There wouldn't be any screaming for help. No violent kick to the shins or attempts to slip out of his grip.

To make matters worse, Nadine was sure she was experiencing some kind of trauma-induced flashback. Something about the way the man pushed her along filled her nostrils with nonexistent smoke and her heart with remembered fear. She could nearly hear the sounds that plagued her dreams. Crackling wood. The incessant beep of hospital monitors. Hushed, worried voices.

She tried to force it aside. To remind herself that a decade had passed since then. She was strong and capable and on a mission to set things right.

But they were getting closer to the man's car now, and Nadine couldn't quell the panic. It increased tenfold. Time was running out, the window for escape—for survival—growing slimmer by the second. Her need for it, though, was doing just the opposite. Ballooning into a desire to drag her heels. To close her eyes and delay whatever was about to come by any means possible.

Like he could sense her blossoming urge to fight back, her captor tightened his already painful grip on her wrists. She bit back a whimper, but she didn't have the same control over her feet as she had over her mouth. In her attempt to keep her eyes forward, she didn't notice the sudden dip in the sidewalk in front of her. Her shoe caught the edge of the concrete. Her knee twisted awkwardly. And down she went, blissfully free. But the euphoria lasted only a moment.

From behind her, the man snarled. "You think a game like that's going to work?"

He thought she'd done it on purpose, she realized.

"No," she gasped. "I didn't mean to—"

She didn't get to finish. An unfamiliar noise—almost the sound of a punch—cut her off. And then something heavy smacked into her back. For a second, she was stunned. The air blew from her lungs as the deadweight of whatever it was flattened her to the ground. She no sooner recognized that it was *someone*—her captor—rather than *something* landing on her than the weight was abruptly pulled off.

"Nadine."

Anderson's voice flooded her so hard with relief that she almost let out a sob. His hand on her wrist—no less strong than that of her attacker—was the most welcome bit of human contact she'd ever felt. Her fingers closed on his, and as he tugged her gently to her feet, she threw herself into his arms, not caring if she seemed needy. Because right that second, she *was* in need. And nothing could've been more reassuring than the solid feel of the big cop's chest against her face.

He hugged her back for a second, then spoke softly in her hair. "We should go."

Nadine exhaled. "What about *him*?"

"I'd love to ask him a question or ten, but I'm not inclined to draw any more attention to us by dragging him down the block. I don't think we have time to wait for him to wake up."

"Time?"

"Look up for a second, sweetheart."

She lifted her head reluctantly, then pulled away with a sharp gasp as she realized that the smoke scent hadn't just been some residual memory trying to come to the surface. Even from where they stood, she could see that a black cloud was pushing through the cracks around the doorframe. Her captor had succeeded in setting his fire. Her mother's house would be destroyed, if not by flames then by the smoke damage. And it would likely take the three shared suites with it.

"The neighbors," she said worriedly.

"Already know." Anderson inclined his head toward a woman who'd just appeared on the lawn in front of the house. "And if we don't go now, we'll probably have to answer more questions than we'd like."

Nadine glanced from the smoke to the unconscious man, then back to Anderson before nodding and straightening her shoulders. "Okay."

He took her hand, and she didn't look back as he tugged her quickly over the pavement. She let him help her into the truck, too, squeezing her eyes shut as he reached over and buckled her seat belt. A few seconds later, the driver's-side door creaked open, and the seat beside her sank down, letting her know Anderson had climbed in, as well. Then the rumble of the engine and the bump of the tires told her they'd started moving, and the wail of sirens made her sure they were heading away from the house. But cataloging it the way she was—with her lips pressed together and a small wall around her heart—could only last so long. And as soon as they were out of her old neighborhood, the flood of emotions trickled through the cracks and forced her to acknowledge them.

The home where she'd spent the first decade and a half of her life would no longer exist. The shoe box full of notes that she'd *just* seen would be ruined. Maybe burned to a crisp. Maybe soaked by the firefighters. Either way, they'd be unreadable. Everything would become a memory. And while memories were all well and good, Nadine thought there were probably few people who knew as well as she did just how tenuous they could be.

"Hey." Anderson's low timbre cut through her silent mourning.

"Hey," she managed to echo with only a slight tremor in her voice.

"It's going to be okay," he said. "You're safe."

She finally opened her eyes and fixed her gaze out the windshield. "It's not that. I mean, yes, I was scared back there. But it's not the first time I've been through something harrowing. And I know what to expect where Garibaldi and his men are concerned. I set myself up to dive right in. I just… I guess I wasn't expecting to lose all those memories. I feel broken all over again. My heart hurts like it did when my dad died. I want the heartbreak to *end.* That's why I came back to Whispering Woods. Not to get destroyed a second time."

Anderson went quiet for a moment, and Nadine wondered if her admission had crossed some invisible line. She didn't really know him, after all. And large, emotional declarations weren't the norm for her, even in the most intimate circumstances. She fiddled self-consciously with the hem of her shirt, trying to formulate a way to withdraw the outburst. But before she could say anything, Anderson flipped on his turn signal and veered onto the shoulder.

"Come here," he commanded.

Nadine blinked. "Come…*where*?"

He leaned over and unbuckled her seat belt. He slid his hand to her waist, then dragged her across the bench seat so that she was flush against him. Then he squeezed.

"What are you doing?" she asked, a catch in her voice.

"Hugging you, sweetheart."

"No. I mean, I know. But…"

"But what?" he said. "You're hurting. I care. Simple as that."

"We don't even know each other." Now the catch had a desperate edge.

"I know your whole family history. I know you're tough as hell on the outside, but that you must have a soft inside because you teach elementary school. I know some jerk convinced you that commitment meant nothing. And right now…I know that you need a hug. I think that's a lot."

Tears threatened all over again, and try as she might, she couldn't quite fight them. "I'm sorry, Anderson."

His free hand came up to wipe the wetness from her cheeks. "For what?"

"For running off this morning. It was stupid."

"Damn right it was."

"Oh."

He chuckled and pressed his chin to the top of her head. "Did you expect me to argue with that? My team of guys had me dedicate myself to keeping you out of harm's way. That right there tells you how much danger we think you're in."

Her heart sank a little, just like it had the last time she remembered that she was a part of his job. She pulled away. For a second, she met resistance, but his grip relaxed quickly, and she slid into her own seat.

"We should go," she said in as cool a voice as she could manage.

"Nadine…"

"Yes?"

"You want to tell me what's wrong?"

"Nothing," she lied.

He raised an eyebrow. "I might not be a complete expert, but I know that 'nothing' means 'something' in woman-speak."

"I'm not exactly a typical woman."

"No kidding." He dropped a wink. "And I mean that as a compliment."

She felt heat creep up her cheeks. "We have work to do."

"Work to do… Some things are more important than work."

"Like what?"

Unexpectedly, his hand shot out and landed on her wrist. Each point of each of his fingers sent a jolt of heat into her skin, then straight to her heart. It was almost dizzying. And when he pulled her back into his arms, it made Nadine want to cry all over again. Because it drove home just how badly she wanted to be more than a job to the big, protective cop.

Anderson was at a bit of a loss. His instinct was to comfort the woman in his arms in any way he could. To offer a shoulder. To hold her as long as it took to wring out all of her tears. To kiss them away, if that's what it took.

Hell. The last bit was what he *really* wanted to do. He

thought it was obvious that he was willing to be whatever she needed him to be. But he also felt like he was somehow getting it wrong. Every time he delved into a bit of emotional supportiveness, Nadine backed off. He couldn't figure out why. Yeah, she had a bit—okay, more than a bit—of a prickly exterior going on. Definitely in place to keep herself from getting hurt any more than she had been already. Except Anderson was damned sure she *wanted* something more tender from him. The way she'd thrown herself into his arms back there at her mom's house. The warmth in her eyes when she looked at him. So what was he doing wrong?

*Things are easier when it's just a job, aren't they, Somers?*

The self-directed question made him pause mentally. He felt something click. He remembered that she'd become defensive when referring to him as her babysitter. He'd assumed it was because she didn't want to be under guard. Except now that he was thinking about it, there'd been a touch of something else in her reaction, too. A bit of hurt, maybe. The expression on her face just a second ago had been the same.

He felt his forehead wrinkle into a deep frown as an explanation occurred to him. "Is that what's bothering you?"

She spoke into his chest. "Is *what* what's bothering me? I didn't say anything."

"I'm reading between the lines."

"Maybe you shouldn't do that."

He leaned away just enough that she had to sit up a bit and look up at him as he spoke. "I'm picking up a not-wanting-to-be-protected-by-Detective-Anderson-Somers vibe. And I can't say I'm crazy about it."

"I know I need your help. That whole thing back there proved it."

"Needing and wanting are two different things," he pointed out.

"I'm aware." Her reply was stiff.

"I don't think you're hearing me, honey. A week ago, my guys gave me this job. I took it because we're a team. And I'd keep doing it regardless of my feelings about you specifically." He paused to clear his throat. "Look. I'm not much of a subtle guy. Straightforward all the way. Sometimes that gets in the way of…I dunno. Emotional finesse?"

"Emotional finesse?"

"No need to mock me."

"No mocking intended. But using the words 'emotional finesse' to describe the lack thereof seems kind of ironic."

"Why? Too poetic?"

"Exactly."

A tiny smile tipped up her lips, and he couldn't resist the urge to lift his thumb to follow the curve of her mouth. She held still as he did it, the only movement the automatic rise and fall of her chest. He dragged his fingers back to first cup her cheek, then smooth back a lock of hair. Her breaths came a little faster, and Anderson knew he was reading her body language correctly. As much as she might try to pretend otherwise, her interest in him went as much beyond the professional as his did for her.

"My point is that you're right," he said softly.

"About?"

"Need and want are different."

"You said that, not me."

"But you agreed. Resentfully."

"I didn't—"

"Just listen for a second."

"Isn't that what I'm doing?"

"Also resentfully," he teased.

"You're going to see some *actual* resentment if you

don't spit out whatever emotionally unfinessed thing you're trying to say."

He laughed. "I'm trying to say that I like this."

She made a face. "You like arguing about nothing?"

"I like the ebb and flow of conversation with you. I like that you say what's on your mind. I like *you*, Nadine, and I'm not going to waste time pretending I don't. And that's where the want versus need comes in for me. I need to protect you because it's my job. I *want* to protect you because I'm interested in you. Unprofessionally."

Her eyes had grown wider with each word, and when he was done talking, she swallowed. "Is that…bad?"

"I hope to God it's not. Unless you don't feel the same?"

"No. Yes, I mean. I like you, too. But is being involved unprofessionally, well…unprofessional?"

He shrugged. "The truth is, I don't care. Life's too damned short to ignore feelings that are so strong after only a day. Hell, Nadine. Not knowing where you were for that little bit of time today made me crazy."

"Hmm."

"What?"

"Is that 'liking' or 'stalking'?" she asked, face pleasantly pink. "Because there's a line."

He grinned. "It's liking."

"How can you be sure?"

"Stalking is an unreasonable need to know every move. My need was a very reasonable one. I was scared that you weren't safe."

"And I wasn't."

"Nope."

"I really am sorry."

Anderson sighed and said, "I can't even muster up the proper amount of anger. I'm just glad you're okay. Which is just further proof of liking you over stalking you."

"What about your boss? And your partners? Won't they

have something to say about you getting involved with a witness?"

"This case is unofficially official. So I'm going to stretch that rule to cover this—you and me, that is—as well."

"Unprofessionally professional?"

"Could say." He studied her unconvinced expression. "Unless you don't want to take the chance. Because I can't tell if you're trying to talk me out of liking you, or trying to convince yourself, or—"

"Anderson?"

"Yeah?"

"I'm going to kiss you now."

"Glad to hear it."

"Shut up."

He fought a laugh—he *really* didn't want to give her an excuse to back out—and closed his eyes as she tipped her face up. The first touch wasn't more than a brush of her lips to his. Exploratory. Almost hesitant.

He waited.

A heartbeat later, her mouth came back. Firmer this time, but still soft. She hovered there long enough to make him ache to grab her. He told himself not to give in. To let her continue to lead. His patience paid off. On the third pass, her tongue joined her lips. It played into his mouth, warm and sweet. Her hands came up, too—one to the back of his head, the other to his thigh. Under the attention, he couldn't stifle a low growl. In response, her hands tightened, and they stayed that way as she laid slow, purposeful claim to every bit of his mouth. When she at last finished, blood was thundering through Anderson's veins. He'd never wanted a woman so badly. And all from a kiss.

He opened his eyes and stared down into Nadine's face. He could see a matching desire reflected in her gaze.

She gave her head a little shake like she was trying to clear it and said, "That was…"

"Worth any and all risk of workplace impropriety?" Anderson filled in.

"Definitely."

"Wanna do it again?"

She laughed—low and breathy. "Yes. But I think we should try and balance the work and fun."

In spite of the way he wanted to dismiss it, his cop self perked up. "Why? You got something for me other than a mind-blowing kiss?"

"As a matter of fact..." She slid a bit farther away, stuck her hand into her pocket and pulled out a small white envelope. "Ta-da!"

He took it from her and read the printed name aloud. "Henderson. Is that familiar to you?"

"Yes. But I can't place it."

"It's familiar to me, too."

He opened the envelope and dumped a small key into his hand, the familiarity growing a little stronger. The key meant nothing to him. It was too small to belong to a door and too big to fit into a typical padlock. He frowned, unsure why just the idea of a key made him think he should know what "Henderson" meant.

"Talk to me for a second," he said.

"Talk to you?"

"Doesn't matter what it's about. Just a trick I used when my brain needs to work through something that's just out of reach. Helps to have some white noise."

"I'm going to pretend that doesn't feel like an insult."

He smiled. "I wouldn't dare insult you."

She shot him a doubtful look. "Uh-huh."

"Tell me about the key."

"So you can tune me out?"

"Trust me. That'd be impossible."

She rolled her eyes, but her gaze was soft. "The key belongs to a jewelry box. The box was a gift from my dad.

A place to keep our secrets safe, he said. I never really put anything important into it, but for some reason I woke up thinking about it today."

"So that's why you pulled the little escape act this morning?"

"It seemed important. But when I got to the house..." She swallowed, her eyes flicking out the window in the general direction of her mom's place.

Anderson reached out and gave her hand a reassuring squeeze. "It'll be all right, honey."

She took a breath. "I know. And it's just stuff. And not even stuff that I've looked at closely in a decade."

"Doesn't make it any less important or make you feel it any less strongly."

"I guess not." She sighed and brought her gaze back to his own, steady once more. "The jewelry box was already gone when I got there. And it was weird, because I don't think it had been gone for long. It looked like nothing else had been touched since we moved, but there was a pretty conspicuous space right where I'd left just that one thing."

"Not a coincidence, then."

"No. But I don't have any idea who took it or why."

"Where'd you find the key?"

"Right outside my mom's room."

"Right where you brother died," Anderson added gently.

She nodded once. "Yes."

"Do you think there's a chance *he* moved the jewelry box? Put it somewhere inst— Damn." He turned the key in the ignition. "I know where we need to go."

# *Chapter 9*

As Anderson pulled a quick U-turn, Nadine buckled up her seat belt and asked, “Are you going to fill me in?”

“Henderson. It’s the name of a storage place in that small industrial area on the other side of town.”

“Oh. That’s right.” She frowned. “But how do *you* know about it? I might never even have remembered it myself.”

“Drove through the whole town when I first got here. I noticed the handmade sign. Had a high school teacher named Mr. Henderson, so it stuck with me. Has your family ever stored anything there?”

“Not that I’m aware of. But there’s a lot of stuff they didn’t tell me, so that’s not saying much. Every one of them could’ve had *three* storage units for all I know.”

“I’ll settle for one if it contains a jewelry box.”

“So you think I’m right about it being significant?”

“I think it adds up enough that it’s worth investigating.”

She stared out the windshield for a second. “Can I ask you something personal?”

"You can ask me anything you like," he said.

"Do you know your family well?"

"You mean well enough that they wouldn't have any secret storage rentals?" He shot her a rueful smile and shook his head. "Sorry. I'm not trying to trivialize this. I know you're upset."

Nadine smiled. "Don't worry. Sarcasm is like a second language to me. I actually feel better when you use it. Then I feel normal."

"Noted." Then his voice turned serious. "To answer your question…I'd say there are plenty of things I don't *want* to know about my mom and stepdad. And my sisters are younger than I am—Riley by almost eighteen years, and Elle by twenty—so there are things we don't connect on. But overall I'd say, yeah, we have a pretty close relationship. The girls come to me for advice that I don't want to give. Walt—my stepdad—and I have a monthly movie night, and my mom is…my mom. I guess that's not what you wanted to hear, though?"

"Actually, I far prefer the honesty."

"You can count on me for that. Always."

"Thank you."

"Hey…look at that."

"What?"

"I think you just conceded a bit of trust."

"I guess I did."

"How does it feel?" he asked.

"Good," she said. "But weird."

"You really have a thing about normal, hmm?"

"I keep wondering if I know what it *is*. I thought I did when I was a kid. Then I found out about my dad's real life so there went that. So I had to start over again. And I tried. I even thought I had it figured out with my education and career and Grant…"

"Have you ever considered an alternative?"

"Like what?"

"Embracing the not-normal."

She snorted. "Settle for being a freak, you mean?"

"Settle?" He shook his head. "No. But embrace? Absolutely."

"And that's worked for you?"

"Uh-uh. *I'm* totally normal."

"Didn't you just literally tell me last night about how abnormal your family was, and—"

"What's wrong?"

"It's not that something's wrong," Nadine replied. "It's just that I can't believe that was only yesterday. It feels like I've known you for a year."

Anderson nodded and went silent as he turned the truck onto the street that led to Whispering Woods' only industrial complex. Nadine worried at her lip, wondering if her last comment was a bit too much. She wasn't sure where the line was between meaningful kisses and blurting out a comment that—in very recent retrospect—bordered on something stalkeresque. And she somehow doubted that she could gracefully sidestep her own words. But when Anderson brought the truck through the chain-link fence that wound around the edge of Henderson Storage, then guided it into a parking space and turned toward her, Nadine realized she wouldn't need to come up with an excuse.

His blue eyes were tender, his words fierce. "You're right. It feels like a hell of lot longer than a day. And I want it to keep feeling like that. In fact, I want to feel even more. Which is why I think we should follow this lead—and anything else that comes from it—and put Garibaldi away so we can focus on us."

*Us.* She liked the way it sounded.

She met Anderson's eyes. "You realize that all of that just makes me want to sit here and kiss you instead of going in."

He shot her a cheeky grin. "Well, I guess if you really want another kiss, you'll just have to catch me."

"Catch you?" Nadine repeated.

He swung open the door. "Yep."

"What if someone's watching?"

"Then they'll get a voyeuristic eyeful."

"I don't mean that kind of watching."

"You mean what if someone's lying in wait?"

"Yes."

He lifted an eyebrow. "You really think I'd let you run around if I had even the tiniest suspicion of danger?"

Nadine swallowed. "No."

"Not a chance."

"But you're not really going to—" She groaned as he hopped out. "You *are*."

"Sure am."

He slammed the door shut and loped off. For a second, Nadine stared after him, unable to believe that he was choosing this moment to be playful. That he expected her to chase him. Literally. With another groan, she climbed out, too. But as she moved on quick feet over the hard-packed dirt, she realized that the levity felt good.

*Maybe Anderson knew it would.*

By the time she reached the gate, she could feel a wide smile wanting to break free. And as she rounded it and found Anderson leaned up against the small office building, it burst through, along with a laugh. She felt lighter than she had in months. If she hadn't thought it sounded crazy, she might've admitted it was lighter than she'd felt in *years*. So when Anderson put out his arms, without hesitating, Nadine threw her arms over his shoulders, pressed her body to his and tipped up her face.

"Thank you," she said.

"For?"

"Making me feel okay in this bad situation."

"That's what I'm here for."

"I thought you were here for a kiss."

"That, too."

She pushed up to her toes, braced herself for the jolt of searing heat she knew would be coming and cemented her lips to his. The simple contact was enough to make her a little breathless. And when his hands came up to the small of her back to pull her closer and his tongue plunged into her mouth, the effect was dizzying. Warmth and desire swept through Nadine. And the intensity grew stronger as Anderson's palms slid up, then down to splay across her hips possessively. She wanted more. She wanted to get impossibly close. She wanted *him*.

"Ahem."

The exaggerated sound of a throat clearing made Nadine draw back fast. Her face flushed as she turned and spotted a man clad in a Henderson Storage golf shirt eyeing the two of them with amusement.

"If you're looking for a room, you've come to the wrong place," he said.

Anderson adjusted to sling his arm over Nadine's shoulders—like he'd done it a thousand times before—and let out a chuckle. "Already got *that* kinda room, thanks. We're actually in search of something else."

"If it's a storage solution, I'm your guy. Hank Henderson at your service."

"Well, we're hoping that it's a solution." Anderson gave Nadine a squeeze, and she knew he was prompting her to say something.

"My brother," she blurted. "I think he had a storage unit here."

"What's his name?"

"His name *was* Tyler Strange," Anderson said.

Nadine didn't miss the slight emphasis on the word *was*, and neither did Hank Henderson.

"Mr. Strange…nice enough kid. Sorry to hear, but…" He gave his chin a quick scratch.

"But what?" Anderson prodded.

"You've gotta be Nadine?"

Nadine nodded. "Yes. How did you know?"

"Weird thing," Hank said. "Your brother just rented the unit a couple of weeks ago. Paid for three months in cash, then told me that if you came by, to let you in because it might mean he wouldn't be coming back. Gave me a spare key, just in case. Sounded like the lead-up to an action movie, you know what I mean?"

"Sorry. We only watch romances," Anderson said in an utterly serious voice.

Hank frowned. "This wasn't a romantic thing. You can trust me on that."

A stab of sadness threatened, and Nadine forced it aside. "But you can let us in?"

"Promised your brother I would. Sit tight and I'll grab that key."

Nadine waited until he'd disappeared into the building before extricating herself from Anderson's sideways embrace so she could shoot him a properly dirty look.

"We only watch romance movies?" she said. "Really?"

"What? It's true. We've watched exactly one movie together and it *was* a romance."

"I fell asleep five minutes in."

"Four minutes," he corrected. "But I'm still counting it."

Nadine opened her mouth to argue, but Hank came back out then, a key on a ring hanging from his finger.

"Here you go," he said. "It's unit eighteen. You want me to show you?"

"I think we'll be fine." Anderson took the key, then took Nadine's hand.

And less than thirty seconds later, they were standing in front of the slide-up metal door.

* * *

Anderson squeezed Nadine's hand reassuringly one more time. He knew she was anxious, and he didn't blame her. He also knew, though, that words weren't going to help. What she needed was to see what her brother had left behind—be that the jewelry box or something else entirely. So he concentrated on that instead.

He released his hold on her hand, bent to one knee and slid the key into the padlock. A quick twist, and it opened easily.

Anderson didn't waste time on being dramatic. He dropped the lock into his coat pocket, then lifted the rolling door up, standing as he did it. Before he could step into the dark room, Nadine's hand snaked out to clasp his again.

"Ready?" she asked.

"I am if you are," Anderson replied.

He let her tug him forward, but they only made it a couple of steps before she stopped again. The light from outside didn't carry more than a few feet in, and they were immersed in darkness already.

"Can you see anything?" Nadine's question echoed a little in the seemingly cavernous space.

"Nope. Not even a damned shadow," Anderson said. "Makes me think it might actually be empty. Don't see a light switch, either."

"I think maybe there's a string hanging there in the middle."

He squinted. "Where?"

"Here." She didn't let his hand go as she pulled him farther in.

Though he couldn't see what she was doing, he did hear the click right before the six-by-six room filled with a yellow light. Sure enough, a thin piece of brown string hung down from a single ceiling-mounted bulb. It held his attention for only a moment, though, because of Nadine's sharply indrawn breath.

"That's it," she said, her gaze fixed on one corner of the room.

He lifted his eyes to follow her stare. A smallish box sat on the floor, its polished wood exterior eerily catching the light. Nadine's fingers tightened around his hand.

"Hey," he said gently. "Your brother left it here for you to find. That's a good thing."

Her exhale bounced off the metal walls. "You think so?"

"I know so."

"Should we open it?"

"Definitely."

"Okay."

It was his turn to give her a little tug, and after the briefest stall, she walked with him to the jewelry box.

"You have the envelope?" she asked.

"Yep." He released her to dig into his pocket so he could hand it over.

She smiled, then sat on the concrete floor and pulled the box into her lap. Anderson crouched down beside her, watching as she opened the lid, then lifted a false bottom and tilted it so he could see the keyhole in the bottom. It wasn't a particularly clever or secretive design, and he couldn't help but wonder why her father would use it in the first place and why her brother would continue.

"The box is wood on the outside, but metal on the inside," Nadine explained, clearly reading his doubtful expression. "Steel encased in blown plastic, actually."

"Like a safe."

"Yes. The same stuff they use to make the little fireproof home safes. For important documents. My dad told me that when he gave it to me. I thought it was cool. A little funny. But it never occurred to me that it might be all that important."

"Well, I guess we're about to find out just how important it really is."

"Yes."

She turned her attention back to the jewelry box. She slid the key free from the envelope, then fit it into the lock. A firm turn made the mechanism inside click, and the false bottom popped up. Nadine pulled it open the rest of the way and pulled out something small and rectangular.

"It's a USB stick."

She held it out and Anderson took it. He frowned. For some reason, he'd been expecting some conclusive piece of evidence. A USB stick could hold anything. Photos. Files. Personal notes.

"I know it's stating the obvious," he said, "but we're going to need a computer."

Nadine didn't acknowledge his words; instead, she spoke in a slightly strained voice. "There's something else in here, Anderson."

She made no move to pick up whatever it was, so he put his own hand in the box. What he drew out was a folded piece of note card addressed to Nadine.

"That's my brother's handwriting," she told him.

"Do you want me to read it aloud?"

"Please."

Anderson lifted the top half of the card. "It says, 'If you're reading this, the news for me is probably bad. I wanted to keep you safe. Always. You're on your own now, so you'll have to use the pictures on this stick to do it yourself. Love, T.'"

Nadine inhaled and nodded. "You're right."

"About what?"

"We need a computer." She pushed to her feet. "I've got one at my apartment, but I guess it's probably not safe to go there. So we'll have to buy a new one. Of course, there aren't any big-box stores in town. Oh. But there's a guy who has an electronics repair shop that sells refurbished stuff. The only problem is that it's on Main Street. Not exactly an unobtrusive location."

He stood up, too. "Nadine."

"Yes?"

"Just hang on for a second. We can talk about this."

"There's nothing to talk about. We really do need to figure out what's on that USB stick." She turned toward the door.

He took her by the elbow and spun her back. "The note."

"I can't change anything in it," she said.

"I need you to know something."

"What?"

"Your brother was wrong."

"He was?"

"Definitely, sweetheart. He said you were alone. But I promise you, you're not. And you won't ever be, so long as I have anything to say about it."

She smiled. "Thank you."

"Don't thank me," Anderson said back. "It's as *selfish* as it is *selfless*. Because I'm the one who's going to keep you company."

"Stalking me again?" she joked.

"Maybe a little."

She placed a soft kiss on his cheek. "Good. Should we go?"

"Yeah."

Anderson waited until they'd rolled the door back into place, thanked Hank Henderson for his time and pulled back out onto the road before speaking again. He knew Nadine wouldn't like what he had to say.

"Spit it out," she ordered as soon as he'd brought the truck up to the speed limit.

"What?"

"I can tell you're trying to work up to saying something. So you might as well just say it."

He sighed. "I think I should probably make the computer pickup on my own."

"Didn't you just say I'd never be alone again?" she countered.

"I didn't mean that literally. And if you're trying to goad me into taking you with me, it won't work. No matter how hard you try."

"So what's your plan, then? You're going to dump me off at the hotel and hope Garibaldi's men don't figure out that I'm there?"

"No. That's not any better than parking on Main Street and strolling into the computer place together."

He strummed the steering wheel with his thumbs. Truthfully, he didn't have a concrete plan yet. They needed the computer, but he needed her to stay safe even more.

They drove on for a few more blocks before Nadine spoke up. "There's a pie place."

"A what?"

"A pie place. It's a tourist hot spot. Even when the season's just starting, like it is now, it's packed full of people. It's a block over from Main Street. Parking is behind a private fence."

"Very public."

"Too public to do anything violent without drawing a lot of attention."

He considered it for a second. She'd be close. A one-minute walk. And she was right—the shield of a crowd would likely keep Garibaldi and his men at bay. He and his partners were sure that in spite of the man's various criminal enterprises, he was doing his damnedest to fly under the radar. Garibaldi had something bigger to protect.

"It might not be ideal," Nadine added, interrupting his

thoughts. "But I think it's the only thing that'll make both of us happy."

Anderson grunted. "I'm not sure *happy* is the right word in this case."

"Adequately satisfied?"

"How about *in*adequately satisfied?"

"How about a compromise both of us can live with?"

He sighed. "Okay. I'll agree to that last one. But only because I can't get away with winding you up in bubble wrap and stashing you away somewhere."

"Funny."

"Whatever it takes to keep you safe."

"Short of bubble wrap."

"Exactly."

He slid his hand from the steering wheel to her thigh, and he gave her a squeeze. "I do like these pants better than plastic."

"Anderson?"

"Yeah?"

"You may want to rewatch some of those romantic movies you like so much. Because that is the *worst* compliment I've ever received."

He laughed and pressed his fingers to her thigh again before bringing his hand back to the steering wheel. For a few seconds, his mood stayed light. The closer they got to Main Street, though, the more it darkened. And by the time they'd reached the pie shop, he was just about ready to pull the plug.

He angled the truck into the last gravel parking space and turned to Nadine without unlocking the doors. "Maybe we can find a different way to retrieve the pictures from the USB stick."

"Like what? Have it couriered to your guy—Harley?—and wait for him to get back to us? That would take at least two days."

"That's not unreasonable."

"Yes. It is. I don't want to wait. I don't think we *should* wait. And on top of that…the pictures are *mine*. They're the only link I have left to my brother and my dad."

"They're a blackmail bargaining chip, Nadine. Not a legacy."

"It's the same thing in this case," she argued. "And even if you don't agree, the time factor's just too much of a risk. I don't want to spend the next two days hiding out while we wait."

"It might not be *all* bad." He shot her his best suggestive smile.

It earned him a laugh. "I'm sure it wouldn't be. But I'm still not willing to wait. I'll see you in a few minutes, okay?"

She leaned over and gave him the quickest kiss in the world, then jumped out and ran up to the crowded little café. Anderson watched her disappear, apprehension growing the moment he couldn't see her anymore. Suppressing a frustrated growl, he swung open his own door and resolved to be the fastest computer purchaser in the world.

# Chapter 10

Nadine forced herself not to turn around and look at Anderson as she stepped into the pie shop. She could feel his eyes on her, and she didn't trust herself to meet his gaze. She was afraid that if she did, her resolve would crumble. She'd dive straight into his arms, hand over the USB stick and agree to stay locked in the honeymoon suite for as long it took for someone else to retrieve the pictures.

*Not all bad*, he'd said.

But the heat that flowed through her when she thought about being alone with him in the room at the lodge told her that "not bad" wouldn't even come close. Between the oversize spa tub, the huge bed and the potential for chocolate-covered strawberries and champagne, they'd have more than enough to distract them from everything else. Which was an even bigger reason not to give in to the urge. She wanted to focus on the case. She knew Anderson did, too.

*Of course, two days isn't much in the grand scheme of things*, pointed out a little voice in her head.

She made her feet stay planted. Anderson hadn't spent the last fifteen years hunting Garibaldi just to turn his back on it now. Not even in the short term. She refused to be the reason for letting that happen. She'd get a coffee. A slice of pie. And then she'd dive back into helping him get what they both wanted—to see the man answer for his past crimes and be barred from committing more in the future.

Resolve in place once more, she moved a little farther into the café. But she no sooner got into the line than a tap on the shoulder just about made her jump.

"Nadine Spencer, right?"

She took a steadying breath and turned slowly to face the questioner, a forced smile on her face as she corrected, "Nadine Stuart."

A plump brunette about her own age smiled back. "Right! Sorry. I've got a million things going on, but I still should've got that right."

"Have we met?"

"Yes. Or, no, I guess. Not officially. I'm Tegan's mom. She's in third grade at Whispering Woods Elementary, so I was at the meeting a few weeks back when the principal introduced you."

"Well. It's nice to meet you, Tegan's mom."

The brunette laughed. "Oh. Sorry. Bad habit. I've been introducing myself that way for eight years. I'm Liz Redford. In addition to being Tegan's mom, I'm also a person. That last bit is a reminder for me, not you."

Nadine couldn't help but laugh. "Doubly nice to meet you, then. It's nice to talk to other humans now and then."

"Speaking of which…" The other woman nodded forward. "I think it's your turn."

Nadine smiled again and turned her attention to the

kid behind the counter. "Two slices of the cherry. To go, please."

"Eight-fifty," said the kid.

It wasn't until she reached for her purse that she realized she had a problem. No purse. No money. With her face already flaming, she glanced around. There were at least five people within hearing distance.

*Just another thing to draw unwanted attention.*

But as she opened her mouth to mumble a retraction of the order, Liz Redford piped up again.

"Here," the other woman said. "My treat. To welcome you to Whispering Woods Elementary."

Nadine didn't argue. "Thank you."

She moved aside as Liz paid for her order and gave her own. Shooting the brunette another grateful look and another mumble of thanks, she excused herself and tried to sneak away. The other woman followed, still smiling.

"So…" she said. "Cherry pie from the Pie Shack. Who can resist it?"

"No one in their right mind." Nadine scanned the parking lot for Anderson while trying not to look obvious. "It's one of the things I missed the whole time I was away from Whispering Woods."

"It's one of the reasons I'm glad I moved here."

"You're new in town?"

"A year now. Sometimes it feels like forever. Especially with the amount of work I've had to put in at the store. Thank goodness for Jesse Garibaldi. I don't know where I'd be without him."

Nadine's eyes jerked to the other woman. "What?"

"He's my landlord. For both work and home. My daughter and I live in that row of houses with the converted main floors? My store is downstairs and our apartment is above. I lease the whole thing from Jesse Garibaldi. The man is practically a saint. He gave me a huge break on the first few months' rent while I did the renovations."

"What did Garibaldi ask you for?" Nadine replied before she could stop herself.

Liz blinked. "What?"

Nadine tried to smile again, but it felt wooden. "That sounded different than I meant it. I just heard from a friend that Garibaldi exchanges favors."

"Oh. I don't know if I'd call it a favor, but Jesse did ask me to stock some high-priced art for him."

"Art?"

"Mmm. That's what I sell at my store. Handmade items, mostly. But I don't mind the bigger pieces from Jesse. He has regular buyers and just takes the standard commission. So if it *is* a favor, I'm guessing it benefits me more than him."

"That's great for you, then, right?"

"Keeps me in business anyway."

Nadine frowned. She felt like there was something significant in what the other woman had just said. But whatever it was, it was just out of reach. Like the buried memories from the day her dad died.

"What about you?" Liz asked. "You're out for pie. Does that mean *you're* back in business, too?"

"Um."

"The principal sent around an email about the car accident. I can't imagine how terrible that must've been."

Nadine started to say that she was fine, then stopped herself as her mind leaped from one thing to another. Her accident was public knowledge. So was her stay in the care facility. People who saw her would naturally ask how she was and when she'd been released. But she *hadn't* been released. In fact, she'd disappeared completely. And right in the middle of an evacuation, as well.

*Shouldn't that have triggered an investigation of some kind? Or at least a phone call?*

She didn't know why it hadn't occurred to her before. Or why it hadn't occurred to Anderson.

*Dammit.*

"Ms. Stuart? Are you all right?" Liz Redford placed a gentle hand on her elbow. "Do you need to sit down?"

Nadine cleared her throat. "No. I'm fine. Really."

"Sorry for prying."

"It's all right. You're not prying. If I wanted to stay incognito, I should've worn a disguise," she said as lightly as she could manage.

But her eyes flicked nervously around the pie shop.

How many people would know her by sight? Until the accident that killed Officer Delta, she'd been very careful to keep her knowledge about Garibaldi's illegal activity a secret. All of the amateur investigating she'd done—before figuring out that Reggie Frost and Brayden Maxwell were on the right side—had been done covertly. Under the cover of night and from behind a black hoodie. During the day, she'd just been an old resident, returning home to take a job. A smiling schoolteacher whose reasons for being in Whispering Woods were fully explainable. Now, though, she couldn't walk around like she knew nothing.

*Coming into a public place was a mistake.*

"Are you sure you're all right?" Liz asked.

"Yes. I'm—" Relief flooded through her as she spied Anderson outside. "I'm sorry. My ride is here. I've gotta get going. It's always nice to meet a parent."

"Nice to meet you, too. Come by the shop sometime. Liz's Lovely Things."

"Thanks. I'll check it out."

Nadine clutched the pie tightly and hurried out to Anderson.

* * *

Anderson could tell something was wrong the second Nadine stepped out of the pie shop. Her face was pale, and she was all but crushing the white box she held in her hands.

"Hey," he greeted. "Is everything—"

"Let's just get back to the hotel." She brushed by him and moved toward the truck, then swung open the door and climbed in. "You coming?"

He eyed the café for a second before turning his attention back to Nadine.

"Please," she said.

"All right."

He waited until they were back on the road before asking, "Something you want to share?"

"Did you call the care facility?" she replied.

"What?"

"Yesterday. After we took off."

"No. Why?"

"Why aren't they looking for me? I mean, I know I wasn't a prisoner, but still…they had the cops there looking for a masked intruder. One of their patients disappears. Shouldn't that have attracted some kind of notice?"

Anderson's gut churned, and he cursed himself for not thinking of it. Making the call should've been the first thing he did. And Nadine was right. The care center and the police would have been—*should* have been—more than concerned about losing a patient in the middle of an evacuation incident.

"Am I wrong?" Nadine asked.

"No. You're completely right."

"Can you think of a reason they might *not* be worried about where I am?"

"If you'd checked yourself out."

"Which I didn't."

"Or someone they trusted told them you'd left voluntarily."

"Like who?"

"Your doctor," he suggested, then shook his head. "But I can only think of reasons for him to worry *more* than anyone else."

"What about Garibaldi?" she replied softly. "He's a major benefactor of the hospital. His name's at the top of that board of contributors they have hanging in the entryway."

"Can't imagine him trying to cover your tracks for you."

"But it would make sense, too," she persisted, "if he thought I wouldn't be there because his guys were going to make sure I wasn't."

The roiling in Anderson's stomach grew thicker, and his grip on the steering wheel tightened so hard that his hands ached.

Nadine ran a hand over his forearm. "Are you okay?"

"I hate feeling like we're at his mercy," he admitted, his voice rough.

"We're not."

"How do you figure? The man's got every damned card, doesn't he? And he's a step ahead, too."

"I think he's a step behind, actually, because he doesn't know who *you* are."

"That we're aware of."

"I'm sure of it," she argued. "If he did, he would've made an effort to get to you, too. At the hospital or at the hotel. But he's still just focused on me."

Anderson flexed his fingers and muttered, "Then maybe I'd *rather* him know who I am."

Nadine laughed, and he turned a surprised look her way.

"That's funny?" he asked.

"Misguidedly romantic," she corrected. "It's not every

day that someone wishes they could be stalked on your behalf."

"In the old days, they called that chivalry."

"You didn't offer to throw your jacket over a puddle, Anderson."

"Go big or go home."

"Tell me about it. We just met a week ago, and we're already engaged."

Now his hands relaxed completely, and he let out his own chuckle. "Maybe you're just that irresistible."

She snorted. "Yeah. That's the word I'd use to describe myself."

"We're not talking about words *you'd* use. We're talking about words *I'd* use."

"I've never in my life been accused of being irresistible."

"Then you've been associating with the wrong people."

"Clearly." She settled back against the seat, a small—definitely irresistible—smile tipping up her lips. "What's so irresistible about me?"

"You're after a little flattery?"

"What woman isn't?"

"Ah. But you told me yourself you're not a typical woman."

"And that's what makes me so irresistible?"

"At least partly," he said seriously. "I like that you're different."

"Into freaks," she replied. "Noted."

He laughed. "You don't put up with crap. You tell it like it is. You're smart and intuitive. You're determined and fearless. And your world's been blowing up again and again, and you haven't given up. Not once. All of *that* is what makes you irresistible. And if it also makes you a freak, then I guess I'm on board with a first-class ticket."

"Ugh."

"Ugh?"

"How am I supposed to top that? Any compliment I give you is going to seem pretty damned lame now."

Another laugh escaped, and Anderson shook his head. "I bet you're pretty damned good at placating unruly third-graders, aren't you?"

"I think I do all right. Why?"

"Because a second ago, all I could think about was throwing myself—chivalrously, of course—onto a grenade for you. Now all I can think about is throwing myself at you directly."

"Hmm." She dragged the noise out, obviously amused.

"What?"

"Well, putting aside the relative smoothness of that segue, I have to admit that I don't get a lot of calls to use my skills to transition from grenades to kisses."

"And for that I'm thankful."

"Oh, really?"

"It means I'm first." He grinned. "Plus, grenades in the classroom aren't a good thing."

"No. Best to keep the two things separate."

He sneaked another glance at her. Her gaze was out the front windshield, that little smile still playing across her face. The sun shone through the side window, catching bits of her blond hair and making it shimmer.

He could stare at her all day, Anderson thought as he forced his eyes back to the road.

"I think I forgot something in that long-winded compliment of mine," he said.

He felt her brown eyes flick his way. "What's that?"

"You're beautiful."

"Thank you."

"No need to thank me. It's just the truth."

"Hey, Anderson?"

"Yes?"

"How come some other girl hasn't already snapped you up? Have you got some dark secret you're working up to telling me?"

"It wouldn't be a very dark secret if I was going to tell you so quickly, would it?" he teased.

She gave his shoulder a playful push. "That was actually a serious question."

"Ah. Your subtle way of asking about my past."

"I'm not very good at subtlety. In case you haven't noticed."

"Oh, I've noticed."

"You're avoiding the question."

He sighed. "We're only about three minutes from the lodge."

"And that's three minutes you can use to confess all the lurid details of your love life," she countered.

"Three minutes, huh?"

"Do you need more time?"

He covered a laugh at her pointed tone. "Three minutes will do."

"I think we're actually down to two and a half," she said.

"That's cutting it close."

"Then I guess you better hurry up."

"Persistent, aren't you?"

"Didn't you say a minute ago that was one of my more irresistible qualities?"

"And your memory's a steel trap, apparently."

"Stalling again."

"Okay. Fine. Here it is. My love life, in under three minutes." He inhaled, then laid out the embarrassingly minimal details in rush. "High school sweetheart moved away right after graduation. Vet school. Never heard from her again. Kinda expected it to happen, so I got over it quickly. I worked for a year, then went into the academy. Dated casually while I trained, but didn't have time for anything too serious. Same for my rookie year at Freemont PD. Second year, though, I met a woman I liked a lot. A clerk at the courthouse. Clara was her name. We went out for eighteen months or so before she broke it off. She told me I was married to my job, and she wanted something more. I resented that for a while. My Mr. Nice Guy attitude even took a back seat to Mr. Bitter. But when I got into my next relationship—a year with a woman who owned a chain of statewide coffee shops—I realized that Clara was right. I chose my work over my relationship at every chance. And even though my new girlfriend either never noticed or didn't care, I knew I wouldn't ever be able to give her anything more than I was at that moment. So I ended it. That was three years ago. And here I am."

"Wow."

"Wow?" he repeated. "I didn't think it was all that impressive—more like underwhelming."

"No. I mean…did you even breathe while you were telling me all of that?"

"You said I had to fill three minutes." He nodded out the window toward the Whispering Woods Lodge, which loomed on the horizon. "And we're here, so I'd say my timing is damned near impeccable."

"Uh-huh. And you always do what you're told?"

"I try to accommodate when I can."

"Riiiight."

"It helps when doing what I'm told serves my own interests."

"And what are your interests in this case?"

Anderson shot her a smile as he took the final turn up to the lodge. "Right now…making you happy, sweetheart."

## *Chapter 11*

As they made their way from the truck to their room, the blooming warmth in Nadine's chest didn't fade. If anything, it grew, spurred on by the fact that Anderson's fingers were threaded tightly with her own. By the time they actually made it to the suite, the warmth was a burn. And when the door shut, it became a raging inferno. Her chest wanted to burst.

As Anderson turned her way, his mouth open to say something, Nadine pounced. She wrapped her arms around his shoulders, dug her fingers into his hair and slammed her lips forcefully to his mouth. She took all of the heat coursing through her and channeled it into the kiss. And yet when she pulled away, it stayed. Banked. Just waiting to blow up again.

She lifted her eyes to meet Anderson's and she saw the same warmth reflected there.

"Success," she breathed.

"Success?" he repeated.

"In your 'right now' interests." She leaned back and smiled. "I'm happy."

His mouth tipped up on one side. "Oh, yeah?"

"Crazy, right? I've been attacked. Had my childhood home burned down. And I'm pretty sure we can agree that Garibaldi wants me dead. But I'm happy. Right now. Right here with you."

He lifted a finger and smoothed her hair back from her face. "That *is* crazy. Some therapy might be in order."

"How about another kiss instead?"

"Don't we have some work to do?"

"All right. If you don't want to kiss me..." She took a step back.

He took a step forward. "That's not what I said."

She took another step back. "No. Not literally. But we can't work *and* kiss, can we?"

He moved closer again. "How can we be sure unless we try?"

Suppressing a laugh, she tried to inch out of reach, but both of Anderson's hands shot up to close on her shoulders. His palms slid down her arms to her wrists, and he lifted her hands to his waist, and this time when Nadine moved back, it was because he was pushing her. Three steps, and the backs of her knees hit the couch.

"Hey!" she protested. "This most definitely is *not* work."

"I know."

His smile turned sly, and with a little shove, he sent her backward. And he followed. He landed over top of her, his thickly muscled arm holding him up. He grinned at her.

"Not a bad view," he said.

"Lamest line, ever, Anderson."

"Well. Maybe I can make up for it."

He tipped his head down, and Nadine let herself be swept away. His mouth was warm, his tongue firm as he ran his mouth first over the length of her throat, then the line of her jaw. He kissed and sucked, teased and tasted. The opulent hotel slipped to oblivion, and the very pressing fears and worries weren't far behind.

Nadine leaned her head back to give Anderson better access, and the move arched her body against his. She couldn't help but appreciate the strong, hard line of him as their still-covered skin met. It made her want to tear off every piece of fabric. To give in to the most basic of urges and to forget all else. And without even being conscious that she was following through on the need, she lifted her fingers to the top button of his shirt. They unfastened that one. Then the next. The third popped open with the barest touch, and Nadine slipped her hand inside. His skin was perfect. Just barely smooth enough to not be called rough. She dragged her fingers back and forth over his collarbone, reveling in the feel of it.

*I want more*, she realized.

But when she reached for the fourth button, Anderson growled something unintelligible against her throat and pulled back.

"Nadine..."

The way he said her name—raw with passion—made her reply come out as a gasp. "Yes?"

He bent again to rub his nose against hers lightly. "I'm a nice guy. But I'm not a saint."

"I'm counting on it." She gave his lower lip a nip.

He groaned. "We should stop."

"Really?"

"Not because I want to."

"Well, I'm willing to keep going. I've only got a few buttons left. Then we can move on to disrobing *me*."

"You're killing me."

"Is that code for something?"

She slipped her hand to the fourth button, but he pulled back. It set him into a kneeling position. Right between her legs. His shirt had parted, exposing his thick chest and displaying a mouthwatering hint of his defined pectoral muscles. Nadine's desire for him only spiked higher. She reached up and pressed her hands to his thighs.

"If you really want to stop," she said, "I'd suggest moving to the other side of the room. Quickly. Because I'm not the only one with a few irresistible qualities."

He looked genuinely torn. So much so that Nadine laughed, then slid back and dragged her legs free.

"Relax, Detective Somers. I'm not about to force you to get naked."

He didn't smile back. Instead, he adjusted his own position, then leaned forward to cup her cheek.

"I want this, Nadine," he said. "I want *you*. But I also want it to be right. I don't want to be in a rush, or to have any other distractions or concerns weighing us down."

The heat in Nadine's chest reared up again, and she smiled. "You're underestimating the effect you have on me."

"Oh, I am, am I?"

"Definitely. The second I get close to your lips, I forget everything else."

"Like this?" He pushed up to give her another kiss—this one soft.

"Exactly like that," she agreed.

"But when I pull away…it all comes flooding back?"

Nadine made a face. "Yes. More quickly than I'd like."

"Well," Anderson said with a smile. "That's what I'm trying to avoid. I want you to focus on me one hundred percent."

"Me focusing on you, huh? What about the other way around?"

"Oh, I have no doubt that I can put everything aside in favor of you."

"Even your investigation?" she blurted, then quickly tried to backpedal. "Sorry, I didn't mean—"

"No need to apologize, honey. Really. I've gotta admit that the case has gone on the back burner since I met you."

"I'm s—" This time she cut herself off with a headshake. "I don't want to get in the way of your work any more than I want to *be* your work."

"You're not. On both things. I promise." He grabbed her hand and brought it to his mouth. "Tell me you believe me."

There went that explosion in her chest. And she finally recognized it for what it was—burgeoning affection. She liked him. A lot. And every time he said something that made her sure the feeling was mutual, her heart swelled.

"Well?" he pushed. "Have I earned that much trust?"

She nodded, not trusting herself to speak.

"Good," he said. "So should we take care of the scary stuff that's getting in our way so we can move on to more important things."

"Okay."

He gave her another kiss, then grabbed the laptop, talking as he pulled it from the bag. "The guy in the store did the setup. Nothing too fancy. Figured we didn't need to break the bank to look through a few files."

Nadine winced as something occurred to her. "I owe you—or the Freemont PD—a lot of money."

"What?"

"The hotel room. The clothes and the food. And now a computer. Maybe not breaking the bank, but it's still a good chunk."

"I'll just take it out of the date credits."

"Date credits?"

"Yeah. What I'd normally spend on movie tickets, dinner, wine and roses. Trust me. The cost is comparable."

"But I'm the kind of girl who normally pays her own way."

"Then you can pay for the next round of purchases related to crime solving." He held out his hand. "Have you got the USB stick?"

She retrieved it from the little pocket at her waistband and gave it to him. "I'm kind of hoping this is the last crime I'll have to solve."

"You want to turn in your gun and badge so soon?"

"I'd like to have gone without the fictional pair completely, actually."

"So why'd you stay in Whispering Woods at all?"

"I'm sure Brayden filled you in on the details."

"He told me that you found out unexpectedly that your mom still had her place here. And I know about the teaching position, and you explained about Grant the Ungrateful. So I get why you'd feel compelled to come. But I'm not sure why you *stayed*." He studied her face, his hand hovering near the USB port. "Closure is all well and good, but most people just let the authorities deal with things."

"I've had a hole in my memory since I was a teenager, Anderson. I've known for just as long that Garibaldi isn't who he says he is. But I never did anything about it. I took his payoff money in the form of hospital bills and my education, even though I really had no idea what it was I was being paid off *for*. My only experience with the authorities taught me that Garibaldi is capable of mass manipulation. My brother died trying to keep me safe. The sheer amount of guilt I have is enough to make me crazy." She managed a half-hearted smile. "And I'm not sure I was all that sane to begin with."

"So I guess I should hurry up?"

"Please."

Without further comment, Anderson jammed the USB stick into the corresponding slot, and in seconds a series of files—each labeled with a date—appeared on the laptop's screen. He set it up to open versus save, just in case the laptop got into the wrong hands, and when Anderson clicked on one, a host of tiny photographs flickered into view. And even as small as they were, Nadine knew exactly what they were.

Nadine's audible inhale made Anderson turn his attention away from the computer screen.

"See something?" he asked.

She nodded. "Every one of those thumbnails is a shot of the car my dad drove for Garibaldi."

He turned back to the laptop. The car was navy, with nothing to distinguish it from a thousand other sedans.

"How can you be sure?"

"Click one."

Anderson complied, choosing a picture at random. Nadine pointed at what looked like a smudge on the driver's-side bumper.

"See that right there?" she said. "You can't tell so much from the photo, but it's pale pink paint. My dad had it parked in the driveway one day, and I crashed into it with my bike. It was brand-new at the time. I thought he was going to be furious—especially because the car belonged to his boss—but he laughed it off. He said the mark was shaped like a heart, and he asked Garibaldi to leave it there so he could think of me every time he got inside."

"Sounds like you meant a lot to your father."

"I thought we were close, right up until the day I found out about his other life."

"A thing like that could make you question everything."

"It did. At least for the two days that I had before the bomb. After that, it was all beeping machines and doctors and trying to make people think I hadn't lost my mind. Then it became something I didn't want to think about."

"No hashing it out in therapy?"

"I've always favored actions over words." She met his eyes. "What about you?"

He felt compelled to tell the truth. "Therapy? Years of it. You remember what I told you about my mom and how she wanted me to remember the good things?"

"Yes."

"It wasn't quite as smooth a transition as I made it sound. I had moments of clarity. Moments of resentment. I was angry and sad. A hundred other things, too."

"A hundred other completely *understandable* things," Nadine replied.

"Definitely," Anderson agreed. "And I couldn't do it alone. I spent eight months working with the counselor at my high school. A summer in group. Then I saw someone casually off and on all the way into adulthood."

"I've never been all that good at discussing my feelings."

"You do all right."

"You're easy to talk to."

"That whole Mr. Nice Guy thing works in my favor sometimes."

"Damaged hero doesn't hurt, either."

"Healed hero," he corrected with a wink. "Wanna do some more hands-on?"

"I'm assuming you mean with the pictures." In spite of her dry tone, a blush crept up her cheeks.

"For the short term." He started to reach for the keyboard again, then thought better of it and stopped.

"What?" Nadine said immediately.

"I'm not really a short-term kinda guy."

"I sort of figured that out already."

He shrugged. "I just think it's important to put it on the table."

The pink in her cheeks became crimson. "We only met

a little over a week ago. And most of that week, I resented you."

"I know. But I also know when something's worth it. I'm not going to be another Grant. I'm not going to pretend that I don't want something committed from you. I'm after forever, Nadine. And even though I'm not in a giant hurry to get there, I *am* going to pursue it." He shrugged again, a little embarrassed at the passion in the admission, then made himself add, "So if you're not after the same thing, you'd better tell me now."

Her mouth worked silently for a second before she breathed out. "Okay."

"Okay?"

"Not as in okay, that's not what I want."

"You do want it?"

She met his eyes. "I do. And it scares the hell out of me, so don't expect me to jump up and down with joy about it."

Anderson felt a sloppy grin split his face. "Good enough."

She offered him an eye roll, but her mouth was twitching, too. "Pictures?"

"Yep."

He dragged the computer a little closer, his smile fading as he switched from the close-up of Garibaldi's car to the list of files.

"These dates..." he said. "I think they correspond to crimes."

"What makes you say that?"

He pointed at one, his voice roughening. "This first one is the day my dad died." He lifted his finger and indicated the last file in the row. "And this is the day of the Main Street bombing."

A heavy silence hung in the air for several long moments before Nadine finally broke it. "If you don't want to open them, then don't."

"It's not a matter of wanting to or not wanting to. I have to. We have to. Or we won't know why Garibaldi is willing to kill to get this USB stick." When he tried to move to follow through, though, his hand froze.

A heartbeat later, Nadine's slim fingers slid past his. "Let me."

"Thank you."

As she tapped through, Anderson let himself close his eyes for a second. What had the photographer recorded on the day of the explosion in Freemont? How bad would it be?

*And how much will it hurt?*

Nadine's voice brought him back to the moment, and her words managed to anchor him. "It's all right to look, Anderson. I promise."

He opened his eyes and— trusting that she was telling the truth—he peered down at the screen. The shots were grainy. Though the car was slightly different from the one from the previous set of photographs, it was similar enough that he knew it just had to be an earlier model, serving the same purpose.

"Another of Garibaldi's vehicles," he stated.

"Yes. The quality is terrible, but I think my dad took these pictures. I remember when he got the camera phone. It was a pretty big deal at the time."

She clicked a few times, and it was obvious to Anderson that the shots were taken outside the Freemont City Police Station. He'd spent enough time there to recognize it from any angle, even as badly pixelated as the photos were. Thankfully, the shots were just of the car and the street. No bomb. No aftermath. The very last one in the group, though, made him pause.

"Is that a person?" He pointed to a blurred corner at the bottom of the screen.

Nadine leaned forward. "I think so. Garibaldi?"

"Possibly. Maybe even likely. I'll get Harley to see about enhancing the image."

"Should I move to the next files?"

"Please."

They moved through the next few sets quickly. They were all similar. A car, presumably driven by Nadine's father and ridden in by Jesse Garibaldi, sat outside varying places. A couple were identifiable as businesses. Some were residences. Others could've been either.

"Did my dad document every single place he drove Garibaldi?" Nadine asked after a few minutes of flicking through the pictures.

"Looks like he did a lot of the time," Anderson replied. "Maybe not literally every time. Maybe only when he thought something illegal was happening."

"Why?"

"Insurance."

"You mean blackmail."

"Working for a man like that...you probably never know whether or not it's safe to turn your back."

Nadine's gaze flicked from him to the computer, then back again. "That was a decade and a half ago. Garibaldi would've been barely more than a kid when he set off the bomb in Freemont."

Anderson nodded. "But your dad knew him before that. Your brother told my partner that before your dad drove for Jesse, he drove for the senior Garibaldi."

"You think he saw something dangerous in him that long ago?"

"He must've." He clicked through a few more of the files—it was the same, though the pictures grew a little clearer as the dates moved up. "I'll have Harley plug in these dates and see if he can line them up with anything else. You want to go over all of them now?"

"Don't you?"

"I like to be thorough. But I have to admit that I'm also in the mood for room service and a hot shower. Harley's far more efficient at computer stuff. He's got algorithms for everything. Location. Facial recognition. You name it."

"Sounds handy."

"Very. Harley's got a degree in fine arts and he's a whiz on the keyboard. Those two things make him pretty damned indispensable."

"Oh."

Nadine's eyes were fixed on the screen, her lower lip tugged between her teeth, and Anderson realized she wasn't really listening.

"Nadine?"

"What about the last file?" she asked.

Anderson followed her stare. "You sure you want to see?"

"Yes."

"Me? Or you?"

"You."

He reached over and clicked open the file. The first few pictures were just like the others. The paint-marked car, this time parked on Main Street in Whispering Woods. There were some still shots of the buildings along the strip of road. Then things changed. The exterior photos gave way to interior ones. They were dark. Blurred. Like the person taking them was trying to capture everything without exposing himself.

Anderson clicked a few more times, and the pictures changed again. Still not much to be said for the quality, which was frustrating, but a few details became evident. The room was big and lined with tall, narrow shelves. The ground seemed to be made of hard-packed dirt. He had no idea what he was looking at, so he clicked again. What he saw next made him frown. In the new shot, two people stood at a table. Even with the poor lighting it was easy to make out that their clothing was something out the ordinary.

"Those look like hazmat suits," Nadine stated.

He couldn't disagree with the observation. Each of the figures in the photo was covered head to toe. Jumpsuits and gloves. Face masks and hoods. The kind of things that belonged in a science lab.

Curiosity made him move to the next picture. It only got more puzzling. The figures in the picture held a wide piece of…something between them.

"What is it?" he wondered aloud.

"I think it might be a canvas," Nadine replied.

"Canvas?"

"The kind you use for painting. In fact, it might actually *be* a painting. It doesn't look blank. And I—" She stopped, her face pinching.

"What?"

"Art."

"What about it?"

"I don't know. I ran into a woman in the pie place today. She owns an art shop, and she mentioned that Garibaldi has her stock some high-end pieces. Does that seem like too much of a coincidence?"

"Damn right it does."

"You're agreeing," she said, bringing her fingers up to his furrowed brow. "But you're also frowning so hard that it looks like it hurts."

"Just seems odd."

"What does? That Garibaldi would be involved in some kind of art crime?"

"Hardly in line with bombings and murder."

"Maybe he branched out."

"Maybe," he said doubtfully.

She picked up on skepticism right away. "But you don't think so."

"Can't say that I do. Art theft. Art forgery. They're a little more specialized than I'd expect from a guy like Garibaldi. He's got his fingers in his share of crime pies, but this seems—I dunno—outside the frame." He smiled. "Pardon the pun."

She shot him an eye roll, then asked, "So if these pictures aren't about something directly art related, then what *are* they about?"

"Not sure. Something we're missing. Or haven't found yet. But there're still a few more pictures."

He reached out and clicked again. The next few shots were similar to the previous, each one showing the next piece of action. The suited-up men lifting the unframed painting higher. Then moving it across the room and finally sliding it into a narrow shelf.

Anderson squinted, trying to discern exactly what it was he was looking at. After a second, though, he didn't have to.

"That's it," said Nadine, her voice soft.

"That's what?"

"The room where the bomb went off and killed my dad."

# *Chapter 12*

The second the words left Nadine's mouth, Anderson started to shift the laptop screen away from her. She immediately shot out her hand to stop him. Inside, she was shaking. Her heart was shuddering faster than a hummingbird's wings. She could feel her nerves vibrating. Her stomach churned, her lungs hummed. But somehow, she managed to stay outwardly calm. Like the inner turmoil provided just enough chaos that her hands and mouth could manage without anything more.

"Don't," she said.

"If you don't remember it, how can you be sure that it's the same spot?" Anderson replied with a stubborn, worried edge to his voice.

"The date is right. The first pictures are outside the spot where the explosion happened. I'm sure."

"Then let me look through the rest of the photos first."

"I don't need a filter. My dad took these pictures, and he somehow managed to export them from his phone before he died. Whatever's on here could put Garibaldi away."

"That doesn't obligate you to look."

"Isn't that what I told you a minute ago?"

"Yeah, it is. But—"

"No. No *buts*. I want to see the rest. I *need* to. Just like you needed to look at the ones from the day your dad died."

"You don't know what's on there."

"Exactly." She met his gaze unblinkingly. "This might be the closest I ever come to accessing those lost memories. Please. Let me look."

He opened his mouth, then closed it and blew out a sigh from between his lips. But he also relented, turning the computer toward her once more.

"I'm ready for this," she said aloud, more to herself than to Anderson.

He answered anyway. "And if it turns out you're *not* ready…I've got you."

With a grateful nod, Nadine clicked the mouse. What she saw made her frown. The angle of the shot was off. Crooked.

*No*, she decided after a second. *Not just crooked. Sideways.*

She tipped her head to the side, trying to see properly. And when she did, she swallowed.

"That's us." The words came out in a whisper.

Anderson leaned closer, peering down at the screen. "Us who?"

"Me and Tyler."

With a few quick clicks, she rotated the photo so that it faced the right way. A few more adjustments, and she'd cropped and enlarged one corner of the picture. It was a little blurry, but it was easy enough to draw a conclusion about what was happening. Her brother stood just in front of her, one arm stretched out to hold her back. Nadine's blond hair stood out like a lightning bolt. Her arms were out, too, seeming to be grasping for some invisible object just out of reach. Her eyes were fixed ahead, fear evident even with the poor quality of the shot.

Though her face was directed toward the camera, Nadine had no recollection of the photo being taken. Was it because she actually hadn't known her father held the phone, or because it was another thing she'd forgotten? Thinking about it made her heart hammer impossibly harder.

"You still okay?" Anderson's arm accompanied his words, slinging around her waist and drawing her a little closer.

"Fine," she said, then thought better of the automatic affirmation and shook her head instead. "I just don't remember it, and it's disorienting."

"Hard to be missing a chunk of time like that."

"So hard. Especially at the beginning."

"You can still stop looking through them."

"I'm okay. Really."

"You wanna talk about what you *do* remember? Might help."

"Ten years ago, I woke up in the hospital in Freemont," she said. "And the doctors kept asking me that same thing. What did I remember? They figured I'd banged my head and blacked out. But when I talked about my brother and Whispering Woods, they backed off. It took me a while to get all the pieces."

"And when you did?"

"It was all wrong. They told me the car had hit a telephone pole. That my dad had been driving and he'd died on impact. Some Good Samaritan dragged me out and called 911. It was a lie, of course. I *knew* that I got into the car with Tyler two hundred miles away. The last conversation we had is still clear in my mind. We'd been searching for my dad for two days, and all of a sudden my brother had a lead through Garibaldi. Garibaldi knew where my dad was." She tapped the mouse and brought it back to the original picture, then pointed. "I'm a hundred percent sure this is the cellar under Main Street. I might not actually remember getting there, but Tyler told me later that it's where he and I were headed."

"And you went there again more recently." He said it with no force and no accusation, but guilt still stabbed at Nadine.

But she made herself nod. "I did. And not just when I took Reggie there while I was trying to figure out if she and Brayden were working with Garibaldi. When I first got back into town, it's one of the first places I stopped. I stood outside for a long time. On multiple days. I just thought it might help me remember. Exposure or something."

"It didn't work."

"No. Nothing came to me. So I took it one step further and I snuck into the basement. I found the renovated room. And I couldn't make sense of it. I mean, I knew the explosion that destroyed the original cellar was real. Garibaldi told me about it while I was still at the hospital. But the setup down there..." She trailed off, thinking of her puzzlement at the odd, underground room.

"You were expecting something else?"

"I honestly don't know." She took a breath and lifted her eyes to his.

"What's wrong, honey?"

She exhaled. "Promise you won't pass judgment because of what I'm about to tell you, okay?"

"How can I promise you that when I don't know what you're going to say?" he teased.

"I'm serious, Anderson."

He touched her chin with his thumb and forefinger. "Hey. You know me better than to think I'm going to pass judgment on you."

"It's just silly."

"Tell me."

She dropped her gaze. "I dream about it."

He didn't release her chin. "About what?"

"About the way it was in that room. The dark. The smell of smoke. And not just occasionally. All the time. The dreams are like fuzzy memories. Flashes that remind me of these pictures, actually. And they're a hell of a lot more real than the story about the car accident."

"Because they *are* real," he said firmly. "And these pictures could be proof of it. There're still a few we haven't looked at, but if you don't want to, we can just ship them off to Harley and let him deal with it."

She didn't even have to think about it. "No. We've come this far through them. I want to see what happened next."

She clicked onto the next shot. It was nothing but a blur. The one after was the same. But the final picture was a whole other story. It made her draw in a gasp and recoil from the computer. Because, startlingly, her own face filled the screen. It was a clearer photograph than all the others and showcased her younger self perfectly. Her hair was shoulder length, her bangs a blunt cut over her eyebrows. Black eyeliner smudged heavily across her lids, and the crimson lipstick she'd always preferred as a teen turned her mouth into a vibrant slash. But the picture was as disconcerting as it was clear.

In the shot, her eyes were closed, her face flat against the packed-dirt ground. Her cheek, which was now scarred from the so-called accident that she couldn't remember, was completely smooth.

Unconsciously, she reached up to touch the rough skin. Anderson's hand followed, his warm fingers closing over top of hers. Comfort flowed from his touch, and Nadine closed her eyes to lean into it.

"Send them to Harley," she said. "There has to be something in here that incriminates Garibaldi. Badly. If there wasn't, he wouldn't be coming after me to get it. He wouldn't have let my dad and my brother use it as blackmail."

"I'll call him now."

Regret at the loss of contact hit Nadine strangely hard. She opened her eyes to study Anderson as he dialed his partner's number, then stood to pace the room as he spoke.

She liked the way his presence filled the room.

She liked how easy it was to fall into a pattern of trust.

She even liked how the intensity of the very new feelings scared her a little.

Because she knew it wasn't really a fear of being hurt or betrayed. Anderson was open and honest. Protective and kind. So the fear was more about letting herself give in to the feelings. Though, if she was being honest, it was more a crash than a gentle slide.

*All I have to do is jump.*

She didn't realize she'd murmured the thought aloud until Anderson paused in front of her, his hand over the receiver on the phone. "Jump into what?"

She opened her mouth, unsure if she was going to brush it off or admit that she'd been thinking about how easy it would be to fall in love with him. But she didn't get a chance to say anything. A loud thump on the door cut her off. Fear—and not the exciting kind this time—slammed into her chest.

Anderson's chest compressed at the fear in Nadine's eyes. He wanted to reassure her, but his gut told him that it was too soon to do it. He wanted to offer her hope. But not false hope.

"Harley," he said softly into the phone. "I've gotta go."

"Everything all right?" his friend replied.

"Not sure yet. Someone's at the door, and we weren't expecting company." As if to emphasize his statement, the solid knock echoed through the room again. "Call you back in a few." He clicked off the phone and turned his attention to Nadine. "Grab the flash drive."

She held out her palm, the USB stick already in her hand. "Got it."

"Good. Head to the bedroom."

"What?"

"Trust me."

"I do, but..." She cast a concerned look toward the door.

"I'll be fine," he promised.

"Okay." She still sounded uncertain, but she pushed to her feet and complied with his request.

Exhaling, and hoping for the best, Anderson crept across the floor to peer through the peephole. What he saw on the other side sent more than a lick of worry through him. Two men stood in the hall. One was dressed in the standard Whispering Woods Lodge staff uniform. The other wore a suit, and his head turned twice as Anderson watched—once up the hall, then down. He held his hand near his hip in a way that implied that a weapon most likely waited there for easy retrieval. And he looked ready to use it.

Anderson eased away from the door, eyeing the swing lock near the top third of the frame. It was in the locked position, but he knew from experience that it was really there for peace of mind. Anyone with five minutes and a bit of patience could jimmy it free. Or kick their way through if patience and time happened to be in short supply.

The real problem was the fact that it was locked at all.

He brought his hand up, grasped the cool metal, and tugged it slowly and silently open. He heard Nadine's indrawn breath, and he turned to find her standing in the bedroom doorway.

"What did you just *do*?" she whispered.

Ignoring her stunned expression, he strode over to the laptop, unplugged it, then tucked it under the couch.

"C'mon." He threaded his fingers through hers to pull her to the bedroom. "I said to trust me."

She freed her hand. "And I do. But you just unlocked the door."

"I'm giving us a fighting chance at staying hidden."

"Hidden?"

He swung open the closet door. "Believe it or not, this is the second time I've been in here today."

"What?"

He gestured for her to step in. "Hid from the maid this morning."

She stepped forward, her frown evident even as the darkness of the closet took over. "You're not making any sense, Anderson."

He followed her, closing the door gently behind the two of them. He took her face between his hands and gave her a swift kiss, then turned her so that she was tucked more comfortably against him, her back to his chest.

"There're two guys out in the hall," he said into her ear. "Could have a legitimate reason for being here. But probably not."

Her voice, the barest whisper, carried back. "So you decided to make it easier for them to get in?"

"If I left it locked, they'd know without a doubt that we're in here. This gives us the tiniest advantage."

"And that's why you hid the laptop, too?"

"More plausible that we'd tuck it away."

"Smart."

"I like to think so."

"Modesty will—"

Anderson brought his hand up to Nadine's mouth as the muffled sound of someone entering the room cut through. The slight noise was followed by silence.

Then a male voice called out, "Housekeeping!"

In the dark, Anderson narrowed his eyes. *Yeah, right.*

"Mr. Smith?" said the voice, using the pseudonym Anderson had given at check-in. "Are you here? Sorry to barge in like this, but someone requested some extra blankets?"

There was a pause.

"I really don't think they're here."

A second, deeper voice—quieter but still easily audible—answered. "His truck's in the underground parking lot. Saw it myself a half hour ago."

"Yeah," said the first man. "But I told you that when the woman left this morning, it was in a cab. Not in the truck."

"And *I* told *you* that I'm damned sure I saw him in town."

"Maybe it was a mistake."

"I don't make that kind of mistake."

"So maybe he went with her in the cab. I didn't see him, but I *do* make the odd mistake."

Shuffling—furniture being moved, maybe?—dominated for a moment.

"What'd you find?" asked the first man.

"Computer."

"You gonna load it up?"

"Yeah. Why don't you check the bedroom?"

"Sure."

Anderson tensed as footfalls got closer and closer. He felt Nadine's body do the same, and he ran his hands up and down her arms soothingly. Instead of the sounds of a search, though, there was just the sound of the bed sinking in. It took Anderson only a second to figure out what was happening. The guy in the hotel uniform had no interest in looking through the room—he was already convinced that the suite was empty, so he was just waiting it out.

Sure enough, a second later, he called to the man in the other room, "Find anything interesting in there?"

The reply came back immediately, frustration evident in both tone and words. "Not a damned thing. Looks like the laptop's only just been set up."

The bed creaked again. "Nothing in here, either. Checked under the bed. In the closet, and the shower. Felt like an idiot doing it."

"Thoroughness never equates to idiocy."

The second man's voice was closer now, and Anderson squeezed Nadine tighter. Without knowing a single other thing, he was damned sure that the man with the deeper voice was the more dangerous of the two.

"Who do you think he is?" The question came from a spot right beside the closet where they hid.

The hotel employee answered right away. "No idea. Boyfriend?"

"She doesn't have one. Not according to her records, anyway."

"They keep that kind of stuff in a file somewhere?"

"Not official records, you idiot. Garibaldi's records. He's kept pretty good tabs on her."

At the sound of the man's name, one of Nadine's hands slid back to Anderson's thigh. He dropped his own hand over top and help on tightly.

"We should go," the first man stated.

"Not yet," said the second.

"Just because they're not here now doesn't mean they won't be back any second."

"Avoiding a confrontation isn't on the top of my list of priorities."

"Mr. Garibaldi said—"

"I heard what he said. And I wouldn't upset his precious little hotel. I just want another minute to look around."

Anderson tensed again. Through the slats, he could see the suited man slowly circling the room.

"Doesn't even look like anyone's staying here," he muttered. "Bed doesn't look slept in. Bag's zipped up. You said they made a request for no housekeeping?"

"Yeah."

"Who rents the honeymoon suite, then doesn't take advantage of all the perks?"

"Guy's been living at the Whispering Woods care center taking care of the Stuart girl, right?"

"Even so."

A drawer slid out, its rolling tracks slicing noisily through the air. Anderson's throat went dry at the idea that the second man might start the search over again, only this time for real. The precariousness of their situation made his chest compress. If something happened to Nadine on his watch, he'd never forgive himself.

*So make sure that it doesn't.*

He closed his eyes for a second, inventorying their situation.

His gun was holstered at his side—he wouldn't make the mistake of leaving himself without it a second time—so that was good. He couldn't say he had the same confidence about Nadine's position. To be better protected, she needed to be behind him rather than the other way around.

*Too late to change now.*

It was true. There wasn't enough room inside the small space to jockey around. Not if they wanted to keep quiet, too. He'd just have to wait. Be ready to react. He'd use surprise as his weapon, and his body as a shield.

*Whatever it takes to make sure Nadine gets out alive.*

Opening his eyes revealed just how close the two men stood. The uniformed hotel employee was near enough that Anderson could see the five o'clock shadow on his face. A shallow inhale brought the sour smell of smoke wafting in, too. The other man was just as close, but he faced away from the closet. Anderson studied him, searching for a hint as to his role or some further insight into his motivation.

The man's hair was cropped short. Dark, but peppered with gray. His jacket was designer—a logo Anderson recognized but not one he could name. He held himself confidently.

*No. Not confidently. Arrogantly.*

That was a more apt word.

He had money or power. Or both.

Then the man turned, and Anderson realized that the logo wasn't the only thing he recognized. The man's face was one he'd seen just this morning.

# Chapter 13

Nadine felt Anderson go rigid behind her, and she knew the change in his demeanor had something to do with the man standing just outside the closet. Nervously she tried to see what he saw. She focused her gaze on the forty-something man in the expensive jacket as he spoke in a low voice to the guy in the hotel uniform. He looked the slightest bit familiar, but she thought that might be because there was nothing terribly distinctive about his features. He had an average face, an average build and an average level of attractiveness. The kind of man who would blend into a crowd.

Wishing she could ask Anderson what had caused him to tense up the second he laid eyes on the man, Nadine drew in a silent breath and then paused. A smoky scent filled her nose, and her mind pricked up with some unidentified hint of memory. Before she could pinpoint its source, the well-dressed man turned. And as Nadine spied his profile, she almost gasped. Though it'd been unnoticeable when he was facing them head-on, the new angle showcased a mottled bruise on the side of his head. A slash of red marked his jaw, too, turning him from average to fearsome.

Nadine inhaled again, trying to calm the syncopated rhythm of her heart. But the influx of air only brought with it more of the smoke-tinged smell. And with the second taste of it, Nadine placed the man. And her pulse surged with renewed fear.

It was him. The man who'd lit her mom's home on fire. She'd only caught the briefest glimpse of his face—and even then, it had been with his head pressed to the ground, his jaw slack and his eyes shut—but she was certain it was him.

What was he doing there? How had he managed to walk away from the scene of the crime?

His next words distracted her from thinking about it. "Be nice if we could get some answers before the police connect the two of them."

The hotel employee's response was tinged with worry. "You think that'll be soon? Because I'd really rather not cross paths with the local cops."

"Relax. I didn't give them a reason to come looking for Mr. Smith or whatever the hell his real name is. I dropped enough hints that the entire thing lies on Ms. Stuart's shoulders. They'll have to put the pieces together themselves."

It was Nadine's turn to stiffen. And even Anderson's gentle squeeze of her arm didn't help her relax.

The man out there hadn't just burned down her mom's apartment. He'd made the police think it was *her* fault. He was still talking about it. Saying that they'd be looking for her. That they'd probably have gone to her own apartment already and asked around at the hospital, too.

But it wasn't fear that made her bristle. It was anger.

She was so mad that she wouldn't have been able to string together a sentence even if she'd been in a spot where she could speak. Her hands balled into fists, and her arms shook.

*He blamed* me, she thought furiously. *That son of a—*

"Nadine."

At the sound of her name, she twitched back in surprise. Anderson's hands came up to steady her, and as she leaned back into his embrace, she realized that the bedroom was empty.

"They're gone," Anderson said softly. "I heard the door close. I just want to give it a minute to make sure they're not coming back."

She breathed out. "That was the man who burned down my mom's house."

"I recognized him, too."

"He told the police it was me."

"I know, sweetheart. But it's not all bad."

"How do you figure? They're going to come looking for me, Anderson. They'll find me and arrest me, and instead of being able to get answers or justice, I'll just end up in jail. Or worse."

His hands slid down her shoulders to her wrists, and he attempted to spin her to face him, the movement making both of them thump noisily against the walls of the small space. For a second, it was almost comical. A small laugh even escaped from Nadine's mouth. But it quickly dissolved into something that bordered on a sob.

"Nadine. Look at me." The order was gentle, and she complied, her gaze seeking his in the dark.

"Tell me how it's not all bad," she said. "Tell me how any of that was okay."

"Because we know their plan. Or at least part of it. They may have set that fire to your mom's place to cover something up—maybe to destroy the USB stick—but they aren't just going to let that be an accident. Which means that whatever they're doing, it's important enough that they'll risk letting the police at you."

"But they're framing me."

"Do you think it'll hold up? You were with *me* this morning."

"Not while the house was being lit on fire."

"Hey. You did *not* light the house on fire."

"I know that. And you know that. But are the police going to believe that I saw some masked man do it?"

"They already know a masked man was in the care facility."

Nadine's shoulders sagged, and she nodded. "That's true."

He bent to kiss her forehead. "It's not a hell of a lot of consolation, but knowing what Garibaldi's men are up to does give us an advantage."

"It doesn't make me any less mad."

"I'm aware." He smoothed back her hair and kissed her again, this time lightly on the lips.

A tiny bit of the anger slipped away, but she wasn't really ready to let it go. "I hate the thought of anyone believing—even for a second—that I would do something like that. I only just found out that this little piece of my mom still existed. I wouldn't destroy it."

He kissed her again. "I'm aware of that, too."

"Are you trying to distract me from being mad?"

"Maybe."

"I think you *are*."

"Is it working?"

"A bit," she admitted.

His mouth found hers a third time, and Nadine couldn't help but push to her tiptoes to sink into it. Anderson's touch was warm. Already familiar. Like coming home. He parted her lips with his tongue and took a quick, shiver-inducing taste before he pulled away.

"Still only a bit?" he teased.

Nadine smiled and pressed her hands to his hips. "You might have to try a little harder."

"You think so?" He pulled her hands up to his chest, dragged them over his shoulders, then backed her to the door. "How's this?"

"Well, it's kind of hard to get truly comfortable in a closet."

"I kind of like it."

"Really?"

"Mmm. Makes it easy to keep you nice and close."

"You think I'm going to run away the second you open that door?"

"I'm hoping not."

"I won't."

"Is that a promise?"

"Yes."

"Then I guess I'll take the chance."

In spite of his words, Nadine couldn't help but notice that he didn't let her go as he pushed the closet open. If anything, he held her tighter, backing her slowly into the room. When the back of her knees hit the bed, she couldn't stifle a gasp.

Anderson kissed her again. Slowly. Thoroughly. Exploring each part of her mouth like he was claiming it as his own. And everywhere that he made contact, a little spark of heat came to life. It only took a heartbeat for the sparks to bloom into full-on fireworks. The explosions of warmth radiated from the inside out, and even though the space between them was only as wide as the clothes they wore, even that seemed like too much.

Nadine pulled back just enough to slide her hands to the hem of Anderson's T-shirt. Her fingertips brushed the smooth, hard ridges of his abs, and he groaned. It only spurred her on. She dragged the shirt up over his head, then tossed it aside. Having him topless left her a little torn. On the one hand, she wanted to stare—to admire the well-formed muscles along his chest and stomach, to run her hands over each sculpted inch. But on the other hand, she wanted to pull him closer again. To *feel* those muscles against her. Her hesitation cost her the chance to make the choice.

Anderson stepped back and spoke in a raw voice. "Nadine."

"Sorry," she said. "I know you said you wanted to wait."

He shook his head. "That's not it."

"What's wrong?"

"Nothing. In fact, being trapped in that closet while Garibaldi's men were just inches away made me want to seize this moment—every moment—with you."

"So we're stopping because…?"

"Because being stuck like that also reminded me how things can change in an instant."

"Okay." She heard the uncertainty in her own reply, and Anderson's smile made her sure he'd heard it, too.

"A week ago, you were a pain in my butt."

"Thanks."

He touched her cheek. "A beautiful pain. But a pain. I don't think you liked me very much."

She leaned into the caress. "Only because you were a pain in *my* butt. No one wants to feel like they're under lock and key."

"No one wants to *be* a lock and key, either." He kissed her nose, somehow making the gesture romantic and sweet and even a little sexy.

"And now you're not."

"And now I'm not," he agreed. "Which illustrates my point even further."

"Which is that things can change fast."

"Exactly."

"That worries you?"

"It scares me a bit, Nadine." He sighed. "Or maybe more than a bit."

"You think I'm going to go back to being a pain in your butt?" she teased.

"I don't think that could ever happen. Just the opposite, actually."

"Hmm."

"What?"

"Just trying to figure out…what's the opposite of a pain in the butt?"

He didn't laugh. He didn't smile. He just met her eyes, his sea blue gaze as serious as anything Nadine had ever seen. And for a second, she actually worried that she'd said something wrong. Then he spoke, though, and she realized that instead of being wrong…everything was right.

"The opposite of pain in the butt," said Anderson, "is falling head over heels in love."

She stared back at him for a second, emotion overriding rational thought. Her heart wanted to explode. Dizzy, heady happiness threatened to overwhelm her.

"It's crazy, I know," Anderson added. "But that's the way this is headed for me, and if we take this further—if we get into that bed together—it's going to change again. Though hopefully not in quite as short of a time frame as an instant."

Nadine laughed at his impish grin. "That's where you're going to take this?"

"Can't help it. I'm a nice man. But I'm still a man." His expression turned serious again, and he reached up to run his thumb over her bottom lip. "I'm not after a one-night stand."

"Neither am I," she replied breathlessly.

"Or a one-week fling."

"No."

"And this..." He gestured behind her toward the bed. "It could have lifetime consequences."

She flushed as she realized what he might be referring to. "I'm on the pill."

"The—oh." He chuckled. "Yeah, that, too. But right now I was more thinking about us. As in making sure there *is* an us."

"Are you asking me to be your girlfriend, Anderson?"

"I guess I am."

"Well, that's probably the easiest thing I've been presented with since the second we met."

"So that's a yes?"

"It's much more than a yes."

His eyes sparkled with amusement. "What's more than a yes?"

She shrugged. "I don't know. Maybe a hell yes? Or..."

"Or what?"

"Maybe this."

She lifted an eyebrow. She reached down to take ahold of her shirt. Then she tugged it off and threw it on top of his. His eyes raked over her, his attention intent and hungry. They rested on the scars that dusted the side of her body—far lighter than the ones on her face but still very much on display—and for a solitary breath Nadine felt self-conscious. But the second his gaze came back up to her face, the feeling disappeared. Burned to a crisp by the blistering heat she saw there.

"More than yes..." he said softly. "I think I like it."

"You *think* you do?" She reached out to the clasp of his belt, still holding his gaze as she pulled it free. "I was hoping for more than think."

"Greedy, aren't you? Always with the more."

"It's give-and-take."

Smiling, she slid the belt out completely, then moved on to the button of his jeans. When she popped it open, the zipper came down, too, and Anderson groaned.

"Speaking of giving..." Nadine said teasingly. "Come here."

"Come where?"

"Down. So I can give you a kiss."

"Give me one? Or take one from me?"

"Let's call it mutually beneficial. Now. Come here. Please."

Obediently, he stepped forward and tipped his head down. His lips touched hers lightly, letting her take control. She kissed him firmly. She tasted him sweetly. But when she dragged his lower lip between her teeth and gave it a teasing tug, his demeanor changed. Any temporary illusion of passivity slipped far, far away.

Anderson's hands came to her shoulders. They slid back and forth, then made their way to her lower back, then slipped down her waist and finally came to rest on her hips. He shot her a wicked little smile before he pulled her forward forcefully enough to make her gasp. And without warning, he lifted her from the floor and hooked her knees over his hips. But she didn't have time to adjust to the new position before he shifted again. This time to propel them both to the bed.

For a second after they hit the feather duvet, he hung suspended over her, his strong arms holding him up as he pinned her to the spot with his desire-filled eyes. "Tell me you're hoping to find forever, Nadine."

She didn't hesitate. "Actually...what I'm really hoping is that I might've found it already."

And, after that, words were entirely unnecessary. They would've just taken up space that was otherwise occupied by the sound of clothes hitting the floor, sheets sliding free and skin meeting skin.

* * *

Anderson rolled over, reaching automatically for Nadine. It surprised him to find her side of the bed empty. He was sure she'd been curled against him just a few moments earlier, her warm skin pressed to his. As he pushed up to his elbow, though, and spotted the bedside clock, he realized that several hours had passed since he'd whispered his last sweet nothing into her ear, then closed his eyes, more sated than he remembered ever being in all of his thirty years.

"Nadine?" he called, a hint of sleep weighing down his voice.

When she didn't appear right away, worry tugged at him. Sliding off the bed, he came up to a sitting position and tried again.

"Nadine?"

"Hey, sleepyhead."

Her voice brought relief, and he tipped his head to find her standing in the bedroom doorway, a mug of something hot and steamy gripped in her hands.

"Coffee?" she offered.

"Please."

She stepped in and held out the ceramic cup. Anderson took it, but now that she was close enough that he could smell her skin, he wanted to set it aside again. To drag her back into the bed and start round two.

"Oh, no, you don't," she said, dancing out of reach.

He took a sip of the coffee and played dumb. "What?"

"I saw that look in your eyes a few hours ago. I'm well aware of what it means."

"You can read me already, huh? I'm obviously far too simple."

"Simple." She rolled her eyes. "Yes, that's the word I'd use to describe this whole situation. But speaking of the situation, Harley said—"

"You talked to Harley?"

"He called your cell phone about ten times. I didn't want to wake you if I didn't have to, but I also figured I shouldn't let him assume the worst. Was it wrong to answer?"

Anderson felt a sloppy grin creep up. "No."

She narrowed her eyes. "Why are you making that face?"

"I just like the idea of you talking to my friends. Of being in every part of my life."

"You're insane."

"Infatuated. On my way to being in love."

"Insane."

He set down his coffee, grabbed his boxers from the floor and slid them on, still smiling. "What did Harley say?"

Nadine took the mug from the nightstand and helped herself to a sip. "He muttered a lot about distraction, confirmed that you weren't dead, then asked me a little more about the pictures."

"Asked you? You didn't send them over?"

She pressed her lips together and shook her head.

Worry sliced through him. "Why didn't you send them?"

"I couldn't. They took the computer."

"And you didn't think that was a good reason to wake me up?"

"I thought about it. But there's nothing on the laptop. So then I thought about *why* they might take it. And I decided that it was a trap."

Anderson relaxed, just marginally. "A trap."

She nodded. "If we call in the theft, we'll probably have to talk to the police. Which works in their favor. It'll also let them know exactly where we are. And Harley concurred."

"Oh, he did, did he?"

"Yes."

"I take back what I said about liking it when you talk to my friends."

"Ha-ha."

"What else did he have to say?"

"That we should get him the pictures as soon as we can. He'll run the dates on them against known crimes. Oh! And he thinks that the room in the photos *is* an art-storage room. And that after it blew up, Garibaldi rebuilt it, only better. To professional grade standards. Harley only made the connection because of my description. He said it was because I had an artist's eye. I think it's just because I'm used to explaining things to eight-year-olds."

Anderson took the coffee back from her. "Pleased with yourself, aren't you?"

She smiled. "A little bit."

"Did you also come up with some genius way for us to get a new computer?"

"Harley did."

"Of course he did."

"You're not going to like it."

"Tell me anyway."

"He thinks the simplest thing to do is to go to my apartment."

"Did you tell him that was out of the question?"

"No," she said. "But he gave me some instructions."

Anderson set aside the coffee again and pinched the bridge of his nose. "What were they?"

"Hang on. I wrote them down."

She slipped out of the room again, and Anderson sank back onto the bed and let himself exhale noisily. Heading to Nadine's apartment was the last thing he wanted to do. The potential for exposure was too high, the risk too great. That crushing feeling returned to his chest, and he knew it was spurred along by one thing—the thought of losing Nadine to Garibaldi and whatever criminal scheme the man had under way.

"Here's the—" Nadine cut herself off as she stepped into the room again. "What's wrong?"

Anderson stood and stepped closer. "We can just leave."

"What?"

"Stuff your things in my bag. Buy a new toothbrush wherever we land."

"Anderson…running away won't make you happy."

"It'll make me happy to know that you're far away from Garibaldi." He ran a finger along her cheekbone.

Her hand came up to close on his. "That'd make me happy, too. But only if it happens after I figure out what happened with my dad. And you want justice for your dad, too."

"Yeah, I do." He sighed. "I've just never considered what I might be giving up in exchange for getting it."

"You're not giving me up to get that justice, Anderson. You're getting me as an ally. Two heads. That's what they say, right?"

"There's no one I'd rather be working with, honey. Hell. I'd deputize you if I could. Give you a gun and some body armor. But I don't have the power. And if something happened to you while we were investigating my dad's death…"

"We're not investigating *your* dad's death. We're investigating *our* dads' deaths. And Garibaldi. Which I was doing before you showed up in Whispering Woods. Which I'd still be doing if you hadn't shown up at all."

He met her eyes. "If I hadn't shown up, that little incident with the car outside the care facility might've ended very differently."

She lifted an eyebrow. "If you're trying to scare me into running, it's not going to work. If you hadn't shown up, the car incident *would* have ended differently. No *might've* about it."

He studied her face, trying to find the right thing to say, but he honestly wasn't sure that there was one. He wanted her close. He wanted her far from danger. He wanted to do what he could to put Garibaldi behind bars. But he wanted a life and a future, too. With Nadine.

"There's no middle of the road here," he murmured.

"Isn't that what you've been saying all along? Both feet?"

"I guess it is." He leaned down to kiss her.

She sank into the attention but pulled away first. "The faster we do this, the faster we can just be us."

"Better give me that list, then. See if Harley's plans have any merit."

"You know that they do."

"*Really* second-guessing that claim that I wanted you to talk to my friends."

"So you said."

Anderson shot her a smile and held out his hand. She was right. Harley's plan would be solid, and the quicker they got through it, the quicker they could move on to all the stuff he hadn't even known he'd needed until she fell into his arms.

# *Chapter 14*

Anderson stuck his head out of the hotel-room door and peered up and down the hall. With the exception of a solitary woman in a pantsuit, the space was empty.

"All right," Anderson said over his shoulder. "We're clear."

"I know," Nadine replied. "Harley said we would be."

"He's not some all-seeing, all-knowing wizard."

"That's actually exactly what *he* said."

"Are you trying to make me jealous, Ms. Stuart?"

"No." She paused. "*Are* you jealous?"

He guided her out into the hall. "Of Harley? Never."

"Why? He seems like a nice guy. Smart."

"Yep. Far too smart to try and steal my girlfriend out from under me."

He kept walking for a few more steps before he realized she hadn't followed. He turned back.

"What's wrong?" he asked.

"Nothing. Say it again."

"Say what again?"

"That I'm your girlfriend."

"Didn't we already establish this a few hours ago?"

She nodded. "Yes. But I just like the way it sounds when you say it."

He chuckled. "Okay. You're my girlfriend."

"Good."

"Can we go now?"

"Maybe just one more time."

"You're my girlfriend."

"Perfect. *Now* we can go."

He took her hand, and they made their way to the end of the corridor.

"Okay, Harley," Anderson said as they turned the corner and pushed through the heavy fireproof doors. "Don't let me down."

According to Nadine, Anderson's friend had looked over the blueprints of the building carefully and from those devised the best route to escape without being detected. So—silently and with hands clasped—they followed the instructions to the letter.

Though the first set of stairs went all the way to the underground parking lot, getting to the truck wasn't on their to-do list. Instead, the notes Nadine had taken said only to use the stairs as far as the second floor. There, they would reroute in the interest of stealth.

They made short work of the two-story trip, pausing cautiously to survey the hall on the second floor before continuing. Once they were sure it was clear, they quickly moved to the opposite end of the corridor and switched to the other set of stairs. At the lobby level, there were two sets of doors at the bottom of the stairwell, just as Harley had said there would be. One led directly into the hotel, but the other was an un-alarmed emergency exit that would take them out to one side of the lodge.

Praying that their good luck would continue—but half expecting it not to—Anderson pushed the second door open. As he stepped out and scanned the area for trouble, a strong gust of mountain air whipped through suddenly, pulling the door from his grasp. Without thinking about it, he yanked Nadine out of the frame and out of harm's way. The door slammed shut.

"Dammit," he muttered, spinning to survey the row of cars for the one that Harley had sent as their final goal at the lodge.

His heart leaped to his throat, and his arm shot up to push Nadine flat against the brick building. At the end of the line of cars was a dark-colored sedan, which in and of itself might not have been worrisome. Dark-colored sedans weren't exactly rare. The problem was the person sitting in the driver's seat—the same, all-too-familiar, salt-and-pepper-haired man who'd been causing problems for them for the last twenty-four hours.

"We need a way out," Anderson said, the words escaping in a low growl.

Nadine's response came back with a quaver. "There's nowhere to go."

"There has to be. The second that thug looks up from his phone and into his rearview mirror, we're as good as caught."

"Harley said this would be the easy part."

"Not an all-seeing wizard," he reminded her.

"No kidding."

Anderson scanned the edge of the building in search of a way to get by the sedan without being spotted. Aside from a few lampposts and the cars themselves, the parking lot was bare. And of course, there was another problem. Even if they managed to get to the car Harley had picked out for them via the lodge's online service, there was no way they could drive it away undetected.

He searched for another option, quickly inventorying their position.

The lodge was a huge building, and the side where they stood was the only one free from crowds of guests and employees. It was assumable that Harley had chosen it for that reason. Right now, it wasn't working in their favor.

They couldn't move forward and head for the front of the building—that path would take them right past the car. Had *that* not been true, there was the added risk that a whole host of Garibaldi-employed hotel staff were currently on the lookout for them.

The rear of the hotel presented the same problem. Though the back faced the wooded mountains—and in fact had well-used paths leading in for hiking or biking—it also housed the outdoor pool, which was overlooked by the patio bar.

*You're going to have to pick one*, he said to himself. *The longer you stand here, the more likely it is that you'll be spotted.*

He surveyed the area once more. No answers leaped out at him. His mouth dropped open to let out a frustrated curse, but Nadine's hand closed on his arm and gave it a gentle squeeze.

"I've got an idea," she said.

"What is it?"

"Do you want to talk about it? Because I'm pretty sure now is the time for action rather than words."

There was no point in arguing—she was right. "Okay."

"C'mon," she replied. "Follow me."

She slunk along the edge of the building, and he stayed close behind her, his eyes on the man in the car. He had zero interest in a making a scene. Especially one caused by a gunfight. If it came to a choice between drawing attention to themselves and saving Nadine's life, though, Anderson would err on the side of the biggest disruption in Whispering Woods history. Thankfully, they made it to the edge of the building without the need for him to pull his weapon. But there was still the issue of exposure. Before he could bring it up, though, Nadine squeezed his arm again, then pointed toward a row of stacked-up plastic chairs that sat just against a small outbuilding.

A quick glance around told him that the spot was sheltered just enough that no one would be able to see them once they were there. As far as actually making the move… He was sure that anyone who happened to be looking up and saw them sneaking off would assume something far sexier than what they were really up to.

"Ready?" Nadine asked.

"Probably not."

"Funny."

"On the count of three?" he suggested.

"One…" she replied.

"Two…" he added.

"Three!" they said together.

He grabbed Nadine's hand and dragged her away from the cover of the building, and in less than ten seconds, they were tucked between the chairs and the outbuilding.

"Well," Anderson prodded. "What now?"

"Don't sound so doubtful," she said. "Have you got your phone?"

"Yes."

"Hand it over."

Amused by her bossiness, his dug into his pocket for the slim device. "Here you go, Sergeant."

She gave his entertained expression a narrow-eyed glare. "No need to mock me. I'm the one with the idea."

He fought a laugh. "True enough."

She grabbed the cell from him, swiped the screen and punched the digital keys a few times, then announced, "Speakerphone."

It rang noisily on the other end three times before a very familiar voice issued a greeting. "Anderson. Everything all right?"

"Hi, Harley! It's Nadine." Her tone was sweeter than he'd heard it before.

"Oh, hey there," said his friend. "Run into a problem?"

"Small one."

"Small?" Anderson repeated.

Nadine made a face. "Shh."

"Me?" said Harley.

"Not you," replied Nadine. "Your friend."

"Anderson's never been too good at keeping quiet."

"Good thing he's cute."

"Says you."

Anderson snorted and raised his voice. "Better looking than you by a mile."

"Cocky, isn't he?" Harley responded.

"A little bit," Nadine agreed. "But I like him too much to complain. You want to help us a bit more?"

"For you? Anything."

It was Anderson's turn to make a face. "Suck-up."

Nadine bit her lip, looking an awful lot like she wanted to laugh. "The rental car didn't pan out. One of our 'friends' decided the parking lot was a good place to lay low."

"Damn," Harley replied.

"Your mom would wash your mouth out with soap if she heard that," Anderson stated.

"What she can't hear won't hurt her," Harley said. "What do you guys need? Another car? 'Cause it wasn't all that easy to hack into the Whispering Woods Lodge system in the first place."

"Hack, Harley?" Anderson interjected. "Did you make us an accessory to grand theft auto? Because I kind of like my job."

"Of course not." His friend sounded appalled. "I *paid*

for the rental. I just had to get creative on the booking because they require two pieces of government ID, a driver's abstract and have a strong preference for forty-eight hours' notice. Plus, they needed some extra convincing to leave the key in that magnetic box under the door. But if you just wanted to walk in and ask for the car…"

Anderson rolled his eyes. "Forget I even asked."

"You make it hard to feel appreciated," his partner stated.

Nadine let out a sigh. "Can we get back to the important stuff?"

"Like I said…anything for you," repeated Harley.

Nadine smiled. "We're still planning on using the car you booked. What we need is a phone call."

"A phone call?" Harley sounded as puzzled as Anderson felt.

"Yes. To the front desk. Since we're not sure who we can trust, I don't think Anderson and I should do it ourselves. But if *you* do it, there won't be any awkward questions."

"What am I saying to them?"

"That you just came from the car rental parking lot, and you—or better yet, *your daughter*—saw a man loitering there. Trust me when I say that the lodge cares enough about its reputation that they'll send security. Quickly. And our friend will clear out just as fast."

"And if security's in on it?" Anderson wondered aloud.

"He'll still leave," Nadine replied. "Because he'll be worried about attracting attention."

"All right." Now Harley sounded kind of pleased. "I do like a chance to be creative. I'll make the call, and request that they call me back when it's done. Then I'll shoot you a text. Sound good?"

"Right as rain, as my grandmother used to say," Nadine said cheerfully.

"Bye, Harley." Anderson took the phone from her and

tapped the hang-up key emphatically before sticking it into his pocket. "I think you *are* trying to make me jealous."

She fixed him with a too-innocent smile. "Who, me?"

"Do I have *another* girlfriend kicking around?"

"I hope not."

"Would that make *you* jealous?" He stepped a little closer.

"Jealous, no." She danced out of reach. "Vengeful, possibly."

"Would you go after me? Or her?"

"Neither."

"Neither?"

"Nope. I'd just have Harley take care of the whole thing."

"I wouldn't smirk quite so hard if I were you."

"Oh, really?"

"No."

"Are you going to stop me?"

"Definitely." He brought both hands up to her shoulders, then backed her to the wall of the outbuilding. "It's not like you can run away from me. In fact…I think you're pretty much stuck."

She pursed her lips like she was trying not to smile. "And *I* think you're taking advantage of the situation."

"I sure am."

He dipped his head so he could press his lips to hers. He meant it to be a quick, firm kiss, but her fingers came up to the back of his neck and dug into his hair, and there was no way he was breaking contact. Especially not when she lifted her foot to the back of his calf and propelled him closer. He deepened the kiss, then grabbed ahold of her bent knee and lifted it up to his thigh. She moaned against his mouth, and for a very pleasant moment, the rest of the world slipped away.

No guest-filled hotel.

No Garibaldi.

No arrogant, ill-meaning man hovering on the periphery, waiting to swoop in and kill them both.

It was just Anderson, Nadine and the best damned kiss in the world.

For as long as Nadine could remember, she'd been after answers about her father's death. But now she was literally in the arms of a man who could help her get them, and it was the furthest thing from her mind. In fact, her mind had given way to her heart. Instead of thinking, she was simply feeling. Because everything about Anderson was right. His kindness. His protectiveness. The way his body fit against hers. The firm, hot touch of his mouth. It made Nadine needy. And while she normally considered herself to be self-sufficient and decidedly independent, this was a kind of need she didn't mind. One she was even sort of reveling in. Which was why, when Anderson's phone chimed to life, she had a primal urge to grab it, throw it to the ground and stomp on it. Judging by the groan Anderson issued as he pulled away, he concurred with the idea.

"Damn you, Harley," he growled.

"Is it wrong to ignore him?" Nadine breathed.

"Unfortunately."

"Well. That sucks."

His mouth turned up. "To put it mildly."

"I guess he's doing us a favor," she conceded.

"Sure is." He tugged his phone out of his pocket, then turned the screen so she could read it, too.

Coast is clear. Some REALLY chatty front desk girl was eager to help. She told me that security would sweep through every ten minutes for the next bit. Better hurry. And don't forget to let me know you're alive.

"I guess our break is over," Anderson said, holding out his hand. "Ready to steal a car?"

Nadine threaded her fingers through his. "We're not stealing it. Harley paid for it. I know you heard him."

"Oh, now that we're not ignoring him, we're back to praising him?"

"He *is* saving our butts."

"So you keep reminding me." Anderson stepped ahead to peer around the outbuilding. "Count of three again?"

"Let's count down instead of up, just to keep it interesting."

"If you insist."

"I do."

"All right. Three…"

"Two…"

"One!"

They made the mad dash again, then slipped around the corner and pressed their backs to the edge of the lodge. As promised, the parking lot was now devoid of a certain nondescript sedan.

"I know you're silently thanking him," Anderson said.

"Don't jump to conclusions," Nadine scolded. "I won't be silently thanking him until we're driving away in the third car from the left."

He chuckled, and she tugged his hand again, and they headed toward the vehicle in question. After another look around and a quick duck to grab the hidden key, he opened her door and ushered her into the passenger seat.

"Just so you know…" he said as he climbed in and started the engine. "When this is done, I'm definitely going to find him a girlfriend."

"You think that'll dull his impeccable expertise?"

"Couldn't hurt. You know any nice local girls?"

"Sadly…no. Well, Reggie. But Brayden might have something to say about that. The only other eligible bachelorette I've met since coming back is that girl at the pie shop. How does he feel about kids?"

"Likes 'em, same as anyone with sense."

She laughed. "But tell me what you *really* think."

He glanced her way. "You don't like kids?"

"Um…"

"What?"

"I'm an elementary schoolteacher."

"Oh, right. Not normally a crime fighter." His brow pinched into a frown.

"Spit it out, Detective," Nadine ordered teasingly.

"You're a teacher. So you like *other* people's kids. But what about kids of your own?"

"I don't have any."

"Nadine…"

"It's kind of a loaded question, Anderson."

"It's the kind of question most people think about."

She studied her hands, feeling strangely shy. Though she'd spent two days straight with the man, been intimate with him and agreed to what she knew was going to blossom into a permanent relationship, this particular topic seemed to take things a step further.

"My experience of family is a little skewed," she admitted softly.

"I know that, honey," he said. "But I like to think of that as drawing board. A place where you can erase the things you don't like, build on the ones you do and work toward something just short of perfection."

"Not actual perfection?"

"It's a family. Perfection doesn't exist."

She stared at his profile, searching for a hint that he was kidding around. But even from the half of his face that she could see, Nadine could tell that he was serious.

"So if I said I wanted *six* kids…" She trailed off and waited for him to jump ship.

His mouth just quirked a little. "Then I'd tell you that we probably need something bigger than my apartment. Or yours. Of course, since yours is a rental, it won't be that hard to give up. And being right in the heart of Freemont City, mine's worth a little something if I sell it."

"That's your plan, then? Meet a girl. Fall in love at first sight. Plan a life before the weekend is even over, sell your apartment and buy a two-story with a white picket fence?"

"Do they have white picket fences here in Whispering Woods?"

"Why? Is this where you want to settle down?"

He shrugged. "I like it here. Aside from Garibaldi, of course."

She exhaled, wondering how Anderson kept making her forget about the man. "Once he's no longer a factor?"

"Your job is here."

"But yours isn't."

"I suspect there'll be a few openings on the Whispering Woods PD when this all straightens out. And there're already some spots at the fire department. I could handle the change."

"How do you even know that?"

"I had to fill the hours I spent sitting outside your door somehow."

"You're completely insane."

"Possibly." He gestured out the front windshield and pulled the car over to the side of the road. "We're here."

Nadine brought her gaze up. Even though they were still one street over, she could easily see the short row of five-story buildings. Their flat gray roofs poked out from over the tall fir trees that lined the road. She had to admit that, compared to the Whispering Woods Lodge, the accommodations had little curb appeal. But they were far cheaper. And functional. Run by a property management company, the apartments were—for the most part, anyway—short-term seasonal rentals. People booked the fully furnished suites by the week or even the month during the two major tourist seasons. Since it was only the end of May, they were also pretty much empty. Nadine herself had only intended to stay until she was able to work up the courage to go through her mom's place. Now, of course, that wouldn't be a factor.

She swallowed against the sudden rawness in her throat, and she was glad when Anderson spoke, providing her with a distraction.

"Remind me of Harley's big plan for sneaking in," he said.

"See the second one?" she asked.

"Yep."

"It's hard to tell from the outside, but it shares an underground parking lot with my building. Harley said the entrance gates are wired together, too, and that my code will work. So we just drive in."

"And we assume that no one will spot us?"

"We assume that they're looking for your truck, specifically, and that they won't know the two lots connect. It was news to me, and I've been renting there for over a month. And on top of everything else, they're looking for a couple. I'm going to be lying flat on the back seat."

Anderson sighed. "I somehow still don't like it."

Nadine undid her seat belt and leaned over to kiss his cheek. "That's only because it was Harley's idea. If it was your own, you'd be thrilled with the whole thing."

He was silent as she clambered into the back seat, but once she was settled, he turned to face her and sighed again. "You know that I trust him utterly."

"I do," she agreed.

"Harley and the other guys…they're like brothers to me. We started out as friends because our dads were buddies at work. But when they died together, our friendship evolved.

No matter what else goes on in our lives, this one thing connects us. It's always superseded everything else. We go for beers. We talk about the case. We have Christmas dinner. We finish it by talking about the case."

Nadine propped her head up on her hand and studied him, wondering why he was telling her this now, in such a serious voice. She didn't have to ask. He let out a breath and spoke again, this time sounding fierce.

"I'm ready for it to be over," he said. "I've put everything I have into this case. Everything into solving my dad's murder. I've never thought twice about that until now. A day with you, and I know I want more than that. It's something I've never considered before. And forgive me for sounding weak, but honestly…my head says I can protect you long enough to make a hundred percent sure it happens. My heart, on the other hand, is a little scared."

Nadine sat up and reached out to squeeze his shoulder. "Anderson."

His other hand came up and closed on hers, his touch as raw as his tone. "What if this is the one time Harley is wrong?"

"He won't be."

"I *know* that. I know he wouldn't risk your life even more than I know he wouldn't risk mine. But my heart…" He let her hand go to press his fingers to his own chest.

Nadine placed her palm over the back of his hand. "*My* heart says everything will be fine. The universe didn't throw us together just to rip us apart."

For a long moment, he was silent. His blue gaze was warm with emotion. Hope and trust. Worry and affection. Everything Nadine felt, reflected back at her.

"I love you, Anderson," she said, the words bursting out before she could think to stop them.

Anderson's eyes widened, and then his mouth tipped up. "Now who's the hopeless romantic?"

Nadine's face heated, but not in an unpleasant way. "Shut up."

"Seriously, though. I was *really* hoping to say that first."

"Then I guess you should've been a little faster."

"I could try being a little more thorough instead."

"I don't think anything gets more thorough than those three words."

He raised an eyebrow, and her blush deepened.

"That's *not* what I meant," she said.

"Uh-huh."

"Are we ever going inside?"

"In a second."

"What are we waiting for?"

"This." He brought their clasped hands to his mouth and issued a gentle kiss on each of her fingertips. "I love you, too, Nadine."

Hearing him say it made her chest expand in a perfectly sweet burst of pure joy. A perfect moment in a far-from-perfect situation.

# *Chapter 15*

Doing things with ease always made Anderson wary, and—even with the fact that he was riding high from exchanging those three all-important little words with Nadine—entering the apartment building with zero interruptions was no exception. By the time they'd successfully punched in Nadine's pass code, made their way through the underground parking lot to her building and stepped from the concrete structure into the elevator, Anderson was tense with apprehension. When the light overhead dinged an announcement that they'd reached the right floor, he all but jumped.

"Let me go first," he said.

"Sure. You're the man with the *g-u-n*," Nadine replied.

Her attempt at levity did nothing to ease Anderson's nagging concern that something was off. He leaned cautiously into the hall, his hand at the gun on his hip. A glance left and a glance right showed nothing but an emptiness. He took a step out of the elevator. Then another.

Nadine followed so closely that he could feel her warmth against his back, and when a light, unexpected jingling noise carried through the air, she bumped right into him with a gasp.

Anderson shifted automatically, trying to position himself so that he could see her and still shield her. "What's wrong?"

"That noise… Those are the bells that hang from my door."

He swiveled his head toward the end of the hall, drawing his gun out silently as he did. Her unit was the very last one on their right. There was no sign of movement at all, but the angle at which they stood allowed him only a view of the frame rather than the door itself.

"Feel like breaking into an empty apartment to hide out?" he asked in a low voice.

"Not in the slightest." Nadine's reply was a whisper. "And even if I *was* in the mood for a little B and E, I have no idea which units are rented and which aren't. Or which ones have cleaning or maintenance scheduled. Or—"

"Okay. I get it. No breaking and entering, no hiding out."

"Good."

"I'm kinda wishing you had your own gun."

"I had a gun. Your friend Brayden took it."

"Probably wasn't strictly legal, then." He continued to stand still, his eyes fixed in the direction of her apartment.

After a silent pause, Nadine asked, "Are you stalling?"

"Yep."

"Why?"

"Hoping that we startle the hell out of whoever's in there. Surprise is always our friend. And the hallway gives me a clear shot. Can't say the same for inside an apartment."

The bells chimed again, this time managing to sound a

little ominous. Anderson tensed and readied his weapon. The tip of a man's dress shoe came into view. It stayed just at the edge for a second, then disappeared again. An odd tapping sound carried out from the apartment.

Then Nadine exhaled, the breath full of relief. "Mr. Fitzgerald."

As she said the name, an older man inched into the hallway, his cane first. Wariness still present, but true concern fading, Anderson quickly tucked his gun back into its holster and followed Nadine toward the stranger, assessing the man's appearance.

Fitzgerald could've been anywhere between seventy and a hundred. From the top of his sparse but tidily combed hair to the pleats in his pants, he was the epitome of graceful aging. His face cracked into a wrinkled smile directed toward Nadine, and he held out his free hand in anticipation of Anderson's approach.

"David Fitzgerald," the man greeted. "Neighbor."

"Anderson Somers. Boyfriend."

Anderson clasped his fingers and was surprised at the firmness of the shake; it seemed at odds with the man's otherwise frail exterior. Fitzgerald seemed to read his surprise perfectly.

"Don't let appearances fool you, son," said the old man. "Got a busted knee, but the rest of me works just fine."

"Especially his brain," Nadine added. "He beat me at chess, crib and Scrabble all in the first weekend that I moved in. But I'm not sure why he's added sneaking into my apartment to his list of clever tricks."

Fitzgerald's smile turned to a frown. "Weird thing. I came out to grab the paper and saw that your door was open. Thought maybe you'd come home from the care facility earlier than expected and left it open by accident. Gave a knock and didn't get an answer, so I stuck my head in. Don't know why, but something felt off. You know that feeling?"

"*I* do," said Anderson.

The old man turned his way. "I'm guessing you probably do. Anyway, couldn't quite shake it. I took a pretty thorough look through the whole place." He brought his attention back to Nadine. "Apologies if that was an invasion."

"It's fine by me, Mr. Fitzgerald. I appreciate the concern, actually," she replied. "But what if someone had been inside?"

"Then I would've taken him down with my weapon." He lifted his cane and shook it a little.

"Or gotten yourself killed," Nadine scolded.

"Well. At least I would've gone down fighting. But not to worry too much. No one's in there. Was still thinking about giving the police a call right as soon as I got back to my place, though. Just in case."

"Thanks, Mr. Fitzgerald," Nadine replied.

"You want me to call now?"

"I think I'll be okay. The door probably just got left open when the cleaning lady came by. I've had some issues with the latch." She patted Anderson's arm. "And besides that… I brought reinforcements home with me."

Fitzgerald gave Anderson another once-over before nodding approvingly. "All right. But if he needs my help, you just call."

"You know that I will."

The old man turned and moved with near-painful slowness up the hall. When he reached his door, he lifted his cane in a salute, then disappeared into the apartment. As soon as he was out of sight, Anderson turned a worried eye toward her slightly ajar door.

He dropped his voice low again. "You think Mr. Fitzgerald is right about there being no one in there?"

"You know as well as I do that there's nowhere to hide

in my place." She shook her head as he started to protest. "Don't deny it. I know you came and helped yourself to a look around."

He offered her a rueful shrug. "Should I apologize for being invasive?"

"I would've said yes to that question a mere forty-eight hours ago."

"And now?"

"I know you were doing your job. And as long as you didn't steal any underwear from my drawer, we're good."

"Whoops."

She rolled her eyes and grabbed his hand. He let her tug him into the apartment, and as she closed the door behind them, he couldn't help but note that the latch had no problem.

She caught his raised eyebrows. "What?"

"The cleaning lady did it?"

"It worked."

"Sure. But why didn't you just blame the butler?"

"Ha-ha. There *is* a cleaning lady," Nadine said. "The property management company has her do all the apartments once every two weeks."

"But not yours."

"No. I prefer to do it myself. I didn't want to worry Mr. Fitzgerald."

She slipped off her shoes, and Anderson followed suit, scanning the apartment even though she was right about the lack of space to hide. The living space was tiny. A bachelor suite. It had no separate bedroom, a single closet that didn't even have a door and all the appliances looked like they'd shrunk a size or two. Even the furniture was bare minimum. There was a futon frame that doubled as a couch and bed, a coffee table that was also a kitchen table and a squat dresser that housed the TV.

"I've made a decision," Anderson stated.

"About what?" Nadine replied.

"We are definitely *not* living here. I think if I cleared a spot on the floor and stretched out, starfish style, I'd be able to touch all four walls at once."

"That's what makes it so easy to clean on my own."

He sobered and ran his eyes over the small space again. "Someone *was* in here. You should probably look around to see if anything's missing."

"I don't have anything really valuable except my laptop."

She sank down onto the futon and dragged the coffee table drawer open, then pulled out a soft-sided computer bag. A quick zip, and she had it open. The shiny black computer sat conspicuously inside.

"If they didn't take this," she said, flipping it open, "then they probably didn't take anything else."

"You don't keep anything about your dad or brother lying around?" Anderson asked.

Nadine tapped her forehead. "All up here. Just like Mr. Fitzgerald."

"That's a good thing." The gut, something's-wrong feeling came back.

Her eyes came up to meet his. "So why do you sound like you just swallowed something awful?"

"How do you feel about taking the computer somewhere else? We should check to see if it's been tampered with before we send the pictures to Harley."

"We can do that from here, can't we? And even if they got into my computer somehow, there's nothing to find. Cat videos and a cleared web browser."

"I still think we should go."

"I don't understand. I can't see Garibaldi's guys coming back to the apartment anytime soon. They've got no reason to think we're here. And they left empty-handed the first time."

"You wanna argue, or trust me?"

She made a face. "I can do both."

He eyed the door. "I've had a bad feeling ever since we stepped into that elevator."

"Do I have time to get changed?"

"Two minutes."

"So very generous of you."

"Hurry."

Anderson waited as patiently as he could manage as Nadine slipped from the hotel-themed clothes into her own jeans and T-shirt. Really, though, he was distracted enough by the churning in his gut that he couldn't even take a moment to enjoy watching her strip down. The need to move quickly overrode even that. It was all well and good to admire her barely clothed form, but he really didn't want it to be the last time he got a chance to do it. When she was finally ready—dressed and with the laptop bag slung over her shoulder—Anderson could feel the tension in every part of his body. He didn't waste any more time.

"Stairs," he said, pulling her into the hallway.

"Okay," she agreed with a frown.

A brisk walk brought them to the heavy fireproof door at the end of the hallway. Anderson held it open for her. Once she'd stepped through, he paused to give the utterly empty corridor a final glance.

Maybe he was overreacting, he said to himself, releasing his hold on the knob.

Then the telltale ding of the elevator came to life. And just before the door swung shut, he caught a glimpse of two officers in uniform, and he knew his gut had been screaming at him for a damned good reason.

"Time to run," Anderson announced.

And Nadine didn't have to be told twice. The urgency in his voice was enough to propel her into overdrive.

Their feet hit the concrete, her steps at a quick, light tap, and his at a thick smack.

Clutching the laptop to her chest, Nadine counted off the flights and landings and stairs in her head, trying to use the reassuring numbers to anchor her staccato heart.

*Floor three.*

*Nine stairs.*

*Landing one.*

Above them, the door slammed open.

*Nine steps more.*

*Floor two.*

A male voice echoed through the stairwell, the words indistinct.

*Six stairs.*

Booted feet landed on concrete, the sound almost drowning out the noise they were making themselves.

*Three stairs.*

*Landing two.*

It was impossible to say if their pursuers were gaining ground.

*Five stairs.*

She almost tripped, but Anderson's grip kept her steady.

*Four steps more.*

*Floor one.*

Nadine moved to keep going—to head down even farther to the underground parking lot where the rental car awaited—but Anderson stopped abruptly on the first-floor landing. With a quick glance up, he released her hand, then pushed hard on the door. It opened with a rush of warm air. But he didn't pull her through it. Instead, he grabbed her hand again and tugged her to next set of steps. This time, they moved slowly. Silently. And when they reached the next landing, Nadine realized that the opening of the door had been a diversion.

She drew in a deep breath as Anderson stopped, pressed

his index finger to his lips in a "keep quiet" gesture, then tipped his ear up. Moments later, the slam of boots stopped just above, perfectly timing with the echo of the door closing.

There was the briefest pause before a man's gruff voice said, "They must've just gone through here."

"You sure that was her?" a second man replied.

"Petite blonde with short hair. What're the chances there's two of them running around in her building?"

"What's the guy's story?"

"Dunno. Guess we'll find out when we catch up to them. Come on. This conversation is a waste of time."

There was another rush of air—buffered this time by the vertical distance between them and the door—and the footsteps resumed, then faded, then disappeared as it shut once more.

Nadine exhaled, and Anderson shot her a nod and second-long smile before he pointed to the rest of the stairs. She nodded back, and they resumed their descent. Their pace was still hurried, but also hushed now, too. Nadine was almost afraid to speak—she didn't want to jinx their momentary success at escaping. But as they got nearer to the car, her worry got the better of her.

"Do you think it's safe to drive out of here?" she asked.

"*Safe* might be too strong a word," Anderson acknowledged. "But going on foot's not any better an option."

"We could sneak away easier."

"And be stuck without a vehicle?" He stopped on the passenger's side, unlocked her door and then pulled it open. "We're not even sure where we're going."

"I guess you're right," she conceded as she climbed in. "But if Garibaldi's guys have more friends outside…"

Anderson frowned down at her. "Garibaldi's guys? You mean from back there?"

"Yes."

"Those weren't his thugs, sweetheart. They were cops."

She felt her stomach drop. "What?"

"Those were policemen."

"Why didn't they identify themselves?"

He shrugged. "Hard to say what they were yelling when they came into the stairwell. Could've been 'Whispering Woods PD.'"

"How can you be so glib?"

"Hang on, all right?"

She waited impatiently while he closed her door, then stepped around to the other side of the car and got into the driver's seat.

"I'm not being glib," he said as he put the key in the ignition and started the car.

"Could've fooled me," she muttered.

"I'm a cop, too," he reminded her. "We don't tend to come in with our guns blazing. Especially if we're not entirely sure of the situation. Those two uniforms were probably here because Garibaldi's actual guys—the ones from the lodge—reported you as an arsonist, remember?"

"Yeah, it's a little hard to forget," she replied. "But now I look guilty because we *ran* from them."

"I'm honestly not even sure if they knew we were running. You heard them arguing about whether or not it was you."

"You have an answer for everything, don't you?"

"My job is to find answers." He stopped the car at the exit and waited for the gate to lift. "Did you want to stop and talk to them? Because if that's really what you want to do…"

She rolled her eyes. "No. I'm not totally insane."

"Good." They started rolling forward again. "Because trying to explain ourselves would slow us down at best, and halt us completely at worst."

"Of course, now they're going to be trying even harder to find me," she pointed out.

"That's probably true."

"I was hoping you would say I was wrong."

"That'd make me a liar."

"So what do we do?"

"Hide."

"I thought we were already hiding."

"So now we hide better."

Nadine bit her lip to keep from blowing out yet another breath, this one frustrated. "I'm tired of hiding."

Anderson reached over and gave her knee a squeeze. "Not my favorite, either."

"So where are we headed now?"

"It's your town. Got any ideas?"

"Not specifically, but I think we should get as far away from— Wait."

"What?"

"When Brayden came in, he rented a cabin out at this place on the edge of town. Garibaldi owns them, but like you said about the hotel… He probably won't be looking under his own nose. And unlike the lodge, the cabins have none of Garibaldi's staff hanging around, waiting to give us away."

"You're right. That's perfect."

He tipped on the turn signal, and for a few minutes they drove on in silence. Not awkwardly. Nadine was sure that no matter what hung over them, it could never be uncomfortable *between* them. But the current quiet wasn't quite pleasant, either.

She cleared her throat. "I didn't mean to sound so hopeless."

"You're frustrated," Anderson said easily. "I get it. I am, too. But we're making progress."

"We are?"

"Yes."

She'd fixed her gaze out the front windshield, but she could feel his eyes on her. "Don't look at me like that."

"Like what? And how do you even know how I'm looking at you?" he wondered aloud.

"Like you think you can make it better. And because I know *you*."

"That statement makes me indescribably happy. Well, the second part, anyway."

"You know what would make *me* indescribably happy?"

"What?"

"If you reminded me of what progress we've made."

"I saved you from being run over. And from being kidnapped."

"Is that progress? Because it just sounds like you're being all proud of yourself for being heroic."

"I haven't finished," he informed her.

She couldn't stop a smile from creeping up. "Well, please. Carry on."

"Thank you. Very gracious of you." He shot her an exaggerated wink that made her want to laugh.

"Just get it over with."

"You can't rush indescribable happiness. So. After I made myself indispensable to you, we recovered the USB stick—proof that your dad and brother were blackmailing Garibaldi. We found out that whatever the man's up to, it has some strange connection to painting. And we learned enough about Garibaldi's plan that we know to avoid the police until this is over. I think we're doing pretty damned well. And if none of *that* makes you indescribably happy, there's the other thing we accomplished. Maybe the most important thing, actually."

"Which thing is that?"

"You really don't remember?"

She frowned. "No."

"We fell in love."

# Chapter 16

As he pulled the car off the long stretch of paved road and onto the hard-packed dirt road that led to the cabins, Anderson noted a sudden change in the sky. It went from cloud-dotted to gray in a matter of moments, and by the time they reached the clearing that housed the rustic homes the rain had already started to come down heavily. The short run from the vehicle to the main cabin was enough to soak them all the way through.

"First things first," he said as he opened the unlocked front door. "I channel my inner lumberjack and get a fire started. You channel your inner pioneer woman and find a way to make us something hot to drink."

"I don't think either of those descriptions truly applies," Nadine responded, "but I'll agree because I'm freezing cold already."

They got to work, and Anderson was pleased that it really only took a few minutes to organize themselves. As the fire—built with pre-chopped kindling, ready-made fire-starter and a couple of thick logs—roared to life, Nadine set down two mugs of steaming liquid.

"Instant soup," she said. "A meal and a beverage."

Anderson kissed her nose. "Perfect. I'll grab a blanket from the closet if you want to get us set up on the laptop?"

"The romance of file sharing?"

"Exactly."

Two minutes more, and they were tucked together under a thick piece of fleece with the laptop balanced on their adjoining knees. Nadine had stripped off her outer layer, and her soft curves pressed into Anderson in a way that made him want to toss aside the laptop, forget about the pictures altogether and kiss her until neither of them had anything else on their minds. It took a significant amount of willpower to keep from doing so.

*Plenty of time after*, he said to himself, pulling her a little closer when she shivered.

He waited until she was done setting it up—using his own cell phone to create a mobile Wi-Fi hot spot—before asking, "How's it look?"

"Good. I think. The history says no one's logged in since before I went into the care center," she said. "Assuming, of course, that whoever broke into my apartment wasn't some kind of crazy computer genius who could override things or hide them or whatever."

"I wouldn't want to assume that they weren't, but I do think it's unlikely."

"Me, too."

"Confident that we can send the pictures to Harley?"

"Mostly confident. And it's not like we really have a choice. We need to figure out the connection between my dad and the photos, and to figure out what it all means to Garibaldi."

"Yep."

"Okay, then. Here it goes."

She plugged in the USB stick, logged in to her email, then typed in Harley's address as Anderson provided it and hit Send.

"How long do you think it'll take him?" she asked.

"He's quick," Anderson replied. "But thorough, too. He'll probably let us know the second he has anything concrete. A good hour, maybe?"

"Okay. So what do we do while we wait?"

"We sit back. We eat our soup. Maybe play a board game?"

"Seriously?"

"No."

She turned a puzzled look his way, and he couldn't help but laugh. "Come here."

"Come *where*?" she asked. "I'm already about as close to you as I can get."

"We both know that's not true," he teased.

A pretty blush crept up her cheeks, and he adjusted so that he could cup her face with his hands and stroke his thumbs over the pink in her skin. He bent to give her a soft kiss.

"The soup," she protested as he pulled away and pressed his forehead to hers.

"I like it cold," he told her.

"You do?"

"I do now."

He leaned in again, tipping his head sideways so he could give her mouth a little more thorough attention. She let out a little gasp as he traced her lips with his tongue.

"I kind of like this cabin life," he murmured between kisses.

"Do you?" she said back, her voice making his mouth vibrate. "How can you be sure? We've only been here for fifteen minutes."

"Crackling fire. No interruptions. Girl of my dreams." He slid his hands to her hips and pulled her down so that her back was almost flat on the couch. "What's not to like?"

Her fingers came up to the bottom of his shirt, and in an impressively adept move, she tugged it up and over his head, then tossed it aside. Her palms landed on his chest.

"I guess I can't complain *too* much," she said.

"But you can complain a little?" he replied. "Please. Tell me what's lacking, and I'll make it up in some other way."

"Well. There's the fact that you're wearing pants. And the fact that *I'm* wearing pants."

"That's easy enough to undo." He reached for the button on her jeans.

"Was that a pun?" she asked accusingly.

"Possibly."

"Great. Now I can complain about your groan-worthy jokes, too."

"Groan-worthy? That sounds dirty."

She wrinkled her nose. "It wasn't meant to."

"Too bad. That's how I'm interpreting it."

He grinned, popped open the button, then dropped down to lift her tank top and plant a kiss just above her belly button. Her responding inhale was sharp, and a line of goose bumps lifted over her skin.

"Still complaining?" he said, yanking her zipper open and dragging his lips to the top of her panty line.

She mumbled something incomprehensible.

He darted his tongue across the lace. "Sorry. I missed that last bit."

"Not complaining," she gasped.

"You sure?"

"Yes!"

"Good."

And he grabbed the waistband of her jeans, determined to make sure she couldn't even *pretend* to be dissatisfied for a moment longer.

* * *

Nadine wriggled backward on the couch, tucking her rear end a little more firmly against Anderson's thighs. Her body ached a little, and her soup was definitely cold. But her heart was full.

"You're right." She said it softly, not wanting to break the spell of contentedness that hung in the room.

"Not that I want to argue…" Anderson replied. "But what am I right about?"

"Cabin life is nice."

"Very nice."

"Maybe we could live like this permanently."

"Mmm. Preferably in something we don't have to buy from Garibaldi, though."

"I just assumed that went without saying."

She frowned. "What happens to the stuff he owns?"

He smoothed the hair off her forehead. "When he's busted, you mean?"

"Yes."

"His assets will be frozen and seized, and he'll forfeit the rights. Then they'll probably be auctioned off. It's a long process that makes me glad I'm not a lawyer. Why are you asking? Does Garibaldi have something you want?"

"No. I was thinking of Reggie and Brayden, actually. Because Garibaldi kind of took the Frost Family Diner right out from under Reggie's dad."

"All those details will come out when he's taken to trial."

"You always sound so sure. You say 'when' every time. Never 'if.'"

He shifted, pulling them both up to a sitting position. "That's because I *am* sure. It took us fifteen years to find him. It took Brayden all of a week to figure out—without a doubt—that the man's business here is shady."

She met his eyes. "Can I ask you something?"

"Of course."

"What happened before? With the first charges?"

"Good cops were killed. Good lawyers got the killer off. Garibaldi was a minor—barely—when he set off that bomb. It made things easier, and the case was actually dismissed because so much of the evidence was ruled as inadmissible."

"Do you know why he set off that first bomb?"

"We didn't before. Not really, anyway. But it was your brother and you who gave us the big tip," Anderson explained. "The info came to Brayden from Tyler. Did he or Reggie tell you much about it?"

"No," she said. "They were tied up in their thing, and then I was injured."

"Well. Your dad and Jesse Garibaldi's dad worked together. Something happened—at a drug bust, actually—and the senior Garibaldi was killed. We think Jesse was going after revenge."

"So *your* dad was in the group that busted *his* dad?"

"That's what we believe. But Harley couldn't find a record of it, and as you're aware…he's damn good at that part of his job."

"And Jesse Garibaldi was just a kid."

"Seventeen when he set off the bomb. He's actually only three years older than I am, but I was most definitely far more of a child than he was at the time. My dad's murder is probably the only reason I grew up when I did."

As he said the words, a heartbreaking, gut-wrenching thought hit Nadine. And she knew it must've shown in her expression, because Anderson's face filled with concern.

"What's wrong?" he asked immediately.

"My dad," she said, the words catching in her throat. "He was Jesse Garibaldi's driver. Those pictures he had… Anderson, he drove Garibaldi to the station to bomb it. My father was an accessory to *your* father's murder."

He reached out, and she jerked away without meaning to. She didn't know why it hadn't occurred to her the second they saw the incriminating photos. Her heart squeezed so hard that she couldn't breathe.

"Nadine."

She blinked.

"Hey, sweetheart."

She blinked harder.

"Nadine."

She couldn't see. But it wasn't until Anderson's thumb came up to wipe away the tears that she realized she was crying. She tried to draw in a gulp of air. Instead, she exhaled a sob.

"Honey, look at me. Please."

She forced herself to lift her eyes to meet Anderson's. She expected to find pain in his gaze. To see at least a hint of it, even if he tried to mask it. Instead, she just found understanding.

"You aren't your father," he stated. "And in a million years, I'd never hold you responsible for anything he did or didn't do."

"But if he *hadn't* driven…"

"Then Garibaldi would still have found a way to do what he did."

"My dad could've turned over the evidence he had."

"He used it to protect you and your brother instead."

"Garibaldi might already be in jail. Your whole life would've been different, Anderson."

"And I might not have met you."

"You can't convince me that you're thankful."

He shook his head. "I'm not thankful that my dad is dead. I'm not thankful for the years of heartache. But thankful doesn't even *begin* to describe how I feel about having you in my life. If everything else was just a prelude to the moment I walked into that room and found you all hooked up to those machines with that defiant, stubborn look on your face…then, hell, I'll take it."

She blinked again, this time in disbelief. "You're serious."

"Of course I'm serious," he replied. "Bad things happen. Really terrible, awful things. But the shining moments are the ones that matter."

"But my dad—"

"Might have left you the evidence that'll close this case for good. And that's definitely something to be thankful for, too."

Nadine opened her mouth, then closed it. She opened it again. But before she could come even close to formulating an appropriate response, the laptop—still open but shoved to the far side of the coffee table—chimed a notification of an incoming video chat.

"It's Harley," Anderson announced with a glance toward the computer. "But we can wait."

Nadine shook her head. "No. We need to know what he's found out."

"You sure?"

In reply, she tugged her T-shirt back on, pulled the laptop closer and clicked on the button to answer the call.

As Harley's face filled the screen, a disgusted look immediately took over his features.

"Bro," he said. "You seriously couldn't get dressed before you answered?"

Anderson laughed. "To be fair, it was Nadine who insisted that we couldn't ignore you."

His friend's eyes flicked toward the petite blonde. "Her, I'm glad to see."

"Hi, Harley!" Nadine greeted cheerfully.

Anderson pressed his palm into her lower back. In spite of her tone, he could tell she was still hurting. He hated the thought that anything about him, however indirectly, would cause her pain.

Vowing to make sure she was going to be all right as soon as they were done, he made himself focus on Harley. "What've you got for us?"

"The dates were easy," said the other man. "I didn't run all of them yet, obviously—there were way too many for even my mad, crazy skills—and lots just turned up a blank. But a few of the ones I did cross-reference came up with known criminal acts. Couple of thefts. Couple of known drug houses."

"Anything that would tie those directly to Jesse Garibaldi?" Anderson asked.

"Not in a way that would make me think of the shots as blackmail-worthy."

"What about the car?" interjected Nadine. "Isn't it his? I know for a fact that my dad always said it was."

"It's weird. There're actually three cars altogether. None is registered to Jesse Garibaldi. But all three *are* registered to the same man. A guy named…" Harley paused and looked down. "Kincaid Walls. I ran him through the system and found nothing. He's just some middle-aged science teacher at a community college."

"You going to call him?" Anderson wanted to know.

"Not yet. If he *is* connected, I don't wanna spook him."

"True enough."

"One other thing, though," his friend said. "There was a picture in with the others. One near the end? It was some guys in protective suits. Something about it was bugging me, so I did *this*."

His fingers clacked noisily on the keyboard, and suddenly an image filled the screen. It was nothing but a grainy blur.

"Great," said Anderson. "That's *much* better than the picture of the men in their weird suits."

Harley's disembodied laugh carried through the laptop speakers. "Whoops. Wrong one. That's a thumbprint. I was trying to see if I could pull up an ID."

"Did you?"

"No. Well, not yet, anyway. It's not what I wanted to show you."

There were some more keyboard clicks, and then a second image took the place of the first.

"I did my best to enhance it," Harley explained. "Can you see it?"

"I can see it," said Anderson. "But it still doesn't mean anything to me. Just two guys dressed for a hazmat party, holding some canvas between them."

"Well," his friend replied, "I originally hoped that their faces would be a little clearer."

"You originally hoped?" Nadine asked.

"Yeah. I couldn't pinpoint why else my instinct was to blow up the picture and make it better. Unfortunately, I couldn't. The masks they have on obscure their faces even in the enhanced shot. But then I figured out that it wasn't really the guys who caught my eye. It was the painting."

"Of course it was," Anderson muttered good-naturedly.

"Hey. Don't knock my artistic nature." The keyboard sounded again, and his friend's face replaced the picture. "What was interesting about the painting was that it's worthless."

"Worthless?" Nadine sounded as surprised as Anderson felt.

"Without a doubt," Harley affirmed.

"Worthless as in bad forgeries?" Anderson asked.

"Nope. Not even that." His friend frowned. "Or I guess they *could* be forgeries. If someone wanted to forge art by some completely unknown, unrecorded, untraceable artist."

"So if they're not worth anything, why is Garibaldi

being so secretive about them?" Anderson mused. "Why destroy a cellar, kill a man, then build a room dedicated to storing them?"

"And why are his hired helpers dressed like they're working with poison?" Harley added. "And what the hell is Garibaldi doing with the paintings?"

"I know," Nadine announced suddenly.

"You do?" Anderson and Harley said at the same time.

"It's really been bugging me, thinking about it. Probably like you and the picture, Harley," she said. "Anyway, it's that mom from the pie place."

Anderson snapped his fingers. "The art store."

"Fill me in," said Harley.

"The woman owns a shop called Liz's Lovely Things, and she stocks art for Garibaldi. When I told Anderson about it, I thought she'd described the pieces as 'high-end,' but now that I'm thinking about it again, I remember that she actually said 'high-priced.' She's an art dealer. She must know it's not worth what the buyers pay for it."

"She's got regular buyers?" Anderson asked.

"Didn't I say that before?" she replied.

"Maybe you did. I guess I was just too hung up on the idea that Garibaldi wouldn't be involved in something to do with art theft."

"Well," Harley said. "Now you need to get hung up on the idea that he *is* involved in it for some reason. Though damned if I can think of a good one."

Anderson ran a frustrated hand over his hair. "We're missing some element."

"Agreed," his partner replied. "I'm going to comb through the pictures a little more and see if I can find a hint as to what it is."

"Maybe look for more than a hint," Anderson said drily.

"Funny, man. I'll call you if I get anything else, all right?"

"Yep." He leaned over to click off the call, but Nadine's hand shot out to stop him.

"Wait," she said.

"What?" replied Harley.

"There's a picture in the first set." She bit her lip, looking nervous. "In the ones from outside the Freemont City police station?"

"It's all right," Anderson assured her.

She nodded, bit her lip once more and exhaled. "The shot shows the car and the street. But in the corner, there's a man. Maybe you could clean that one up, too."

"Good call, Nadine." Harley sounded genuinely pleased. "I was so fixated on the one of the painting that I didn't think to check it out."

"Okay," said Anderson. "We'll make a plan on our end, you keep us in the loop on yours."

After an affirmation on his partner's end, he reached over and clicked off the call, then closed the laptop. He took a breath and turned to Nadine, bracing for an argument.

# *Chapter 17*

Nadine could tell from the look on Anderson's face—wary but determined—that she wasn't going to like whatever he was about to say.

"Just tell me," she said, already crossing her arms over her chest defensively.

"I want to go back down to the cellar so I can check out the art-storage room."

It took her a second to process why his statement got her back up.

She narrowed her eyes. "You didn't say 'we.'"

"No," he agreed, "I didn't."

"You can't really expect me to stay here."

"I haven't decided yet where I'd like you to stay."

"That's not up to you, Anderson."

"Nadine."

As he reached for her arm, she pulled away and stood up instead. She paced the room, frustration making her seethe.

"I'm not some china doll you can just put on a shelf," she snapped.

"I know that. And I'm not trying to—"

"I can fight. I've taken self-defense classes. I can fire a gun. Accurately, I might add."

"I believe you."

"Then why the hell are you trying to make me stay behind?"

"Because I'm terrified!"

It was yelled, and it made Nadine jump back and blink in surprise. So far, she hadn't seen Anderson lose his temper even once. In fact, if she'd been asked just thirty seconds earlier, she might've said he didn't *have* much of a temper to lose. She stared down at him, unsure what to say. Before she could come up with something, his face crumpled.

"I'm sorry," he said, his voice rough. "I shouldn't have hollered like that."

She inhaled, tears unexpectedly pricking at her eyes. "It's okay."

"No. It's not. I'm just so damned scared."

"Of what?"

"That something's going to happen to you."

Nadine sank back down beside him. "Anderson."

He looked down at his hands. "What?"

"That is *disgustingly* romantic. And I love you even more for it."

"But you're going to fight me on it."

"Absolutely."

"What can I say to convince you?"

"Nothing. *I'm* going to convince *you*."

He looked up. "You can't convince me that it's safer for me to take you into Garibaldi's line of fire than it is for me to find you somewhere to hide out until I'm done looking around."

"Stand up," she replied.

"What?"

"Stand up. And strap on your weapon. I'm going to disarm you."

"You aren't going to disarm me."

"Yes, I am. Then I'm going to knock you down, take the gun outside and fire it accurately at some faraway target of your choice."

He shot her a look like he was going to argue some more, but shook his head instead. "Fine. Good luck."

Trying to keep her smirk to herself, Nadine watched as he readied himself. T-shirt back over his head. Holster strapped to his side. Gun in place.

"Might as well put your shoes on," Nadine said.

"You want me to crush one of your toes?" Anderson replied.

"I'm just trying to give you every advantage."

"Fine." He stepped to the door, where he laced his boots, then straightened up and shot her a smug look. "Anytime."

"Attack me," she ordered.

"No."

She started to argue, but suddenly he was on the move. Crouched low and headed straight for her. Startled, she didn't have time to do much more than dodge his assault. And she barely had time to recover before he was on her again.

Nadine dived forward as Anderson's hands came out in a grabbing motion. Her shoulder hit the coffee table, and she bit back a cry as she rolled out of reach.

"You okay?"

She looked up to see that Anderson had stopped advancing to ask the question. She immediately took advantage. Propelling herself along the floor, whipping out one leg as she did it, Nadine gave Anderson a sharp kick in the shins.

"Hey!" he protested.

"You let your guard down," she replied, pushing to her feet.

He took a step away. "You kicked me."

"That's what you get."

She breathed in, then came at him again, feinting to the left, then adjusting to hit him from the left. He anticipated and used his arm to shoot an expert block her way. Quickly he twisted the same arm around to close his fingers on her wrist. For a second, Nadine let him think he was going to be able to maintain the upper hand. But only for a heartbeat. Then she fought back using the sequence she'd learned in the self-defense class she'd taken years earlier.

First she took a tiny step forward while twisting her hand at the same time. Anderson, of course, maintained his hold. But the move toward him rather than away from him meant that his grip loosened just enough that he couldn't stop her from turning her palm to the ceiling. The move created just the right amount space between his hand and her wrist. Next, Nadine slipped her other hand up between their bodies and gave the soft, fleshy part of Anderson's palm a jab. His fingers opened. And before he could regain his hold, she grabbed his wrist. With a twist, she locked his elbow joint in place. And, finally, she took a step back and rotated her body 180 degrees. The result was just as she intended—Anderson was off balance. With a little shove, he went down.

"Don't move," Nadine said, "or I'll break your arm."

He narrowed his eyes and shifted ever so slightly. In response, she twisted a little harder. She pushed aside a stab of guilt at his wince. She had something to prove; she couldn't afford to feel bad. Especially if he was trying to trick her.

"Give me your gun," she commanded.

"Or you'll break my arm?"

"Yep."

With his free hand, Anderson flipped open his holster and tugged out the weapon. With a self-satisfied grin, Nadine took it from him.

Then she stepped back and smiled sweetly. "This is the part where I'd aim at you if you were a bad guy."

He sat up and studied her from the floor. "Pleased with yourself, aren't you?"

"I thought it was pretty impressive. And I was holding back," she informed him, her tone deliberately pert.

His mouth twitched into a half smile. "Oh, really?"

"I didn't break your arm for *real*, did I?"

"I suppose not." His smile turned to a frown. "But tell me something."

"What?"

"With moves like that, how the hell did the guy at your mom's apartment manage to get to you?"

"I knew you were impressed."

"That's not an answer."

"I just didn't get a chance to escape on my own before you got there, and—" She bit down on her lip to stop herself from finishing.

Anderson wasn't that quick to let it go. "And what?"

"I panicked a little."

"You panicked." His voice had gone flat.

"A little," she repeated. "And it's not going to happen again."

"How can you be sure? How can *I* be sure?"

"I guess you can't. Not a hundred percent, anyway. But I'm confident that I won't. And besides that, I've got a gun now."

"That's my gun," he pointed out. "Police issue. Even if I wanted to hand it over, I couldn't."

"Then I'll just grab the one Brayden hid on the top shelf

of the bedroom closet," she replied. "Come on. Let's go outside so I can prove to you just how good I am."

"It's not going to make me want to put you in harm's way," he said. "And I'm actually not convinced discharging my weapon out there is the best idea."

"Guess you'll have to catch me if you want to stop me."

"You're not seriously going to—"

She missed whatever else he was about to say as she bolted for the door. She flung it open and stepped out onto the porch. An unexpected blast of wind and rain hit her, and she came to a shivering halt. But she heard Anderson mutter a curse, then heard his feet hit the floor as he started his pursuit.

Nadine descended the stairs in a wild leap. She managed to land with barely more than a stumble, and she continued her crazy run. She made it around the back of the house, then to the edge of the forest. There she realized her mistake. She'd forgotten to grab her shoes. And a glance toward the increasingly jagged terrain stopped her short. Her hesitation was just enough time to allow Anderson to catch up. His hands landed on her body, and, instead of fighting him as he forcibly scooped her from the ground, she let herself sink into him, then tipped her face up to meet his eyes.

"Hi," she greeted breathlessly.

"Hi?" he said back. "That's what you're going with?"

"You wanted something more?"

"I let you beat me up. Don't I deserve a reward?"

"You *let* me?"

"That's my story if anyone asks."

"Chauvinist."

"Name-calling isn't going to help you."

"No? Well, how about this?"

She brought a hand to his cheek, tilted his head down and pressed her lips to his in a brief but passion-filled kiss. When she pulled back, his gaze somehow managed to be a third amused, a third unimpressed and a third desirous. Nadine couldn't fight a laugh at the contradictory expressions.

He kissed her nose. "You do realize that you're a serious pain in the—"

His words cut off abruptly as the sound of tires sloshing soggily over the dirt road carried through the air.

In spite of her verbal assurance that she wouldn't panic again, a heavy, heart-squeezing, air-stealing feeling immediately took hold of Nadine's chest. She was glad that Anderson retained control. He didn't put her down right away. Instead, he tucked her even closer to his body, then carried her from their spot behind the house to a particularly thick patch of trees just on the inside edge of the forest.

"If I ask you to wait here for a second, are you going to kick me and take away my gun?" he asked in a low voice.

Nadine shook her head. "No." Then she winced. "And I think I dropped your gun back by the house."

Anderson dropped a curse. "On this side or on the other side."

"This one."

"All right. Sit tight."

He finally set her down, planted a light kiss on her lips and then took off at a slow, silent run. Nadine waited with as much patience as she could muster, watching with her heart in her throat as Anderson reached a spot near the rear of the wood building, then paused and bent down. As he stood again, the telltale flash of silver in his hand let Nadine know he'd located the weapon. Some of the pressure in her lungs released. But when Anderson turned her way and started jogging toward her, it all came back, worse than before.

"What are you doing?" she asked as soon as he was close enough to hear.

"Giving you this." He held out the gun.

"You might need that."

"You might need it more."

"You said it was police issue."

"It is."

"Anderson."

"I'll be right back." He kissed her again, then pressed the cool metal into her hands and loped off.

This time, Nadine didn't watch him. She wasn't sure she trusted herself to not bolt after him. So she pressed her back to one of the surrounding trees and counted to thirty in her head to make sure he was gone before she dared to open her eyes again. But when she did, the rain-filled air and empty space in front of her seemed nothing but ominous.

It took a significant chunk of Anderson's willpower to keep from just running back to Nadine. He would've preferred to grab her tightly and pull her farther into the woods. Out of reaching distance from whatever trouble lay on the other side of the cabin.

*But you don't know what the trouble is*, he reminded himself as he slunk along the log siding of the house. *And that's why you have to do it this way.*

He just hoped that Nadine wasn't going to give in to her stubborn need to stick by him at every turn. Not that he minded in most circumstances. In fact, he liked it. Loved it. Wanted it. When there was an undefined threat in play, though, he had a strong preference for keeping her at a safe distance.

*So stay put*, he ordered silently.

He reached the edge of the house then and paused. He could hear—just barely over the ever-thickening downpour—the indistinct rumble of voices. He knew he had to get closer.

Wiping the rain from his eyes so he could see better, he leaned forward and sought a way to get nearer to the front of the cabin without exposing himself. An option presented itself immediately. A woodshed sat just a few feet away. The squat worn-down structure was just the right size for a hiding place, and at just the right vantage point to give him a perfect view of whatever was happening in front of the cabin. The only problem would be getting there.

*Not just getting there*, he amended. *Getting there unseen, unheard and undetected.* He eyed the shed for another second, then mentally added another "un." *Unrealistic.*

As he tried to come up with a solution, the voices grew louder, and he was sure that the men attached to them were approaching the front porch now. He could even catch the odd word.

"…think it's a…"

"Dunno. That car is…"

"…false alarm…"

Anderson strained to listen. The sound of the storm beat away any chance at understanding. Cursing the weather, he closed his eyes and instead tried to picture where the men might be standing. If they were *on* the porch, their line of sight would be blocked by the hanging screen at the end. He could probably hazard a run toward the woodshed without too much concern. If they stood below the porch's steps, though, even a few steps out would expose him completely. He still had to find a way to do it. Not knowing who'd followed them—and not knowing how they'd done it—wasn't an option he wanted to take.

After another moment of considering it, Anderson dropped low. Right to the ground. Mud immediately soaked through his clothes, but he made himself ignore the discomfort as he shimmied closer. Though he still had his mental sights set on the woodshed, he quickly realized that he might not need to head that way, after all. The two men *were* on the porch, and his wriggling had brought him to a position just below that. He couldn't see them, but he could suddenly hear every word perfectly.

"We've knocked twice. Still no answer," said the first man, his voice a thick rumble.

"You really think that means no one's home?" replied the second, his tone skeptical.

"I dunno," said Rumbly Voice. "I'm kinda starting to think this whole thing is a wild-goose chase."

"The fire was real," pointed out The Skeptic.

"Yeah, I know. But I don't believe for a second that the Stuart woman set it."

"Even though she ran when we went by her apartment?"

The last question was enough to clue Anderson in to the identity of the two men. They were the police officers who'd given them chase at Nadine's apartment. Their presence at the cabin sent Anderson's head into a bad space—there was no way they'd been followed directly, so how had they tracked them down? Gritting his teeth, he shook off the unease and tried to pick up a clue from the men's continued argument.

"Who knows if she even saw us?" Rumbly Voice was saying right then.

Anderson wanted to heave a sigh of relief, but he refrained—especially when The Skeptic voiced yet another doubt.

"What other reason would she have for running?" the man asked.

"Just about anything, I'd say. Late for an appointment. Late for a reservation. Eager to get somewhere with her man friend."

"Man friend?"

"Boyfriend. Male companion. Whatever."

"Did we find anything else about him, by the way?"

"Blake Smith," said Rumbly Voice. "Visiting from Freemont City. No priors. Not even a speeding ticket."

"One more knock?" suggested The Skeptic.

There was a pause in the conversation, and the sound of a fist hitting the door firmly echoed noisily over the rain. Silence hung in the air for a few seconds longer before Rumbly Voice broke it once more.

"Face it," he said. "No one's here."

"The car?" replied The Skeptic.

"Yeah, we knew how to find it, though, right? Convenience of a rental company paranoid enough to install a GPS tracking system. But there's no sign of the girl or her friend, and the car's rented to the same name that's attached to the current lease, so it makes perfect sense for the vehicle to be here."

"So you're willing to just dismiss the whole thing?"

"Not to dismiss it. Just to take a step back and consider whether or not the tips might be a hoax."

"For what purpose?" The Skeptic wondered aloud.

Rumbly Voice's reply dropped to an even lower timbre. "The woman was in an accident that killed a cop. Maybe someone didn't like it. Maybe someone thought we wouldn't like it, either."

In spite of the permeating moisture, Anderson felt his throat grow dry. He was unreasonably glad that Nadine wasn't anywhere near enough to hear what the policeman had just said.

"Not to speak ill of the dead," Rumbly Voice added, "but I never much cared for Officer Delta myself. Always kinda rubbed me the wrong way. But that doesn't mean he didn't have friends."

"Friends who're willing to break the law on his behalf?" The Skeptic asked.

"He didn't give you that vibe?"

"Yeah." The admission was grudging. "Maybe."

"Just think about it. Someone sees a guy in a mask at the care center. We didn't have a reason to be focusing on Ms. Stuart at the time. But it happened on her floor. So let's just say that was someone wanting to scare her. They failed because she'd been discharged."

Anderson relaxed as the man rehashed the details and shared his opinions with his partner. His conclusions were similar to the ones he would've made himself if he'd been investigating. It was reassuring, too, to know that—unlike Chuck Delta, who'd been working for Garibaldi when he was killed—these two officers were clean.

And The Skeptic seemed to be wavering, too. "Maybe you're right. I know it's not a forgone conclusion that a schoolteacher isn't capable of committing a crime, but from what I've seen, it does sound like a leap in this case."

"Exactly," agreed the other man. "And she'll turn up eventually. If she truly set the fire for financial gain, then she'll come after the money. If she had nothing to do with it, she'll just carry on as usual. Either way, I think we should tell the boss that the tips might be phony."

Seeming satisfied—at least temporarily—the two officers traipsed back down the stairs, their voices fading into the storm as they got farther away. Anderson continued to press himself to the ground until he heard their engine fire up. When he was sure they'd driven down the driveway and were out of viewing distance, he pushed to his feet and made his way back to Nadine.

The second she spotted him, her face filled with relief. "They're gone? I heard the car, but why did they take off so quickly?" Then her eyes traveled the length of his body, and she frowned. "And why are you covered in mud?"

He glanced down. Sure enough, his torso and legs were caked with it. "I guess I decided to take getting my hands dirty to the next level."

"That might be an understatement."

"Come on." He extended his hand. "I'll explain what I heard while I get cleaned up. Then we can talk about how we're going to get back into town without getting noticed."

"We?" she said. "As in, you're taking me with you to Garibaldi's underground storage room?"

"Sure as hell can't leave you here now," he grumbled as she threaded her fingers through his.

He led her to the front of the cabin, summarizing the conclusion made by the other cops and telling her that he concurred. He didn't know if whoever had tipped off the police about the rental car was also going to use it to follow them, but he wasn't willing to take the chance either way. They needed to leave the cabin with reasonable quickness.

Inside, he hurriedly stripped down, trading in his own muddy clothes for a pair of jeans and a button-up shirt that Brayden had left behind. It wasn't until he was almost fully dressed that he realized how quiet Nadine had gone.

"Hey," he said, moving closer so he could cup her cheek with his hand. "That part was supposed to be the good news. The local cops don't think you're responsible for the fire, and they're not in on whatever Garibaldi's got going on."

"No," she replied. "I know."

He dropped his hands back to his buttons, doing them up but keeping his eyes on Nadine. "So why the face?"

"Just thinking."

He could tell that she was holding something back, but decided not to push it. "It kind of looks like it hurts."

Her mouth tipped up. "Was that a dig? Are you doubting my intelligence?"

"Never. I'm more concerned about your pretty little face."

"Is that right?"

"Seriously. You've got a wrinkle in your forehead that's about an inch deep."

"Ha-ha."

He smiled. "Tell me what you were thinking about."

"You said we need a way out of here without the car?" she asked.

"That's right. Don't want to risk getting tracked again."

"Well, I've got an idea. But I'm not sure how reasonable it is."

"I guess we won't know until we try."

"Okay, then. Grab your boots and follow me."

And after allowing himself a single, indulgent moment of admiring her as she turned and strode toward the door, Anderson grabbed his coat and hurried to catch up.

# *Chapter 18*

Nadine's body was humming with an urgent need to act. To be on the move. To take control of whatever was coming next.

She didn't know which thing, specifically, had triggered the intense need. Maybe it was the brief, intense anxiety she'd experienced when Anderson had disappeared from sight. Or maybe it was the realization that until Garibaldi was stopped, *he* would be the one in control of her life. Though she supposed it could also be a combination of the two things. An awareness that so long as the situation remained unresolved, the control also extended to keeping them apart.

And the thought of that was something she couldn't stand.

She walked even faster, striding from the cabin's porch to the muddy ground, then crossing down to the clearing that held the other, smaller cabins. She knew Anderson was beside her. She could feel him keeping pace. Everything else seemed secondary.

When she came to a stop just in front of her destination—a dilapidated shed behind one of the smaller cabins—Anderson lifted his jacket up over their heads and stepped close enough that it shielded both of them from the thumping rain.

"This is it?" he asked, his voice barely carrying over the storm.

"I hope so," she replied, reaching for the handle on the shed's door.

Her hand found its mark, but a jab of something sharp in her palm made her pull it back with a cry. A glance down showed her the source of the sudden pain. A long splinter stuck out from the soft padding of her palm. Anderson's hand dropped down from its position above them to gently pluck away the offending piece of wood. Before he got the jacket back in place, the rain sneaked in sideways, and Nadine watched as it washed away a little bead of blood as quickly as it formed.

"You okay?" Anderson asked.

"Fine," she replied, dragging her attention back to the door.

"You know that I don't just mean the splinter, right?"

Nadine lifted her eyes to meet his, and she could see unguarded worry in his gaze.

"That was a pretty intense little walk," he added.

"It's pouring."

"I don't think you even *realized* it was raining."

"You know that you're not supposed to be reading my mind, right?"

"Wouldn't if I could. I only want to know what's going on in your head if *you* want me to know. But I'm a willing listener."

She started to deny that anything was going on under

the surface, but when she opened her mouth, the truth came out instead. "I was just considering how easy it is to wreck someone's life from the inside out."

"Garibaldi."

"Yes. If he'd succeeded in killing me—"

"I won't let that happen."

"But if he did—"

"Nadine."

"Just listen for a second, okay?"

"Fine."

"If he'd killed me back at the care center, I'd have been out of the way. Whatever he thinks I know about the stuff on the USB stick would've been gone. Erased with me. But then you came into the picture. And you would've still been alive, and maybe you'd know what I know, so he'd have to kill you, too. And where does that end?"

Anderson looked like he was trying to force himself to keep from clenching his teeth together, and his words were strained with the apparent effort. "Where are you going with this?"

She took a shaky breath. "Garibaldi could kill everyone who knows something—even everyone who he *thinks* knows something. Except every 'accidental' death would make it harder for him to keep hiding. But he's not stupid. So he's choosing a more subtle route—planting evidence, creating doubt—and that takes the focus off him completely. I mean, he did it with my brother. Framed him for the Main Street bomb."

"But Tyler was never convicted of the crime," Anderson pointed out.

"Did it matter? They let Tyler go because there wasn't enough evidence to make a charge stick. But his life was destroyed. He knew what really happened, and he couldn't do anything about it."

"Your brother had other issues, though, sweetheart. You know that."

"But I'm not without issue myself."

"Only in the same way that none of us are."

"Do you want to know another of the reasons I stayed away from Whispering Woods all those years, Anderson? Something I've never admitted aloud?" She paused, drew in another breath as he nodded, and then she said in a soft voice, "It was doubt."

"About what?"

"Myself. About people's reactions to me. About who would know about my memory loss and my dad's death. Would they think I knew something else? Would they accept a story that I didn't even believe myself? Don't get me wrong. I'm confident in who I am, but with my history, I was honestly surprised when they offered me the job at Whispering Woods Elementary."

He started to respond, but she put up a hand before he could actually speak.

"Garibaldi *created* that history. And his way of doing it was insidious. Just like this. So I'm damned sure that he's trying to make it happen again." She stopped for a second, her emotions running through her fiercely. "And I won't let him."

Anderson stepped forward, letting the jacket drop as he reached for her face with both of his hands. He planted a kiss onto her mouth. For a second, she let him linger there. His lips were warm and firm and reassuringly concrete in the otherwise unpredictable situation. Then she pulled back and straightened her shoulders.

"I'm ready to go back to being a schoolteacher," she said.

Anderson reached for her again—this time to grab her hand. "Just a schoolteacher?"

She frowned. "There's nothing 'just' about being a

schoolteacher. I mean, I know it's not crime fighting and running for my life, but—"

"That's not what I meant." His thumb ran over her fingers.

"What did you— Oh." She felt her face warm as she clued in.

She looked down. He was holding her *left* hand. And he wasn't just running her thumb over her fingers—he was rubbing it over a *specific* finger. She lifted her gaze again. Anderson was wearing a face-splitting grin.

"No pressure," he said.

"No pressure," she repeated dubiously.

He shrugged. "Okay. Some pressure. But I'm willing to hold off until after you've unveiled your secret plan."

Nadine exhaled, but the excited beat of her heart didn't slow even when she turned her attention back to the shed door.

*Marriage.*

Two days ago, she'd been lying in a hospital bed, afraid for her life but seething at the fact that the big, blond detective felt it was his job to babysit her. Now she was having a hard time even thinking about a life that didn't involve him.

*But getting* married...

It was crazy.

*And yet so very right.*

"You going to open that door or just stand there staring at it?" Anderson's voice made her jump, and she flushed all over again.

"I'm opening it." She shook off the tingle in her ring finger and yanked the wooden handle.

The door creaked open, and a blast of odd scents assaulted her nose. Mustiness. Gasoline. Dirt. And a few other things that were unidentifiable.

Nadine pointed into the dark. "There it is."

Anderson leaned over her shoulder. "There what is? All I see is a sheet-covered blob."

Nadine swung the door as wide as it would go. The stormy sky didn't do much to illuminate the interior of the shed, but it seemed to give Anderson enough to discern what it was that hid under the large piece of fabric.

"Is that an ATV?" he asked.

Nadine nodded. "When these cabins were in their prime, the old owners had a little fleet of them for their guests. I think this is the only one left."

"How did you know it was here?"

"From when I was stalking Brayden and Reggie. I did a pretty thorough search of the property."

Anderson chuckled. "Normally I discourage illegal behavior. But right now, I'm thankful for your law-breaking ways."

"Do you think it'll work?"

"That'll depend on how well it was stored. But lucky for us, my stepdad's a mechanic and taught me a thing or two."

She gestured forward. "Well, have at it, then, Detective."

He was already moving, muttering about the relative dampness in the dim space. His tone turned more hopeful, though, as he yanked off the cloth and began examining the off-road vehicle. Nadine didn't understand any of the technical jargon, but what she *could* decipher was that someone had done things right. The ATV's battery was stored separately, the tank left empty. A well-sealed can of gasoline awaited use, and, miraculously—except for a small amount of rust—the vehicle had no damage. So in what seemed like just a few minutes, Anderson had the thing out in the rain with the engine not exactly humming, but at least sounding like it stood a good chance of carrying them the required distance.

"No helmets, though," he complained.

"Don't worry," Nadine replied. "I'm an excellent driver."

"You want me to be your passenger?"

"Do you have a lot of off-road, all-terrain-driving experience?"

"None."

"And do you know the backwoods way from here into town?"

"I think you're aware that I don't."

"So, I reiterate. I'm an excellent driver." She smiled sweetly. "And I'm ready whenever you are."

He shot her a suitably dirty look, but less than five minutes later, he was positioned behind her as the rumbling machine propelled them through the dense, wet forest.

As the trees whipped by, the rain tapered off to a light drizzle, and Anderson found himself actually enjoying the wild ride. Nadine's claim of expertise was more than a boast—she navigated the woods like a pro, slowing in anticipation of any particularly large bumps in the terrain, avoiding low-hanging branches and somehow managing to avoid the slick mud that dotted the forest floor. Anderson caught sight of the odd flash of colored metal tacked against the surrounding trees, and he knew that at some point the path Nadine had chosen must've been a marked trail. And recognizing that fact clued him in to something else. He hadn't even asked her where, specifically, she was taking him. Back to town was obvious. The ultimate goal of getting to the underground storage facility was also a given. Beyond that—between those two things—he had no clue. It was an unnerving realization.

*Reckless*, he chastised himself, his grip tightening unconsciously on Nadine's waist.

He was supposed to be in charge. Not because she wasn't competent but because Anderson was the cop. The one sworn to protect and serve. The one with the training. Yes, the woman nestled against him was smart and capable. She'd proved her abilities time and again over the last two days. That didn't mean she'd spent years training like he had. Anderson rarely even trusted his fellow detectives to just lead the way and they had just as much experience as he did. More, sometimes. There were only three other people he followed blindly, whom he trusted so utterly that he didn't need an explanation.

*Brayden, Harley and Rush.*

Anderson blinked, and it wasn't because the rain was making him do it. It was because he trusted Nadine so very thoroughly. As much as the men that he thought of as brothers. The men who'd gone through the same loss he'd gone through, and who had proved, time and again, that the trust was well deserved and reciprocal.

His hold on her tightened again, this time purposely. Somehow, the explicit trust seemed more meaningful than the love at—almost—first sight. It was one thing to fall head over heels in time of high tension. That had been easy. Nadine was everything Anderson wanted in a woman. She was even things he hadn't *known* he wanted. Beautiful and tough. Unique. Somehow worldly but still unjaded. She made his heart ache.

*But this level of trust... It's more than that. It's like... what?*

Anderson tried to think of an appropriate comparison. The nearest he could come up with was that it was like knowing you'd take a bullet for someone, then realizing that they'd do the same for you. It wasn't a great comparison—not hearts and rainbows like it ought to be. But somehow it was most fitting anyway.

"You okay?"

Nadine's voice cut over the hum of the engine and jolted him back to the moment, and he saw that they'd slowed down and were approaching a thinner patch of trees.

"I'm good," he replied, then chuckled a little to himself as he realized it was the grossest understatement he'd ever made.

He was still smiling a few moments later when Nadine brought the ATV to a halt. Without waiting for her to turn off the machine, Anderson swung himself off the ATV, planted himself firmly on the ground and turned to face her. Her eyes widened with surprise as he clasped her face in his hands.

"I'm crazy about you, Nadine," he said, unsurprised that the words came out in a gruff, emotion-fueled growl.

Her eyes grew even wider, and her response was a little breathy. "I thought we'd already established that the feeling is mutual."

"Mutual," he repeated, thinking of his own take-a-bullet analogy just a few minutes earlier.

"Yes."

"Mutual's good." He tugged her closer and dropped a swift, hard kiss to her mouth. "So long as your 'mutual' includes an over-the-top, lifetime-of-happiness, heart-racing, permanent kind of deal."

She reached up and brushed away a piece of hair that had stuck to his forehead. Her touch was gentle—but not hesitant—and imbued with the same longing he felt coursing through his veins.

Her next words confirmed it. "Of course it does, Anderson."

"I want you to meet my family."

"Okay."

"And get to know the guys."

"All right."

"And to pick out place settings with me."

"Place settings?"

"Yep. Fancy ones that we keep in a glass-fronted cabinet."

"Well…if that's what you want…"

"It is."

"Okay."

He let out a breath and kissed her once more. "Good. Now that that's settled, maybe you can tell me where the hell we are."

She laughed and turned to cut the engine. "We're exactly where you wanted to be. Or almost, anyway." She pointed through the trees. "A two-minute walk will take us to the road that leads up to the movie theater."

"The theater?" He frowned for a second before he remembered. "Oh. The one where you took Reggie. It doubles as an entry point for the tunnel to Garibaldi's art room."

"That's the one," she confirmed. "Ready?"

"I feel like it's my job to ask you that question."

"You can, if you think it's really necessary."

He grinned. "Ready?"

She lifted an eyebrow, then turned back to the ATV, lifted the lid off the small storage compartment at the rear and dragged out a canvas bag from inside. Anderson had stowed the bag himself—a safe, dry place for his electronics and weapons. Nadine left the latter in the bag, but pulled out both Anderson's service gun and the one Brayden had stored in the cabin. She handed the first to him and tucked the other in the rear of her waistband.

"Now I'm ready," she announced. "Let's go."

"You're the boss."

She rolled her eyes but started to walk, leading the way along the edge of the woods. Within a few steps, nervous tension threatened to take over. They were headed straight into the mouth of the beast, and Anderson had a sudden need to hold on to what small amount of lightness he could. When they reached the edge of the road and stopped just in view of the theater, he took her by the elbow and pulled her to a stop.

"Hey, honey?" he said.

"Yes?"

"You really do know how to fire it, right?"

"You're doubting me? Even after I so easily disarmed you back there?"

"Easily?"

She paused to send him a look that made him lift his hands.

"All right, all right," he conceded. "You can obviously hit a moving target from a hundred yards away. Possibly blindfolded. While hopping up and down on one leg."

Her mouth tipped up in a smile, then opened like she was going to say something. Except she froze without uttering a word, and her eyes fixed on something just over his shoulder. It took Anderson only a second to figure out what it was. First came the telltale click of a cocking gun. Then came the press of cool metal against the back of his head. And, finally, a voice that was even colder than the barrel of the gun.

"Maybe she can do all of that. But what about risking a shot at a man who could kill *you* with one slip of his finger. Can she pull that off, too?"

# *Chapter 19*

A sick, light-headed feeling hit Nadine like a punch. She pressed her hand to her stomach in an attempt to control it, but all that happened was a shift in the positioning of the sickness. It moved from her gut to her head, making her sway with dizziness. And yet she couldn't tear her eyes away from the source of it. Because she recognized the man who stood just behind Anderson, and not just because he was the one who'd burned down her mom's apartment or because she'd seen him again through the slats of the closet at Whispering Woods Lodge. *No.* Something about the way he stood where he was, about the way he studied her face with clinical detachment, threw her back a decade. And as his mouth moved, she didn't hear what he said in that very moment. Instead, she heard the words he'd spoken to her years earlier as he'd stood beside her hospital bed.

*"There's been a mistake, Ms. Stuart," he said.*

*"A mistake?" Her voice was a croak brought on by smoke inhalation.*

*"Dr. Dhillon thought you'd been in a fire. She was wrong."*

*"What?"*

*"It was a car accident, Ms. Stuart. Do you remember it?"*

*"Where's Dr. Dhillon?"*

*"She's no longer with us."*

*The words had an ominous undertone. Puzzled and scared, Nadine struggled to sit up, but her body was bound by tubes and blankets and gauze, and after a second, she let herself flop backward again.*

*"I* was *in a fire," she said.*

*The doctor shook his head. "No, you weren't. Do you remember?"*

*"I don't remember anything."*

*"Not a thing?"*

*"No."*

*He looked satisfied, and for some reason his expression made her want to shiver. After all, shouldn't a doctor* want *her memory to work? Shouldn't he be rooting for her recovery? She closed her eyes for a moment, and when she opened them again, he was gone. But the disturbed feeling stayed with her.*

And here it was again. Here *he* was again. The same satisfied look on his face.

"You recognize me now, don't you?" he said.

"Dr. Salinger." She wished her voice had come out stronger—as it was, the quality was so raspy that she might as well have just inhaled a mouthful of ash all over again.

"You know him?" Anderson sounded genuinely surprised.

Nadine nodded. "He was my main doctor when I was at the hospital in Freemont. The one who told everyone I got my injuries in a car accident."

Both of the big detective's eyebrows lifted, but the doctor didn't give him a chance to respond. Instead, he spoke quickly and kept his eyes trained on Nadine.

"Tell me something, Ms. Stuart. Anything else come back to you recently? Inquiring minds want to know."

Her head swam again. Phantom smoke filled her senses, and she felt herself teetering into a memory that she'd always been sure would never come back. And now that it sat on the edge of her consciousness, she didn't want to embrace it.

*Not yet*, urged a voice in her head.

She drew a breath, trying to force her mind to steady itself. She glanced toward Anderson. He was her rock. Her anchor.

"Drop your gun," the other man commanded, jerking Nadine's attention away again.

She eyed the weapon in his hands, and she loosened her grip on her own gun.

Reading her intentions perfectly but without hazarding a move, Anderson spoke up again. "Do *not* drop it, Nadine. Shoot him instead."

"She won't do that." Dr. Salinger sounded utterly sure. "Look at her face. She cares far too much about what might happen to her boyfriend. Don't you, sweetheart?"

Her hand wavered. She *could* shoot. Or disarm him. She knew she was capable of either. But the doctor was right; she couldn't—wouldn't—risk Anderson's life. She'd find another way.

"I'm sorry, Anderson," she said, and she tossed the gun to an open space beside them.

"Good girl." The doctor made the satisfied face again. "Now I need you to hand over whatever it is that you're using to blackmail my friend."

"Your friend?" Anderson scoffed.

"Don't bother," Dr. Salinger said back. "We both know

who I'm talking about. No need to dig myself a hole by announcing it aloud."

"I'm just surprised to hear you call him your 'friend,'" Anderson replied. "I would've assumed the word 'boss' to be more applicable."

Nadine noted the way the doctor stiffened as he answered.

"Doing someone in his position a favor doesn't make me an employee," he said through nearly clenched teeth.

"No?" Anderson's reply was infused with disparagement.

*Why is he goading him on while he's got a gun to his head?* Nadine wondered.

But as the exchange continued, she figured it out. Anderson was trying to buy them a little time.

"Do *friendly* favors usually involve breaking the law?" he asked next.

*C'mon*, she said to herself. *Use the time to come up with something.*

But she was drawing a frustrating blank, and it was impossible to mute the conversation.

"Interesting." Dr. Salinger's tone was heavy with sarcasm. "You're okay with blackmail but draw the line at me offering my medical services to those who might otherwise not be able to get help."

"Tell yourself whatever you need to in order to sleep at night," Anderson replied. "Yanking out bullets from crooks and fabricating stories about car accidents aren't exactly things I'd label as answering to a higher calling."

"My well-lined pockets keep my conscience clear. And before you get all self-righteous, you might want to consider the fact that I'm the reason your girlfriend's alive at all." He smiled darkly. "You can ask her yourself if you don't believe it. Without me, she would've found her way to a quick grave."

The arrogant statement tickled at Nadine's mind. An idea—rough but picking up traction quickly—was starting to form.

She cleared her throat, drawing the doctor's attention with the interruption. "I'm thankful that I didn't die in the hospital, but I'm not going to give you credit for it."

He narrowed his eyes. "Someone else give you an amnesia diagnosis that I don't know about?"

She shook her head. "No one else gave me a diagnosis. But it wasn't you who kept me alive for the last ten years. It was my brother. Knowing what he knew..."

"Knowing what he knew," he repeated.

She dropped her gaze to meet Anderson's eyes for the briefest second, hoping he'd read her again and know that she had a plan, and that—even if he couldn't possibly pinpoint what it was—he'd play along. He offered her the barest nod, and she breathed out.

"Yes," she said to Dr. Salinger. "Blackmail is what kept your 'friend' from killing me. Not your word. And the fact that my brother was smart enough to record it is what's keeping you alive now, as well."

Anderson gave a more noticeable nod. "It's true. The second your so-called friend gets his hands on the evidence, he'll destroy it. Then he'll kill you, too."

"Stop messing around," the doctor snapped. "Whatever it is, hand it over."

"It's a USB stick," Anderson told him. "And it's in the left-hand pocket of my jeans. Don't shoot me when I reach for it."

"Slowly," Dr. Salinger cautioned.

Nadine inhaled. For a second, she thought her plan was going to work. Anderson would shift just enough that the doctor would need to pay extra attention to what he was doing. Nadine would feign a stumble. The two things would divide their captor's focus for just long enough that one of them could make a move. But before she could even let out the breath she held, the doctor spoke again.

"Wait."

Anderson paused, the tips of his fingers just at the edge of his pocket. "What?"

"Why are you willing to give it up so easily?"

Nadine wanted to cry, but she forced herself to speak calmly. "You said it yourself. I care about him too much to risk letting anything happen."

"You're not a fantastic liar, Ms. Stuart. It's one of the reasons I was so sure your memory loss was real." The doctor jabbed the gun against Anderson's head a little. "It's not about *him* this time. It's something else."

The ominous silence that hung in the air after he said it allowed just enough time for a light buzz to cut through. Nadine frowned. She noted that their captor did, too. But Anderson's expression wasn't puzzled at all. Instead, it was the facial manifestation of a groan. Annoyed and regretful and a touch of guilt all at the same time. And when the buzz sounded again, Nadine knew why. It was Anderson's phone, sounding from the very same pocket where his hand rested.

The doctor figured it out pretty quickly, too.

"Who the hell's calling you?" His snarl was laced with well-warranted suspicion, and Nadine braced herself for things to unravel.

Anderson stood very still, cursing his stupidly bad luck. He kept his phone on silent. Always. Why the hell it had managed to shift from its usually still mode to the vibrate function was beyond him.

*No time to dwell on it now. Only time to act.*

He made himself speak calmly. "I was expecting a call from a friend. He wouldn't know that he was interrupting a negotiation."

"This isn't a negotiation," Salinger snapped. "Give me the USB stick. And the damned phone, too."

Moving slowly—and with another apologetic look in Nadine's direction—Anderson stuck his hand the rest of the way into his pocket. He dragged out both his cell and the thumb drive, then extended his arm so that the doctor could take them. The other man snatched them away.

"Don't move," he ordered.

"Wasn't planning on it," Anderson muttered.

"Shut up."

Salinger stepped to the side, and for the first time, Anderson got a good look at him. He'd recognized the guy's voice, of course, from listening to its pretentious tone at the lodge. Now that he could see him, he wanted to curl his lip in disgust. Anderson didn't mind wealth. He appreciated nice things as much as anyone, and had a list of things he'd buy if he ever won the lottery. Something about the way Salinger wore it, though, bothered him. The way the too-expensive shoes dug into the mud without care. The way he had just a hint of tan, which was just as likely to have been acquired from a tropical vacation as it was to have been gained from a salon. Even the way he continued to hold up his weapon as he lifted the phone and studied the screen set Anderson's teeth on edge.

"See anything you like?" he asked irritably.

The other man lowered the phone. "I want to know who you are."

"Blake Smith," Anderson stated.

"Yeah. And I'm the queen of England."

"I've got a driver's license to prove it."

"Ninety percent of the teenage population has a fake ID," Salinger pointed out.

"Do I look like a teenager who needs a fake ID?" Anderson countered.

"The problem is…I can't figure out *what* you look like.

There's no doubt in my mind that you're involved with Ms. Stuart here. It's just that I can't decide what came first. Your relationship or your involvement in my friend's business."

The slight cock of the other man's head made Anderson realize what it was that irked him so badly. It wasn't the arrogance itself. Or even the smugness. It wasn't even the fact that the doctor was doing just the opposite of what he'd sworn to do with his life. It was the casualness. The man was a cavalier know-it-all who really ought to know *better*.

Anderson's jaw tried to clench as he forced out an equally blasé response. "I don't care at all about your friend's business. So if that's your only concern..."

Salinger narrowed his eyes and glanced at the phone again. "Would Harley agree with that statement?"

"Yes."

"So if I called him and asked, he'd have no idea what I was talking about."

"That's right."

"Harley doesn't know anything!" The words burst from Nadine like she couldn't help it. A far too obvious lie. Anderson turned to shoot her a warning look—a silent plea to keep quiet, too—but when he met her eyes, he saw that her gaze was clear. The denial was a ruse. And Salinger was buying it.

The gun pointed at Anderson's head relaxed marginally as the other man addressed Nadine.

"Stop lying to me," he said. "Tell me what *Harley* knows."

"I'm not lying," Nadine replied, her voice infused with clear deception.

"You're underestimating my ability to see through you. Keep it up, and I might just decide that shooting your boyfriend is the best way to get you to talk." At odds with Salinger's words, the gun slipped even more.

Nadine wobbled, and her next statement came out in a matching, wobbly tone. "You wouldn't."

The doctor was all the more smug. "I would."

Nadine swayed. Anderson tensed. Nadine wiped her brow.

"I don't feel so—"

Her words cut off as she toppled to the ground. A hundred percent certain that it was a trick, Anderson continued to hold still. The same couldn't be said of the other man. Salinger stepped forward—maybe in response to some ingrained doctor habit that he hadn't yet weeded out—and started to bend toward Nadine's prone form. The gun dropped to hip level, its muzzle pointed away.

*Now!* urged a voice in Anderson's head.

He leaped into action. The weapon was his primary target. Without it, the only tool Salinger had was his wits, and Anderson was sure those were dulled by overconfidence. So he dropped low and sprang forward, his hand aiming an open-palmed jab at the doctor's gun-wielding side. At the last second, though, the other man clued in. He flung his arm backward—just out of reach.

Anderson came at him again, this time with a fist trained on the man's solar plexus. The blow grazed the doctor's stomach, and Salinger stumbled. Frustratingly, he still managed to retain a hold on the weapon. Even though he was flailing to stay on his feet, his expression was triumphant. It was also fixed on Anderson, and that was a miscalculation. Just as he made a move to swing the gun around, an attack came from below.

Anderson fought his own need to be smug as he took a small step back to watch as Nadine took down the doctor. The other man didn't stand a chance. Her lithe legs were already wrapped around his shin and, with a twist, she sent him toppling over. The gun flew free. It sailed through the air and landed with a *thunk* in the mud a few feet from the aftermath of Nadine's maneuvers.

Trusting Nadine to keep Salinger at bay—Anderson had personally seen the effectiveness of her moves, after all—he strode across the ground and snagged the weapon. When he had it in his grasp, he turned and pointed it at Salinger, who was now lying with his arms over his head while Nadine pressed a knee to his throat.

"What I wouldn't give for a set of handcuffs," Anderson muttered, his eyes flicking around in search of some alternative.

"Your belt?" Nadine suggested.

"Genius. Can you keep holding him while I take it off?"

"One wrong move and his windpipe'll be crushed."

"Perfect."

Anderson made short work of freeing the leather from his waist, then stepped closer to the fallen man. In a few quick moves, he flipped the doctor over, secured his hands behind his back and dragged him to his knees. Fixing his darkest smile at Salinger, he opened his mouth to speak, but a noisy buzz cut him off. His phone was vibrating, the slim electronic device sliding along a flat rock just a yard from his booted feet. Even from where he stood, he could see Harley's name flashing across the screen.

"I feel like you should get that," Nadine said.

Anderson sighed because his gut was telling him the same thing. He held out the gun.

"Point it at his head. I do want to ask him some questions, but if he so much as breathes the wrong way…"

"I'll shoot," she promised.

He aimed a look at Salinger. "I wouldn't test her." Then he bent to grab the still-buzzing cell, clicking it on as he lifted it to his ear. "Better be good, Harley."

"Why?" replied his friend. "Is this a bad time for some semi-decent news?"

"Wish I could say no, but I'm covered in mud, have a guy tied up with my belt and my girlfriend is in charge of a firearm."

"I can't even digest all of that. Do you have the upper hand?"

"For the moment," Anderson said drily. "So you better just hit me with the news."

"I was able to trace those tip calls that came in to the Whispering Woods PD." Harley sounded so pleased with himself that Anderson couldn't help but smile.

"Do I even wanna know how?" he asked.

"A combination of charm and skill."

"So where did the tips come from?"

"The Whispering Woods care center."

Anderson glanced toward the doctor, who was sitting obediently still, his eyes not leaving the gun.

"I wish I could say that surprises me," he told Harley.

"I feel kind of let down that it doesn't. Especially considering how damn quickly I put it together. How did you figure it out?"

"It kind of snuck up on me with a gun. Literally. Now he's sitting here, waiting oh so patiently for me to question him. So I should probably—"

"Wait. *Him?*"

"Yeah. I've got a Dr. Salinger here. He was one of Nadine's physicians after the Main Street bombing."

Harley next words were infused with a mix of confusion and concern. "That's all well and good, but the person who left the tips was female."

Anderson frowned. "You're sure?"

"A hundred percent. You're sure the person you have is a man?"

"Funny, Harley."

His mind was already working through explanations and dismissing them as implausible. Had Salinger hired someone? It seemed too risky. So was it another person working for Garibaldi? That seemed more likely. But a little too obvious, maybe, to call from the care center.

Holding the phone away from his ear a little and keeping his voice neutral, he turned to Salinger. "Let me ask you something."

"Ask whatever you want. Doesn't mean I'll answer."

Anderson fought a need to point out just how ridiculous the response was, and instead said, "This is an easy one, Salinger. You working with a woman?"

The man's face went from sullen to confused. "What?"

"A woman. You've heard about them, right? Sugar and spice?"

"I know what a damned woman is. Why the hell would I be working with one?"

Satisfied that the doctor was genuinely baffled, Anderson made a dismissive noise, then brought his attention back to Harley. "The tipster isn't someone he knows."

His friend paused before answering. "Something about that rubs me the wrong way."

"Me, too."

Anderson's mind started working again, trying hard to grasp pieces of a puzzle that seemed just out of reach. Then a thought jumped out, and it stuck.

*Salinger's a scapegoat. And whoever's trying to frame Nadine is trying to frame him, too.*

"Anderson, you still there?"

Harley's voice seemed very faraway, and in spite of the fact that they were in a somewhat-covered area, Anderson was filled with a feeling of exposure. A need to run from some unseen, unknown force. Most importantly, to get Nadine out of sight.

"I have to go," he said into the phone.

He clicked it off before his friend could get in another word and jammed the device into his pocket quickly. He tugged Nadine a couple of steps away—still well within view of Salinger, but far enough that he could speak so only she could hear.

"We need to get out of here," he said in a low voice.

Her pretty brown eyes filled with puzzlement as they flicked from him to the doctor and back again. "What? Why? What about him?"

Anderson ran a hand over his hair. He was genuinely torn between dragging the man along with them and simply leaving him behind. The latter was potentially dangerous. The former would slow them down, and there wasn't exactly a place for him on the ATV.

"We'll have to leave him," he finally said, and reached out his hand.

She still looked puzzled, but nodded anyway.

He turned to face Salinger. "Sorry, Doctor. Trust me when I say I'd like to continue this conversation, but we've run out of time."

"You can't be serious," Salinger said from his position on the ground. "You're leaving me here?"

"Got more important things to worry about."

As soon as the words were out of his mouth, Anderson realized just how true they were. For the first time in fifteen years, he'd found something far more important to do than seek justice for his father's murder.

With that at the forefront of his mind, he threaded his fingers through Nadine's and resolved to pass on everything he knew about the case to Harley and Rush. They would have enough to work with. Enough to push on. Not that he would walk away completely. He just wanted time enough to elope. To honeymoon. Maybe to pick out a cabin in the woods somewhere that they didn't have to keep looking over their shoulders.

"Anderson?" Nadine pushed.

"I love you, honey." He gave her hand a tug. "Let's go."

But they made it no more than five steps before a deafening gunshot echoed through the woods.

# *Chapter 20*

The single sharp shot was loud enough that Nadine's ear rang and her eyes watered. She knew the shooter had to be very, very close. And for a second, the terrifying realization made the world do its best to grind to a halt. Even though Anderson's arms slid around her just a heartbeat after the gunshot sounded, their dive to the ground felt like it was underwater.

Anderson cocooned her body with his, so warm and comforting that she wanted it to last forever. Vaguely she could hear his voice. But she couldn't make out the words no matter how she strained. Then he peeled away and everything sped up again.

Nadine lifted her head, blinking frantically in search of something—she didn't know what, anything maybe—to restore order to the chaos. Instead, her new view only made things worse.

Just a few feet away sat Dr. Salinger.

*No*, Nadine realized quickly. *Not Dr. Salinger. Dr. Salinger's body.*

His form was slumped sideways, his jaw slack. His eyes were wide and vacant, the life gone from them completely. As Nadine stared at him in horror, she couldn't quite drag her gaze away from the crimson splotch in the center of the doctor's chest. It had overtaken most of his torso, spreading its inky stain over his white shirt.

A little moan carried to her still-ringing ears, and it took a second to recognize it as her own. She tried to bite back the noise but couldn't. Not until Anderson's strong hands took ahold of her again. Then she sank into them—into *him*—in relief, glad to let him have complete control of the situation. He pulled her forcefully along the ground. They crawled, belly down, for what felt like a hundred yards. Nadine knew it was probably more like ten, but every inch of her burned with the exertion. Legs. Abs. Arms and chest. Even the muscles in her neck ached. But just when she thought she couldn't take any more, Anderson at last stopped tugging her hand.

Nadine sagged to the ground. Catching her breath seemed like an impossible task, and the hot tears that poured down her cheeks made it worse because they were accompanied by near-sobs. But once again Anderson came to her rescue. His palms landed unceremoniously under her arms, and he dragged her to a sitting position, then pushed her back against something cool and bumpy. Automatically trying to discern what it was, she lifted her own hands to feel its ridges.

*A rock.*

It was a huge one. More of a boulder, really, that jutted up from the soil and formed an almost shell-shaped barrier between the two of them and whoever had killed the doctor.

*Oh, God.*

In spite of the man's atrocious past and association with

the man who'd killed her father, Nadine couldn't help but feel a pang of sorrow for the way his life had ended.

Anderson's fingers on her face made her aware that she'd closed her eyes, and as she dragged them open again, she saw that he was crouched down right in front of her, his mouth working in what looked like silence. Nadine shook her head, sure that she was experiencing some kind of post-traumatic-stress symptom. Frowning, she ordered herself to focus. And after a few seconds of intense concentration, she was able to make out the fact that he was saying her name. Asking if she was okay. She even managed a nod, and the slight up-and-down movement seemed to help clear away the residual effects of the last few minutes.

"Say something, sweetheart." Anderson's request was almost a plea.

"I'm all right. Really." Saying it made it feel true, and she cleared her throat and added, "Who was shooting at us? Where are they?"

Anderson's face flooded with relief, and he kissed her forehead, then sank back on his heels. But his words were anything but reassuring.

"I don't know where they are," he said, "but I don't think they were aiming for us. Not right then, anyway."

The last part of the statement confused her as much as it unnerved her. "Who were they shooting at?"

Anderson's eyes flicked to the side of the boulder. "Directly at Salinger."

"At Salinger?"

"You want me to explain what I think, or try to find a way back to the ATV?"

"Both," she admitted.

In spite of the situation, Anderson smiled. "Demanding, aren't you."

"We established that." Nadine inhaled and swept her

gaze over what she could see of the forest. "Can we make a straight run for it? Do you know how far we are?"

"Not far. But, Nadine…"

Something in his tone made her heart squeeze nervously. "What?"

"If we're running and we get fired at, you need to know that I'm going to do everything in my power to shield you. Even if that means using my own body."

All the air sucked out of her lungs, and her reply came out in a squeak. "You can't do that."

He shook his head. "I won't be able to help it."

"Why are you even telling me this?"

"Because I want your promise that if that happens, you'll keep going."

Now Nadine's lungs burned. "You want me to *leave* you if you get shot?"

Anderson cupped her cheek. "It's only as a last resort, honey. But I need to know that you'll keep going if I can't be saved. I love you and I have to know that you'll save yourself."

"Would you do it if it was me?"

He opened his mouth. Closed it. Then opened it again. "No," he admitted. "I sure as hell wouldn't."

Some of the pressure in her chest eased. "So then don't ask me to do it."

"Then at least promise me you'll try."

"If you promise me you'll do the same."

After a weighted silence, Anderson finally started to nod. But he stopped before he could finish the gesture.

"I can't," he said softly. "I can't promise you that I'll try to leave you. I can't even wrap my head around thinking about it."

Nadine swallowed. "Same here."

"All right, then. I guess we'll just have to make sure it doesn't happen."

She nodded, but a sense of deep foreboding had managed to worm its way into her heart, and even when they started—careful to move slowly and stay covered by the pieces of naturally occurring cover—she couldn't quite shake it.

Though they reached the ATV safely and quickly, Anderson couldn't make his muscles relax. Mostly because it seemed far too easy. Which—as usual—made him suspicious. So as Nadine swung her leg over the vehicle, he couldn't stop himself from taking a slow look around.

Except for the drip of rain, the forest stayed quiet. No snap of twigs, no rustle of branches. Just the water and the sound of their nearly in sync breathing.

"Are you getting on?" Nadine asked, drawing attention to the fact that she was already in position, her hand poised over the ignition.

"Yep," he said, but paused once more to listen for any sign that they'd been tracked.

"You're wondering why no one followed us?"

"Exactly that."

"I'm going to stick to the whole gift-horse-and-mouth thing."

"Guess it's hard to argue against that." He gave the wooded area another look around, then climbed on behind her.

"Where to?"

"Take us farther up the mountain for now," he said.

"Just far enough to put more than walking distance between us and the shooter?" she replied.

"Yep. Hard to travel subtly on the back of this thing."

She turned the engine over, its rumble proving his point.

"Ready?" she called.

"Whenever you are."

He slung his arms around her waist and tucked her

close, glad to let her have the lead so he could let his mind go to work.

*Where to start?*

The rush of events over the past few minutes had added a whole new pile of questions to his already crowded concerns. Had the person who shot Salinger really only been after the doctor? Was the shooting unrelated to Garibaldi's activities? Had he been wrong in his supposition that Salinger was a target in the same way as Nadine? He knew he'd leaped to that conclusion pretty quickly, but he generally trusted his gut on things like this. Years of experience had honed his ability to think on his feet. Right then, though—for the first time since he was a very new detective, really—he wished he had an office. Somewhere to lay out his thoughts on paper. Maybe a stack of sticky notes to keep them straight.

Instead, he settled for pressing his chin to Nadine's shoulder and going over it silently.

Salinger worked—*had worked*, he corrected silently—for Jesse Garibaldi. That much wasn't up for debate. His goal had been to retrieve the blackmail and turn it in to his boss. Probably to kill Nadine in the process.

His grip on her waist tightened at the thought, beyond grateful that the endeavor had failed.

"You okay back there?" she called over the engine and the wind.

"Fine," he said into her ear. "Keep driving."

The ATV picked up speed, and he forced his mind back to the details of the case.

In addition to the blackmail aspect, it was also a fact that the man had tried to set up Nadine to take the fall for the fire at her mom's place. He'd stated as much while searching their room at the lodge. Because of that, Anderson had assumed that the tips to the police had also come from him. Harley's info proved it wrong. And, in retrospect, having the police take Nadine in for questioning put the whole blackmail-retrieval scheme at risk anyway.

*So who else has the motivation to draw police attention to what we've been doing? More specifically, what* woman *has the motivation?*

He racked his brain, trying to come up with an answer. He didn't even recall encountering a woman over the last few days. Of course, he had to admit that even if he *had* talked to one, he might not have noticed much about her because his attention was so steadily held by Nadine.

*Nadine.*

He frowned. *He* hadn't encountered any memorable women.

*But she had. In the pie shop. The woman who owns the art store and stocks the items provided by Garibaldi.* It took Anderson a second to recall her name. *Liz.*

It kept coming back to the art. To those paintings in the underground storage facility. He wished like crazy that they'd managed to get inside. The chances of that happening anytime soon were looking slimmer by the second. They needed a new plan, but Anderson suspected that coming up with it while whipping through the woods wasn't the way to do it. A change of venue was in order, and when Nadine brought the ATV to a halt, his mind was already working toward a solution.

"How close do you think you can get us to the lodge?" he asked as the engine cut out.

"You want to go back there?"

"We need somewhere to regroup. I think the cabins are too close to our shooter for comfort," he explained.

She scrunched up her face for a moment before she nodded. "I guess it won't be the first place they look, either."

"Not to mention the fact that we're both sorely in need of a bath." He gave her muddy clothes a nod, then added, "I'd like to be close to my truck, too. I know it's identifiable, but I'd still rather be a hundred percent sure that we have access to a vehicle if necessary. It's a bad idea to be without transportation."

"Okay. The lodge isn't all that far, and we've got almost a full tank of gas. It's not a straight shot there, though, so it'll take a while. We might run out of fuel and have to walk the last bit."

"That's fine." He studied her face. "I sense a but."

"We should be fine most of the way because tourists don't come up quite this far, especially when it's not peak season. But closer to the lodge…a lot of the trails are pretty well-used. We risk running into other people."

"I think we can take the chance. Garibaldi won't go after us out in a crowd."

"All right." Her hand moved toward the ignition but paused without turning it. "Anderson?"

"Yeah?"

"Did I hear you ask Dr. Salinger about working with a woman?"

"You did. Harley said the person who tipped off the police was female."

"Is it crazy to wonder if it was that woman from the pie shop?" she asked. "She talked about Garibaldi. Maybe she was feeling me out for what I knew."

"My mind went there, too," he admitted.

"So should we be trying to find out if it's true?"

"We *are* trying to figure out if it's true. But we can't just go in and ask, can we?"

"No, I guess not."

"We'll figure it out."

"Okay." Her fingers turned the key, and once again they were on the move.

The ATV started spluttering about three-quarters of the way down the mountain, and though Nadine pushed it to run on fumes for as long as she could, the vehicle finally gave out. And they weren't as close to Whispering Woods Lodge as she'd anticipated.

"Guess we're on foot from here?" Anderson said from over her shoulder.

He sounded annoyingly okay with the idea, but as Nadine climbed off, she found herself fighting an urge to give the machine a kick. Or maybe a few kicks. And a punch or two for good measure. Reasonably, she knew they weren't stuck because of the ATV. But reason didn't seem to apply to most of what they'd been through in the past few days.

She shot the expired vehicle a dirty look. "You couldn't just take us *one* more mile?"

"You all right?" Anderson wanted to know. "Relatively speaking, I mean."

"Yes," she said with a heavy sigh. "I guess I just feel like… I don't know. Since the guy who was chasing us is dead, the rest of it should be over, too."

He reached up to give both her shoulders a reassuring squeeze. "It won't be truly over until Garibaldi's behind bars. But I promise I'll get you out of this as soon as I can."

"We can't walk away."

"I don't know how many more times I can handle worrying that you're going to get hurt. Or worse."

She stepped forward and leaned the side of her face into his chest. "Me, too. But I meant that kind of literally. Garibaldi's not going to just let us go. And if he figures out who you are, the other guys will be in danger, too."

His hands ran in a circle over her back. "I'm sorry for dragging you into this."

She couldn't suppress a laugh. "I'm pretty sure I jumped straight in before you ever showed up."

"Maybe."

"Truly."

"Then I guess I'm sorry *you* dragged *me* into it."

"You were already invested, too."

"Oh. Right."

She laughed again, then leaned back to stare up at him. "Is it bad that I'm not even sure I've accomplished what I wanted to, but that I'm over it anyway?"

He smiled back and lifted a finger to tuck away a stray lock of her hair. "No. I know what you mean."

His blue gaze held her, warm and loving, and she knew she would never get tired of seeing that look.

"Is what we've found enough?" she wondered aloud.

"It's enough for now," Anderson said. "We know why your dad was killed. We retrieved the evidence your brother left for you."

"Then promptly lost it in the woods," she pointed out.

"But not before we sent it off to Harley," he replied. "The next step is about interpreting that evidence. And keeping you safe, of course."

She opened her mouth to tell him that he was not exempt from being kept safe, either, but a vibration at her hip cut her off.

"I think you're buzzing again," she said.

"What?"

"Your phone."

"Oh. I don't know what's wrong with the stupid settings." He yanked it out his pocket and glanced down at the screen. "Harley."

"Better answer it," she said.

Anderson nodded, then tapped the screen twice, and Harley's voice crackled through the air. "Salinger has an ex-wife."

Nadine felt her own eyes widen, and she saw the same startled expression on Anderson's face as he replied, "Had. Salinger's dead."

Harley went silent for a moment. "Is that good news, or bad news?"

"Wish I knew," Anderson stated humorlessly. "Tell me about the ex."

"She's got a pretty troubling history. List of petty thefts in her late teens. Then a little break. Then an assault case that was dropped. At twenty-five, she became a nursing student down in Freemont, but was released from the program a year in for stealing prescription drugs from the hospital. She spent six months in court-mandated rehab and a year doing community service."

"Her illegal activity could explain the not-so-good-doctor's connection to Garibaldi," Anderson said.

"Could've been the initial contact," Harley replied. "But guess who turned her in?"

"Salinger?" Nadine hazarded.

"Exactly," replied Harley. "Divorced her right after her sentencing. If I was a betting man, I'd put all my money on her as the female tipster. She's got more than enough reason to want to see the man suffer. And guess what else? She's got an address in Whispering Woods, acquired just a couple of weeks ago."

Nadine exchanged a look with Anderson, who asked, "Where?"

"I'm sending you the address. And a picture, too, so you can be on the lookout for her."

"Thanks, man."

"No problem. And, hey, I'm still working on finding a connection between Garibaldi and the guy in that photo, by the way. But one other thing…you mentioned an art shop? Liz's Lovely Things?"

Nadine's heart rate doubled. "That's right. I met the woman who owns it."

"Well, I know this goes without saying, but I'd step lightly around her," Harley cautioned. "In the picture you sent that has the guys holding the canvas, there's a little tag attached to the bottom. When I enhanced it, it was clearly a price tag from her store."

"All right, my friend," said Anderson. "You're a genius, as usual."

"I do what I can."

The line clicked and went dead, and a second later, the phone buzzed with an incoming text message. Anderson held out the phone, and Nadine tensed in anticipation of seeing a picture of Liz. Instead, a mug shot of an unknown blonde woman's face popped up.

"That's not Liz," she said right away.

"No," Anderson agreed. "It's not."

Nadine looked up at him, surprised at how sure he sounded. "You've never met her."

"I haven't. But I'm sure that's not her, because that's the nurse at the care center who told me about the masked man running through the halls." He met her eyes, concern playing over his features. "You recognize the address? Eight-oh-one Peak Street."

"I know it. But only because it's along that block that's slated to be torn down in the summer. My brother was holed up near there before Chuck Delta shot him." She paused, thinking about it. "Could it be a fake address?"

"I guess there's only one way to find out."

# Chapter 21

Anderson slipped a twenty-dollar bill into the palm of the taxi driver. "Thank you."

"You sure you don't want me to wait?" the other man offered.

Anderson shook his head. It was risky enough to have taken the taxi in the first place, and he didn't want to put the guy in any more danger than he already had.

"All right," said the driver. "You two enjoy your day."

Anderson climbed out of the taxi, helped Nadine do the same, then slid his arms to her waist and pulled her in for an overly enthusiastic kiss on her lips, hoping it would send the cabbie away quicker. It worked. The tires crunched on the well-worn road, and when Anderson freed his lips and opened his eyes, the vehicle was gone.

"You think he'll remember us too well?" Nadine wondered aloud.

"Probably," Anderson admitted. "But that's why we had him drop us a block over."

She shivered and drew her fresh Whispering Woods Lodge sweatshirt closer to her body. Guilt tickled at Anderson. He'd set a fifteen-minute limit on their time in the hotel room, and her hair was still damp from the quick shower they'd shared. The air was cool from the recent rain, and judging by the clouds overhead, it wasn't going to warm up anytime soon.

"Let me give you my coat," he offered.

"Then you'll be cold."

"But *you* won't, and that's what matters to me."

She made a face. "And then I'll feel bad. And I don't like feeling bad."

He chuckled. "Okay. Let's get moving instead. Maybe that'll warm you up."

She nodded, then led the way up the road. With a quick glance back and forth, she grabbed his hand and tugged him to a paved path between two houses. When they came out the other side, Anderson was surprised to see what a change just those few hundred feet made. On the one street, the homes had been well cared for, the lawns nicely mowed, the walkways in good repair. On this street, everything was different. Roofs showed moss, windows were boarded up, and more weeds than grass grew on every lot.

"This is one of Garibaldi's projects," Nadine said. "He bought out all the homeowners and has plans to tear everything down and rebuild. Twice as many houses on half as many lots. He'll make a mint."

"Good," Anderson replied grimly.

"Good?"

"He's going to need it to pay for his defense team."

She rolled her eyes. "Come on. Let's find the right house."

They stepped along silently. Anderson was careful to stay close to Nadine, using his body to shield her as best he could. If any unseen forces lay in wait, he wanted to be the first line of defense. But the street remained as quiet as they were. The barricade at the end kept cars out, and there was no hint that anyone was moving around in the run-down homes.

"That's it." Nadine's voice sounded unnaturally loud in the otherwise still air.

Anderson frowned at the house she was indicating. It was in even rougher shape than most of the rest. A chunk of shingles had blown off, and the wreckage sat in a pile on what was left of the lawn. The front door was missing completely, and the paint everywhere else was peeling so badly that raw, rotten wood could be seen underneath.

"No way is anyone living here," he muttered.

"Should we look inside anyway?" Nadine replied. "Just to make sure?"

He considered it for a second, then nodded. "We're here. Might as well have a look. Carefully."

Still shielding her—and now with his hand on his weapon—Anderson guided her up the crumbling steps. Wary of an attack, his senses were on high alert. As they stepped inside, he cocked an ear and strained to hear any evidence of someone inside. His body tensed with anticipation of someone jumping out at them. What hit him as they approached the stairs, though, wasn't a physical assault. It was a nasal one. A peculiar, unpleasantly tangy scent that wafted through the air and filled him with unease. Both things—the pungent aroma and his disquiet—grew stronger as they started their ascent, and when they reached the top stair, Nadine noticed it, too.

"What's that smell?" she whispered.

Anderson drew in a breath. It was familiar, and he knew he ought to be able to place it. It wasn't until they hit the landing, though, that he finally made the connection. And the second he did, his mind screamed at him to grab Nadine and run. When he reached out his hand, though, she'd already stepped out of touching distance.

"Nadine." He heard the urgency in his own voice, and couldn't understand why she didn't come hurrying back. He tried again. "Nadine. That smell is accelerant. We need to get out of here. Fast."

Instead of turning his way, she inched farther into the room.

"Nadine!"

"My God."

The tremulous exclamation finally distracted him from his need to run. He took two wide steps to join her, and as he followed her gaze, he realized why she hadn't been listening. Across the living room, propped up in a grimy chair, was a body. And not just any body. One he knew. One *they* knew. They'd last seen it slumped over in the forest with a gunshot wound to the chest.

"What the hell?" Anderson muttered.

"Look." Nadine inclined her head to the other side of the room.

A second body—this one a woman's—was on the couch. A pill bottle lay to her side, its lid off and its contents spilled into the folds of the microfiber. A gun sat on the coffee table, and there was no doubt in Anderson's mind that it would be a forensic match for the hole in Salinger's chest.

"Someone wanted this to look like a murder-suicide, didn't they?" said Nadine.

Anderson nodded his agreement, but as he took another look around, he knew something was off.

"They weren't very careful," Nadine stated. "You can see the drag marks where they brought the doctor in."

She was right. A faint streak led through the dirt. It started at the stairs and ended right at Salinger's feet.

"It's like they just wanted to create the idea superficially," Nadine added.

Anderson thought that was a pretty apt description, but it made him shake his head. "Why go to all the trouble of setting the scene when anyone who's watched an episode or two of the latest crime drama could see that it's fake?"

"I think I know."

Something in her voice set every fiber of his being on alert. "What?"

She pointed. "That."

There, in the otherwise empty fireplace, sat what looked like an oversize piece of dynamite. Anderson knew what it really was, and it was no better. Inside that plasticized tube was a regular old kitchen timer, the kind used when boiling an egg or making the perfect chocolate chip cookies. Innocuous on its own. The other pieces were what made it deadly. A battery. A detonator. And an incendiary substance.

"We have to run," he said.

Nadine was two steps ahead of him already, her hand outstretched to grab his as she ran toward the stairs. They hit the top step. Then the third one down. Then the world exploded.

*All around Nadine, thick, black smoke pressed in. The scent of charred wood and plastic mingled in the air, making her choke.*

It's the nightmare.

*The thought made sense, but its cool logic seemed out of place in the chaos.*

*She drew in a breath and willed herself to move. She couldn't. She was sluggish, as she knew she would be.*

*A scream built up in her throat.*

*Her mouth dropped wide.*

*She threw back her head.*

*Her mouth drew in soot and smoke, and the scream didn't come because it couldn't come.*

*But her eyes opened.*

And the nightmare didn't end.

Her head was throbbing and spinning simultaneously. She was lying on her back and, overhead, along the edges of her vision, she could see smoke and orange flames licking at everything above her.

"Oh, God," Nadine croaked as she realized it was all real, all over again. "This is happening. Anderson, it's—"

*Anderson.*

Where was he?

She turned her head one way, then the next. He wasn't anywhere in her sight lines. She said his name again, but she wasn't surprised that he didn't answer. She'd barely been able to hear her voice herself over the ringing in her head.

*You have to find him.*

Nadine rolled over and pushed to her hands and knees, and the movement made her ache. Her stomach heaved, and though there was little in it, everything that *was* there came back up. But she didn't let it stop her. She wiped her mouth and sat up, trying hard to focus on where in the rubble Anderson might be. It wasn't an easy task. Pieces of drywall and wood littered the space that surrounded her.

"Anderson!"

The attempt to yell sent a fresh burn down her throat. Automatically, she tried to combat it with a breath. But it just made the pain worse, turning it from almost bearable to dizzying. She collapsed back down, this time to her side. The whole thing reminded her of the dream all over again. The details were far too similar. Right down to the pipe bomb.

*Pipe bomb?*

She wanted to shake her head. The dream had never

had a pipe bomb. Just the awful smell of the world on fire and everything that went along with it.

But she remembered it anyway, and not just because of the one she'd seen in the fireplace. The plastic tube went along with something else—a terrifying realization that she wasn't simply going to walk away from the inferno all around.

Her vision swam for a second, and strangely—eerily—her half brother's voice carried through the increasing fogginess of her mind.

*"You've got this, Nadine. I've got you, and you've got this."*

If she hadn't been so fearful of dragging in another breath, she would've gasped. The words were so very real and so very clear that she knew they were more than a thought manifesting itself as Tyler's voice. They were a memory. And as soon as she realized it, another one came swimming to the surface. She closed her eyes, relishing it because it had been so long since she'd been able to claim it.

*"Tyler," she said between her teeth. "This doesn't feel right."*

*"Mr. Garibaldi said for us not to mind the mess," her half brother replied.*

*Nadine's gaze skirted around the dirt-packed walls. "This isn't a mess. It's a...dungeon."*

*"Don't be melodramatic. Dad's down here waiting for us."*

*"Says Garibaldi."*

*"He's Dad's boss."*

*"I know, but..."*

*"But what?"*

*"I don't know."*

*"You know that you don't know?"*

*"Shut up."*

*He smiled, and she caught a glimpse of their father in the curve of his lips.* Their father. *It was a strange concept, considering that just days earlier, she hadn't even known she had a sibling.*

*He gave her a playful shove as they stopped in front of a wooden door. But as he pushed it open, any hint of joviality disappeared.*

In the memory, she'd been puzzled at why Tyler's demeanor had changed so abruptly. Now she could recall the next sequence of events, albeit hazily. She knew what was coming, and the dread of seeing it played out again in her mind made her open her eyes.

But the current situation was no better.

In the few moments she'd taken to embrace the unexpected recall, the space around Nadine had gone from smoky to near-black. She had a feeling that if she lifted her hand, she wouldn't be able to see it. And the heat had risen ten degrees.

*The only thing that's saving you is the fact that the burn is upstairs, and the blast threw you down.*

But the heat and the blackness told her that wouldn't keep her alive much longer. She had to move. And she had to find Anderson.

Groaning at the pain and nausea it caused, Nadine forced herself to try again. She inched up from the ground, paused in a seated position, then continued. She pressed a hand to the wall and used it to pull herself to a crouch. She paused again. Took a shallow breath. And straightened up.

From overhead, the heat beat down on her. But she made herself ignore it in favor of sweeping her gaze through the smoke-laden room. She couldn't see anything. Not even the rubble that she'd spied before.

Despair threatened. She closed her eyes, trying to ward it off. Instead, more memory rushed to the surface.

*Nadine pushed past her brother to see what lay waiting*

*in the room. As she stepped in, the bizarreness of it struck her as much as the horror.*

*Their father sat tied to a chair, his mouth bound, and something that looked like a stick of white dynamite duct-taped to his feet. His hands were taped to something, too, and it took Nadine a second to recognize what it was.*

His phone.

*Shoving aside the strangeness of it, she tried to make her way in farther, but Tyler's arms came up to stop her, and her father shook his head frantically, the motion making the phone flash as it somehow switched to the camera function.*

*"Let me go!" Nadine gasped.*

*"That's a bomb!" her brother replied.*

*"So we just leave him here?"*

*"I— God."*

*Tyler released her, then stepped past her. He ripped the gag from their dad's mouth, and immediately the older man urged them to go.*

*"Leave me," he said. "I'm a dead man either way. That bomb's on a timer, and I think Garibaldi only gave himself enough time to get him and his men out."*

*Nadine's eyes pricked with tears. "We can't just—"*

*"You can," said her dad. "And you will. Tyler. Get her out. Now!"*

*Her brother grasped her by the shoulders and tried to drag her away. She fought back, slamming an elbow into his chest hard enough that he cursed and released her.*

*"Tell me what's going on, Dad," she pleaded.*

*Her father looked at Tyler again instead, and spoke in a long, quick rush. "Listen to me. I sent you something in the mail. It's insurance. Information that will keep you and your sister alive. I don't know what Garibaldi said to you, but whatever it was, it was a trick to get you to come down here so he could take us all out at once. You need to get out of here and you need to make sure he knows you’re alive and that you have it.”*

*Tyler looked uncertain. “Dad.”*

*“Whatever else I’ve done, I’ve always protected you,” their father stated. “Go. Take your sister.”*

*Tyler nodded, then reached for Nadine, but she once again sidestepped him. She knelt at her father’s feet and started to free the bomb.*

*“Nadine,” her dad growled. “Stop.”*

*She ignored the order and kept working.*

*“Nadine,” her dad repeated.*

*Her brother’s hand landed on her shoulders, and she shrugged it off. “You might be willing to leave him, but I’m not.”*

“I want *you to go,” said her father. “I want you to* live. *To have a normal life and to forget about all of this.”*

*“Forget it? That’s never going to happen.”*

*“You’re going to have to force her, Tyler.”*

*And her brother’s hands found her again, this time with far more force. She tried like crazy to fight him off. But he was too strong and seemed oblivious to the way her fists beat at him. She screamed and begged as he lifted her from the ground. She kicked and bit as he swung her over his shoulder, then sagged helplessly as he started to move toward the door. Her eyes were fixed on her father as Tyler carried her back through the door. But they only made it a few steps into the hall before the bomb went off and rained fire all around.*

The devastation was the same now. Searing heat and an overwhelming feeling that all was lost.

From deep in Nadine’s chest, a sob built up. She could feel it wanting to escape. But then—against every odd she could imagine—a sound gave her hope. It was weak, but she was sure it was a cough.

“Anderson!”

She strained to hear a reply above the crackling flames. There was nothing.

*C'mon*, she said to herself. *No one's going to save you this time. Tyler's dead, and Anderson needs you.*

Drawing from some inner determination that she didn't even know she had, she dropped down to her knees and crawled toward the cough.

"Anderson?"

Another choked noise met her ears, and she adjusted her course. A few shuffles forward, and her hand slammed into a boot. She fought a need to sob with relief, and ran her fingers from his foot to his leg, then to his chest, which rose and fell with a reassuring steadiness.

"Thank God." She crawled up to press her mouth to his ear. "Can you hear me?"

Her question got no response, and neither did a shake of his shoulder.

"Okay," she said. "I can still get us out of this."

She lifted her eyes and thought she saw a faint break in the smoke. She blinked, trying to ascertain if it was an illusion. As she stared, she realized that it wasn't just a break—it was path. The smoke was trickling *out*. Hope flooded through her again.

"Okay, Anderson," she murmured. "Here's hoping that a couple weeks off Pilates hasn't totally dulled my strength."

She slid around to position herself in a crouch at Anderson's head, then hooked her forearms under his armpits. She took a smoky breath, anchored her body as best she could and then pulled. Hard. And remarkably, Anderson skidded along under her exertion. Nadine cast up a silent prayer of thanks for slick linoleum floors, then pulled again. Every inch made her shoulders ache more, and the effort and the heat sent sweat down her back and forehead in rivulets. And just when she wasn't sure if she could make it any farther, the air grew cooler and clearer.

Freedom was within reach. A final tug sent her tumbling backward. She thumped to the ground, taking Anderson with her. And even though his body was almost crushing in its weight, Nadine was still able to draw in a sweet, oxygen-rich breath, and instead of pushing him off, she slid her arms around his waist and held on tightly.

"Nadine?" Anderson's smoke-rough voice made her want to cry, but his next words made her laugh instead. "You're kind of hurting me."

"Ditto," she replied.

"Sorry." He groaned, rolled off and sat up. "What happened?"

"There was a bomb. And the house is burning down."

"You sound awfully calm about that."

"That's because it's over."

"Over?"

"For me," she confirmed, thinking of her dad's wish that she forget and move on.

Somehow, Anderson managed to read her expression yet again. "You remembered."

"Yes. And I'll tell you about it, but I think right now we should worry about getting out of here."

He followed her nod toward the burning house. "Sounds like a good plan. Can you walk?"

Another little laugh bubbled up. "Can *you*?"

"Think so." He grunted and swayed a little as he did it, but still managed to push to his feet.

Nadine stood, too. "You know that when I say 'get out of here' I'm not just talking about going back to the hotel, right?"

"I hope to God you mean the other side of the world, actually."

"You're sure?"

"Why wouldn't I be?"

"Because Garibaldi's still in control of the town."

"I know. But everything that matters to me is covered in soot, standing outside a burning building, telling me it's over. I believe her. And all I want is to have a normal life. It's kind of all I've ever wanted, actually."

Nadine's heart skipped a beat at the echo of her father's last words. "Me, too."

"Good. Then let's make that happen."

As the wail of sirens started in the distance, Anderson slung an arm over her shoulder. And as they started their mutual limp away from the wreckage, Nadine wasn't sure who was supporting whom, and for some reason, that fact filled her heart with more joy than she knew what to do with.

# *Epilogue*

Anderson squinted against the sun, smiling at the sight of Nadine's blond head thrown back in laughter. She was about ten feet in front of him at the market, clad in nothing but a sarong and a bikini top, and she stood out like a short, fair-haired beacon. It didn't help that her skin couldn't seem to soak up the sun. Five days under the Mexican sun, and she was still as creamy as a sheet. She'd confessed a little ruefully that she didn't burn, but didn't tan, either. Anderson's own face and shoulders were crimson. By the end of the week, he'd be the color of the sunset. A week after that, he'd be as toasty brown as an almond. Though, at the moment, a week seemed awfully far into the future.

He felt a frown crease his forehead. *What's taking Harley so long to check in, anyway? We agreed on seventy-two hours.*

Like his thoughts brought it on, his cell phone buzzed to life in his pocket. A glance at the screen told him it was the man himself.

"'Bout time, Harley," he greeted.

"Hey," the other man replied. "Better late than never. Just a second."

"Just a—"

On the other end of the line, the phone clattered noisily enough that Anderson had to pull his own cell away from his ear. The jarring sound was followed by a child's squeal of laughter, then his friend's responding chuckle. Anderson heard some muffled conversation, a question about locating someone's mother, then another laugh, and finally a sigh right into the receiver.

"Sorry about that," said Harley. "Not sure where Liz disappeared to."

"Liz?" Anderson repeated.

"The woman who owns the place where I'm staying."

"Yeah, I know who she is. Proprietor of Liz's Lovely Things, aka one of our suspects. Why aren't you at the apartment?"

"Change of plans. Been a little hectic here. Settling in, though. Cover story's going well. Just that Tegan—Liz's kid—has been at me all morning to play some card game. Who knew that third-graders were so demanding?"

"Everyone?" Anderson replied drily.

"Really?"

"Yeah, Harley. Kids are pretty much a full-time nuisance. But I hear they're worth it."

"Probably true."

Anderson let out a sigh. "Do you have news about the actual case? Or have you just been babysitting for the last five days?"

"I've got news."

"All right. Hit me."

Harley's voice dropped low and turned serious at the same time. "They closed the case on the fires."

Anderson couldn't keep the surprise from his reply. "Really?"

"Did you seriously doubt me?"

"I guess I did."

"You should know better."

"Tell me how it worked."

"Easier than you think, probably," his friend said. "I was able to pull some strings and call in a favor with the National Park Service. My guy came in and declared jurisdiction. Even passed off the fire at Nadine's mom's place as being set by the same people. And I gotta say…locals were actually kind of happy to hand over two arsons and a murder-suicide to someone else."

"That doesn't sound easy at all," Anderson replied.

"All about who you know."

"And what are the papers reporting?"

"Not much. My NPS guy made a show of being tight-lipped."

"And me and Nadine? Are we accounted for?"

"Your lack of faith in me is astounding."

"Just spit it out, Harley."

"Someone tipped off the gossip section of the papers that you headed to Canada for a quickie wedding. Maybe there was a surprise baby involved, maybe not."

"You're sure the locals actually believe it? Or is it more manipulation by Garibaldi?"

"Heard it directly from an old guy at the barbershop."

"Well. I guess I needed a little bit of reassurance. Though I don't know whether to be annoyed or grateful."

"Stick with grateful. You'll live a happier life."

Automatically Anderson's gaze sought Nadine. "Can't say I disagree about that."

"Sucker," Harley cajoled.

"Shut up. Tell me about Garibaldi."

"Nothing yet. I would guess he's got someone looking for you up north. But I think you're safe. I've got this, Anderson. You just worry about using up those accrued hours of yours. Have a margarita for me and give Brayden a slap on the back while you're at it. I'll call you when I have news."

"On time?"

"I'll do my best."

"Stay safe, buddy."

"Always do."

Anderson pressed the hang-up button, then started to lift his eyes toward Nadine again. A hand on his wrist stopped him.

"You touch, you buy," said a gruff voice.

"I think the saying is actually 'you *break*, you buy,'" he corrected, looking from the ring box he'd accidentally picked up to the grizzled man who was stationed at the table.

"My shop, my rules," said the old guy. "Or you wanna correct me about that, too?"

Anderson fought a smile. "I wouldn't dare. But I suspect the ring isn't my size. Fat knuckles."

The man snorted, but gave Anderson a sharp look. "Don't you even want to see inside?"

"No."

"Won't hurt to look."

"Fine. But I'm not agreeing to a 'you look, you buy' policy, either."

"Wait and see."

Anderson flipped open the lid, preparing to nod politely. Instead, he stopped and stared. The ring was silver. Small, as he'd suspected. And topped with a reddish-orange stone that caught the sunlight just right. There was nothing else like it on the table. In fact, it was the only piece of jewelry in sight.

"It's a firestone," the merchant told him. "Very rare."

Anderson ran his thumb over it. "Firestone?"

"Yep. Think you might know someone who'd like it?"

In spite of the way he willed himself not to—it would be bad for negotiating a good price—he lifted his head to gaze at Nadine again. The old man picked up on it right away.

"Not your traditional gold and a diamond," he said shrewdly. "But perfect for someone as unique and fiery as this ring."

Anderson started to argue, then shook his head. "Name your price."

The merchant frowned. "It's real silver. I was hoping to get—"

Anderson cut him off. "I'm not going to argue. So you might as well go high."

He barely heard what the other man said. He just yanked out his wallet and handed over a stack of bills. Everything about the ring was perfect. Except, of course, for one thing—the fact that it wasn't yet on Nadine's finger. But he'd fix that. Quickly.

* * * * *

*Find the next book in the thrilling*
UNDERCOVER JUSTICE *series in Fall 2018!*

*And if you're looking for more stories from Melinda Di Lorenzo, be sure to find these titles:*

*CAPTIVATING WITNESS,*
*the first book in this series,*

*and the stand-alones*
*SILENT RESCUE*
*LAST CHANCE HERO*
*and*
*WORTH THE RISK*

*Available now wherever*
*Harlequin Romantic Suspense*
*books and ebooks are sold!*

SPECIAL EXCERPT FROM

HARLEQUIN®

# ROMANTIC suspense

*Bea Colton is the only living victim of Red Ridge's Groom Killer, and Micah Shaw will do everything in his power to make sure she stays that way—even if he's risking getting his heart broken all over again.*

*Read on for a sneak preview of the next installment in* ***THE COLTONS OF RED RIDGE*** *continuity: COLTON K-9 BODYGUARD* *by* Lara Lacombe.

Micah leaned forward, his hand tightening on hers. "You're the first person to encounter the Groom Killer and live to talk about it," he said quietly. "I want to put you in protective custody, to make sure you're safe in case the killer targets you again."

Bea's heart began to pound. "Do you really think that's a possibility?" The Groom Killer went after men, not women. And she hadn't seen anything in the dark—surely the killer would know Bea couldn't identify them.

"I think it's a risk we can't afford to take." He gave her hand a final squeeze and released it, and Bea immediately missed the warmth of his touch. "I can start the paperwork—"

"That won't be necessary."

Disappointment flashed across Micah's face. "Bea, please," he began, but she lifted her hand to cut him off.

"I'll agree to a bodyguard, but only under one condition."

"What's that?" There was a note of wariness in his voice, as if he was worried about what she was going to say.

"It's got to be you," Bea said firmly. "No one else."

"Me?" Micah made a strangled sound, and Bea fought the urge to laugh. She knew how ridiculous her request must seem to him. They hadn't seen each other in years, and after the way he'd ended things between them, he probably figured she wanted nothing more to do with him.

Truth be told, Bea herself was surprised by the intensity of her determination. But she felt safe with Micah, and she knew he would protect her if the Groom Killer did come back around. Besides, maybe if they spent more time together, she could finally get him out of her system and truly move on. The man had flaws—he was only human, after all. Hopefully, seeing them up close again would be enough to take the shine off her memories of their time together.

It was a long shot, but she was just desperate enough to take it.